Love
Songs &
Other
Lies

Love Songs & Other Lies

JESSICA PENNINGTON

A TOM DOHERTY ASSOCIATES BOOK

NEW YORK

LOVE SONGS & OTHER LIES

Copyright © 2018 by Jessica Pennington

A Tor Teen Book
Published by Tom Doherty Associates
175 Fifth Avenue
New York, NY 10010

www.tor-forge.com

Tor® is a registered trademark of Macmillan Publishing Group, LLC.

Library of Congress Cataloging-in-Publication Data

Names: Pennington, Jessica, author.
Title: Love songs & other lies / Jessica Pennington.
Description: First edition. | New York : Tom Doherty Associates, [2018]
Identifiers: LCCN 2017049765| ISBN 9780765392275 (hardcover : alk. paper) | ISBN 9780765392282 (ebook : alk. paper)
Subjects: LCSH: Man-woman relationships—Fiction. | Reality television programs—Fiction.
Classification: LCC PS3616.E5567 L68 2018 | DDC 813/.6—dc23
LC record available at https://lccn.loc.gov/2017049765

Our books may be purchased in bulk for promotional, educational, or business use. Please contact your local bookseller or the Macmillan Corporate and Premium Sales Department at 1-800-221-7945, extension 5442, or by email at MacmillanSpecialMarkets@macmillan.com.

First Edition: April 2018

Printed in the United States of America

0 9 8 7 6 5 4 3 2 1

TO MY PARENTS—MY VERY OWN SUPER
FANS—FOR RAISING ME TO DREAM BIG.

Love
Songs &
Other
Lies

CHAPTER ONE

NOW

VIRGINIA

It's black, almost liquid looking, and gleaming in the LA sun, like a sleek, horizontal skyscraper. I've only ever seen a tour bus on the highway and I can't believe how gigantic it looks, looming over us. Maybe my fears of being cramped with eleven guys were completely unfounded. Maybe it'll be like a rock 'n' roll palace inside, everything studded and rhinestoned and shimmering. I saw a band special once, where the bus even had a crystal chandelier and a hot tub. *How did I even get here?* I mean, aside from the four-hour plane ride from Chicago and the completely insane cab-ride-from-hell.

"Are you freaking out?" My best friend Logan's voice breaks me out of my thoughts. "I can't wait for you to see it," he says, pushing me out of the car and into the hot afternoon air. "I dropped my bags off already, but I was waiting on you for the big tour."

For the nine hundredth time since Logan called me two weeks ago, I wonder if saying "yes" to this crazy idea was the right choice. *Who just up and leaves everything to join a band tour for three months? And on national television.* The thought of the cameras that will soon surround me sends a flush across my face. "The cameras . . . they're 24/7 or just for interviews and stuff?"

"Dunno," Logan says, hauling one of my bags over his shoulder as I follow him across the parking lot to the last in a row of five identical buses. "But filming doesn't start for a few days, once all the bands are settled in."

I'm positive Logan is sick of my questions, but I just want to know what I'm getting myself into. I bet I know more about this tour than he does. Logan probably packed his bags two minutes before picking me up at the airport this morning. I'd be shocked if he even knows which cities his band, Your Future X, will be competing in. I, on the other hand, have been quizzing him for the last two weeks. It's the most we've talked in the last year, since he left school midsemester and moved to LA. I even looked up bios for the other two bands sharing our bus—the four members of Caustic Underground (a hipster rock band out of Seattle), and a folk-rock trio of brothers from St. Louis called The Phillips. Which is not their last name. Or anyone's first. Go figure. I'm praying they're nice, even though they're technically the competition. I wonder what *they'll* think about me. Probably that it's weird an intern is buddy-buddy with another band. "So when do I get this surprise you promised?"

Logan taps twice on the glass door of the bus, and it opens with a loud, breathy sigh. "Right now," he says, grabbing my hand. Climbing up the stairs into the bus, he pulls me in behind him. "Get your asses out here," he yells into the empty space. "I've got a surprise."

Before even clearing the last step, the unmistakable shriek of Anders—drummer extraordinaire, childhood friend, and resident loudmouth—assaults me. "The strippers are here!"

Strippers? God, what are they planning to do on this bus?

"Sorry to disappoint you," I laugh as his scrawny body comes barreling down the aisle toward me. "No strippers, just me."

Anders's body collides with mine in the front lounge of the bus, almost toppling me over into one of the leather couches. "I can't believe you're here," he says, holding me in a bear hug. My nerves finally start to settle as I'm engulfed in familiarity. I've known Anders and Logan since elementary school—of course this will all be fine. Anders has barely let me out of his grip when I notice someone sitting on the couch next to us, long legs stretched out like he's been here a million times. Eyes that are *so* brown. And a smile that would probably draw me in, if I didn't know who it belonged to.

"Hey there, Vee." I've never actually met Your Future X's bassist, Reese, but from everything Anders and Logan have told me since he joined the band last year—*flirt, player, man-whore*—I'm not surprised by the look he's giving me right now. "You're probably exhausted after your flight." He looks at me apologetically. "I saved a seat for you, if you wanted to get off your feet," he says, patting his thighs as he winks at me.

"Seriously?" I say, laughing. "That's just lazy."

"Is that a no?" Reese says, giving me a gigantic grin as he pats his lap once more.

That grin probably would have done something for me once. I bet it does the trick for ninety-nine percent of the girls he meets. Maybe when I was seventeen I would have melted for the teasing look he's giving me right now—or those brown puppy dog eyes. Not today. Seventeen-year-old Vee feels like a different century, even if it was only a year and a half ago. "That's a no."

Behind me, Anders is laughing. Logan lets out an exhausted grunt. "She's like our sister, dude."

"I guess," Reese says, shrugging his shoulders. "If you've made out with your sister before."

"Logan Samuel Hart," I say, turning back to the front of the bus, where my bigmouth best friend is mouthing "sorry."

"I'm never telling you anything," he says to Reese, who looks happy with himself.

"You can make it up to me by giving me my surprise," I say to Logan. "Let's get it over with, already."

"Turn around," Logan says, looping his finger in the air.

Anders is standing between me and the long line of blue-curtained sleeping cubbies stretching out before me, and something about his face changes, like he just remembered something he forgot. "Don't be mad," he mumbles, leaving me confused.

I'm not sure what I'm supposed to be looking for in the back of the bus. Then it all starts happening: I see a pair of long legs hanging over the edge of the bunk. My body freezes as I look into *his* eyes, seeing my own confusion mirrored there. For the first few seconds it doesn't register. Maybe I'm in denial. Or shock. I hate surprises, but this isn't anything like what I had expected. *It's so much worse.* His hair is a darker blond now, cropped shorter than before. His shoulders are broader, the lean lines of his muscles visible under his shirt, and a faint line of hair prickles along his defined jawline. He's definitely not the boy I knew.

No. No. No.

I can't breathe. As melodramatic as it might sound, if Logan weren't standing between me and the door, I'm pretty sure I'd be sprinting out of this bus and across the parking lot right now. My arm twitches as I contemplate knocking him down to make my escape. *This can't be happening.* Logan is looking past me, at *him*, and I can't even bring myself to think his name. I don't want even that tiny part of him in my head.

"Surprise!" Logan shouts, to no one in particular, and for a moment I have to wonder if my best friend actually hates me. Seeing *him*—the last person I ever expected to lay eyes on again—

wasn't in even the top twenty possible scenarios that crossed my mind when Logan called me three weeks ago, promising me a job that would save me from spending summer break back at home with my parents.

"You know you'll be bored," he said. *"Come help us promote the band,"* he said. *"We need you,"* he said. *"It'll be fun,"* he said.

Right. I can't believe how much *fun* I'm having right now. As I contemplate what I'm going to do about my *dear friend* Logan, the guy staring at me from eight feet away is headed my way. Time has run out and I have to figure out what I'm going to do. *Just get off the bus.* Except the reality is, I don't even have enough money for a ticket home. No, like it or not, I'm going to be trapped on this bus for the next three months. Even if I made it home, there's no way my parents would pay for me to stay in Chicago for the summer. I already moved out of the freshman dorm. And at home, I have zero chance of surviving a small-town summer after a year in the city. Stirring up trouble before this bus even leaves the parking lot is the last thing I want. Because I'm out of options. And this is ancient history, anyway.

All I have to do is act normal. He's just some guy—a friend for a few months, almost two years ago. *Two years!* I'm not the girl he knew then, and he's definitely not going to affect me the way he used to. I need to fake it and not give him the satisfaction of anything more than that.

My eyes are on his brown leather shoes, my voice soft. "Hey, Cameron." I'm trying my best to smile but it feels like my face might crack.

His voice sounds strained, like I said something wrong. "Hey, Vee."

"Your band's in the tour too?" I'm unsure of what to say but I need to fill the silence. I force myself to look him in the eyes just for a moment as I mutter, "Small world."

And really it is, because what are the odds?

"Uh, Vee—" Anders is looking at me like I've got two weeks to live and he doesn't know how to break it to me. "Cam's in *our* band?" It's not a question—he's gauging my reaction.

Of course he is. The universe hates me.

I'm unable to form a coherent thought. "Oh." *You've got this, Virginia. Slap on a smile and get through this.*

Logan moves next to Cameron and throws an arm across his back. "We needed to add a fourth guy. We picked him up a few months ago."

This is the *new guy* Logan has been mentioning for months?

Logan's smile is still assaulting me. "Just like old times, huh, Vee?"

I want to smile, to be happy, because I need to believe that Logan really did believe me when I told him Cameron and I weren't a serious thing. And he thinks he's reuniting long lost friends; bringing back joy-filled memories. Because if it isn't that, then he lured me onto this bus for three months, knowing I'd be trapped with an ex-*whatever*. Logan and I have been friends since we were nine. He knows how to push my buttons, but I don't believe he has an actual death wish.

I'm trying to smile, but I'm not sure if my lips are actually cooperating, because my eyes are locked on Cam and my brain is screaming, "Punch that asshole in the face!"

God, it's hard not to notice that face.

All of the lines that used to be soft are hard. His eyes seem greener. Gone are the preppy polo shirts and khaki cargo shorts, replaced by a tailored, dark blue button-down rolled up his taut forearms. A pair of perfectly worn jeans hangs low on his waist. He is stunning. *And I want to punch him in his beautiful fucking face. Is it thumb-in when you punch someone or thumb-out?* Too bad twelve-year-old Vee didn't pay attention to any of Dad's self-defense lectures.

Logan strides toward me. "Aren't you glad you came, Vee?"

His eyes glow with excitement. "This is going to be epic." Logan lunges at me, throwing his arms around my waist and hoisting me in the air. Our chests press together as he lifts my feet off the ground and bends backward. He has the biggest grin I've ever seen, and it looks like it may split his face in half. Logan thinks he's making me happy. *Poor, delusional Logan.*

CHAPTER TWO

THEN

CAMERON

It hurts to move. The beach is nearly empty, my skin is hot and tight, and the walk back to the apartment is beginning to feel like an epic pilgrimage. My sand-covered surfboard, Lucy, is scraping between my ribs and bicep with every step, slowing me down. I could dump her in the woods along the sidewalk and cover her with some leaves. *Maybe no one will notice her. I can just grab her tomorrow on my way back.* I hesitate along the trees, but can't bring myself to do it. Lucy feels like the closest thing I have to a friend in this town. Or at the least, the closest I want. It's a dick move to abandon your only friend in the woods.

I've spent the last two months in Riverton doing pretty much nothing. During the day, I walk from my apartment down to the beach that edges the town. A lot of my time has been spent making failed attempts at freshwater surfing. I was sucked in by the bastards who sell the fancy, airbrushed boards downtown. I bought myself Lucy as a belated eighteenth birthday present. "Lake surfing is the next big thing," they'd claimed.

Those assholes are delusional.

The store is covered in pictures of surfers standing on top of rolling waves. Every one of them looks carefree. Like the two guys in my junior-year Trig class who always had weird half smiles and reeked of weed every time they came back from lunch. From what I've personally seen of Lake Michigan, those photos aren't the real deal at all. Despite spending most of my time staring out at that giant blue puddle, I haven't seen anything close to a surf-able wave. I should know—I'm from California. I've surfed before, on *actual* waves. Not freshwater hopes and dreams.

Still, I spent six hundred bucks on the board, so the least I can do is drag it down to the beach with me every day. That way I feel like I'm actually using it. Even if I'm just lying out on the water paddling out of view. If I can't ride a wave, then I figure lying under the sun—feeling the swells roll under me—is as close to happy as I'm going to get. Just me, the board, the waves. Life's a lot less complicated out on the water, away from everything. I can shut my brain off for a little while and I'm normal; I feel almost numb out there. Maybe it's just the chill of the water, but I don't think so.

My new apartment isn't far from the beach, but by the time I take a shower and change into a fresh pair of board shorts and a polo, it's nearly seven o'clock—hours past my normal visiting time. Lake Terrace Assisted Living is only a few miles away, sitting along Riverton's busiest street. It's a long, curved cluster of gray three-story buildings flanking a kidney bean pond. Tiny evergreen trees line the winding sidewalks. There are small patches of flowers scattered throughout the large yard, and wooden benches are everywhere.

I've come here exactly sixty-three days in a row, and I've never seen *anyone* outside. Not walking the sidewalks or at the picnic tables. Or sitting in the rowboat that lies suspiciously next to the pond (which I'm pretty sure is just a wooden prop to make it look like people actually go outside). It probably makes families feel better to think their loved ones are wandering around in fresh, colorful gardens, rather than lying in stale, white beds. A wave of cool air engulfs me as I enter the double doors and goosebumps spread across my sunburned arms. Behind the half-moon reception desk, a nurse absentmindedly waves me on. Everyone visits on the weekends. It's always quiet—almost eerie—when I come on weeknights, and it's my favorite time to be here.

A nursing home has become your own personal sanctuary. You're pathetic, Cameron.

Down a long hallway—covered in a flowery red-and-green wallpaper my mother would hate—room 207 smells like eucalyptus, baby powder, and lavender. It's a mixture of the two women who share the room—my Gram, and another elderly woman named Evelyn, who, like Gram, seems to be asleep ninety percent of the time.

I sit at the far end of the room next to the bed, facing the blue fabric curtain that acts as a wall, breaking the room into two halves. Gram has one side of the room, farthest from the door but closest to the window, and Evelyn occupies the other. Gram doesn't talk much, especially in the evenings, but when she does it's usually to call me by my father's name.

She usually wakes up to find me sitting beside her bed, scribbling in a notebook or with earbuds in. "Trevor?"

"No, Gram, it's Cameron."

Every time.

"Oh. That's my grandson's name too." Her face lights up whenever she says this, and I just nod, holding her hand. When I first started visiting, I tried to explain to her that I was *that same Cameron* she seemed so fond of. But as the weeks went by and she never caught on, it got depressing. So I keep quiet. I hold her wrinkled hand in mine, and I nod and smile. Nod and smile. Nod and freaking smile. Like a bobble head.

The reasons I moved to Riverton are simple:

1. Gram is here.
2. Lake Michigan is the closest substitute to the ocean.
3. Anonymity.

I'm in Riverton for a fresh start, and anonymity isn't an issue when it comes to my visits to Lake Terrace. If there's one place I can count on not being recognized—in a town full of people who don't know me—it's in room 207. Even though she doesn't remember me, I still enjoy visiting. I like having this piece of my old life. Knowing Gram was here made Riverton a logical choice, over the thousands of other cities I could have fled to, where I'd be equally anonymous.

We never visited Gram much when we lived in California. We came for the occasional holiday, and for a week every summer until I was twelve. We were always saying we'd make the trip more often—that eventually we would visit more. And like a million other promises, that one was broken when my parents died last year. We ran out of eventuallys.

On days she's feeling talkative, Gram likes to tell me stories. About how she met my grandfather when she was sixteen, or the girls' softball team she played on in her twenties, when she was "quite a looker." She talks about growing up on a farm with eight siblings, which always leads to talk of animals, which somehow devolves into her views on vegetarianism. Gram is no friend of PETA. They probably have her picture on a watch list some-where.

"Do you know there are people who don't eat meat?" she says incredulously, as if these are the same types of weirdos who kidnap children or skin kittens. "It's not natural. You're not one of those vegetable-eaters, are you?"

"No, Gram."

Sometime after bashing vegetarians and recalling her glory years as an editor at a local newspaper, Gram falls asleep. This is usually my cue to leave. But today a soft voice on the other side of the curtain distracts me as I gather my things. It's the first time a visitor has come while I was here. She sounds young—her voice is peppier than the nurses', not as tired and formal—and the way she speaks is so intimate that it feels wrong to barge through. So I sit back down. I can wait a few minutes to leave; I have nowhere to be and no one to answer to—another perk of living in Riverton, I think bitterly.

"Sorry I'm late, Nonni." Her voice is barely a whisper, and the sliding of the metal chair overpowers it as it grates across the floor. "I lost track of time after work, I'm sorry I woke you."

"Oh, honey, come here." I hear the wet snap of kisses. "You look so skinny. Are you eating?"

"Oh, please." She lets out an exaggerated sigh. "Of course I'm eating. Would you look at these legs, Nonni, they're like oak trees!" She laughs and it's a loud, musical sound that bounces around the room and makes me smile. "Are they still treating you okay in here?" Her voice is light and jovial. "They haven't tried to put you to work yet, have they? I hope they don't have a quilting sweatshop set up somewhere." Her voice is deadpan now. "You better pull your weight, or they might make you sleep out on the lawn."

When I hear Evelyn gasp, I have to bite my lip hard to keep from laughing.

"You think they have a sweatshop?" she asks.

The girl's bouncing laugh makes its trip around the room again.

"No, no, I'm just being silly. There's no sweatshop."

"You know, I stayed in a sweat lodge in the desert for two days when I was your age, Ginny." Evelyn states this like it's a fact you can find in a history book.

"You were in school when you were my age, Nonni. Or married, probably. And a sweat lodge isn't the same as a sweatshop."

"Well, close to your age then."

I'm hunched forward in my chair, elbows on my knees, as I listen like one of those cross-legged kids in front of an old-timey radio in a black-and-white movie. *Or like a stalker.* It's a matter of perspective, I guess. I should have left earlier, because I can't do it now without looking like I'm hiding. I don't want to leave, though; this conversation—that I'm not even a part of—is the first thing that's interested me in months.

"That's what you should be doing, Ginny," Evelyn says.

"I should be hanging out in a sweat lodge?"

"It's not warm enough for that here, dear."

That laugh again. Something about it makes me want to join in. It's compelling.

"You should be young and wild, out having fun. Meeting boys. Not hanging out with old ladies."

"Well, you're not just any old lady, are you? I love our Monday nights together. And I was at the beach earlier. With boys."

Have I seen her before?

"Plus, I have band practice after this. So that's wild. *And* crazy." Her voice is sarcastic, almost theatrical. "Bands are very wild and crazy, Nonni, you have no idea. If you did, you probably wouldn't even approve! Tomorrow I'll bring my guitar, and we can be wild and crazy together, okay?"

I think of my own guitar, neglected since moving here, and wonder what kind of band she's in. There's a picture of her being pieced together in my mind.

Noticeably thin.

Tree trunk legs.

I've been in bands before, but never with girls. I don't even know any girls in bands, but I picture neon tights, short shorts, and a ripped T-shirt that hangs off of her shoulder. Something with a skull on it, maybe. She's confident, sarcastic—she seems like the kind of girl who could pull that sort of thing off. The kind of girl who comes to school in leather pants with purple hair, and then three days later it's green.

Ginny stays for another hour, telling Evelyn all about her week. Her band, The Melon Ballers, got a gig at a local bar in two weeks. She's excited about it, but they still need to find a new guitarist to take the place of someone who moved over the summer.

Playing at a bar. She's obviously older.

She's excited for school to start tomorrow.

Maybe not.

A lot of the conversation is about music. One of her favorite bands, The Icarus Account, is playing a concert a few hours away, but she can't afford tickets. I've never even heard of them. *How expensive could tickets possibly be?* It's quiet for a minute, and then I hear acoustic guitars. The music is faint at first—probably playing on her phone. The four of us sit in silence as the singer joins in, describing a girl who "always wears yellow on days when she feels like herself." It's one of those songs that sounds happy and sad all at once, and when it's done I find myself hoping she'll play another. She doesn't.

"I'll see you Friday for the big First Week of School Recap. Same place, same time, Nonni." The door squeaks open, and the hallway sounds infiltrate our quiet room. "But I'll be on time. Promise!"

I'll see you then, I silently reply.

With a final click of the door, I know she's gone. It feels like that moment when the end credits run at a movie, and you wish there were just a few more minutes left before you have to dump your popcorn in the trash. A few more moments before you return to your real life, leaving the imaginary world and characters of the movie behind, trading them in for your own reality.

VIRGINIA

Mom pushes a sticky yellow puddle of eggs around the pan, eyeing me hopefully as I sit across from her on the kitchen island with my glass of orange juice. "You want some?"

I shake my granola bar in front of me. "I'm good."

"I'll just pretend like I didn't see your car missing this morning." She's looking at me the way most moms probably would, if they were about to launch into a full-fledged Gitmo-style interrogation of their seventeen-year-old daughter. Except my mom isn't most mothers, so she just cracks a smile and keeps stirring.

My mom only wishes there was a story of wild adolescent rebellion attached to the disappearance of my green Ford Focus. While she doesn't outright say it, deep down I think my mom, like my Nonni, wishes I had followed in her free-spirited, "try anything once," leather-bound sandal footsteps. Instead of my father's more practical loafers. It's hard to complain. I have a ridiculous amount of freedom. I rarely use it, but it's there. And she isn't one of those weird, incompetent moms who think they're an overgrown teenager, either. She's just got a lot of things to worry about, so I try to make sure I'm not one of them.

"I really don't ask for much, Virginia, just—"

That you come home drunk once.

Get your heart broken.

That you be more like me when I was your age.

"Full disclosure." I say it with a cheesy grin, in my most mocking voice.

"Yes." She's pointing the spatula at me like it's a weapon, but she's smiling. "And I don't think that's so much to ask." She still has her light blue scrubs on, and there are tiny flecks of color on them. I wonder if it's the result of a meal tray malfunction, or some sort of bodily fluid.

Gross.

"Nothing to tell. Steve got wasted at band practice. Again." I sigh. "I left my car at Logan's so I could drive him home. So I'm stuck with his car. Case closed, Detective Miller." I think I can actually hear my mother's hopes fall with each boring word out of my mouth.

"So Logan's picking you up for school?"

"Like usual." My best friend Logan has picked me up for school every day since before he could actually drive. All through middle school Logan's older brother Drew forced us to sit in the backseat and drove us chauffeur-style. *Logan should actually be here by now.*

"I haven't seen him around much lately. Everything okay?"

I nod. "Must be running late." Because of Labor Day, school starts on a Tuesday, and Logan and I have a two-year-long Tuesday ritual. Donut Day. He shows up at my house way too early in the morning and we drive to Bunn's—Riverton's only bakery. We fill a box with donuts of the jelly-filled, twisted, glazed, and sprinkle-dunked varieties. We're basically the donut-saviors of our first-period class. But today—the first day of the third year of our donut-buying ritual—there is no red Honda honking in my driveway five minutes too early. No answer to my seven phone calls and fifteen texts.

It's official. I'm nervous.

"Do you need a ride?" My mom works third shift at Lake Terrace Assisted Living, where my Nonni lives, and she gets home every morning just in time to make me breakfast. I know she'd rather listen to her residents sing show-tune karaoke than stay up longer than she has to, but she still insists on breakfast with me. Even though I only eat a few bites of whatever she makes. It's one of the few times we actually cross paths during the week.

"I'm set, Mom, you don't have to worry about it. I can drive Steve's car if I need to." *Please, please, please don't let me need to.* "When will Dad be home?"

Her eyes are trained on the gooey yellow mess in the pan. "Sunday morning. He's staying for a meeting on Saturday." She's trying not to sound irritated, but I can see it all over her face. Mom has these tiny little wrinkles around her eyes that pinch together when she's frustrated.

Monday through Friday my dad works in Chicago. He lives in a tiny condo outside the city and commutes to his law firm every day. Two years ago—when my parents' arguing escalated to new heights—they sold our house by the beach. The house I grew up in. Mom started working again, and Dad took a job at a big firm in the city. He traded time with his family for a bigger paycheck. And we don't actually talk about it, because any mention of Dad's strange living situation means Mom's eyes start to burrow into their wrinkly sockets. Without my dad here the arguing has stopped, but so has any semblance of what our family used to be.

I finally drive myself to school. Logan must be dead in a ditch. Or dying of some sort of brain-eating disease that you get from sharing a shower with too many dirty guys after gym class. *No one* misses the first day of school. That's insanity. And more to the point, Logan doesn't miss out on a chance to eat donuts.

Boys are lucky like that, with their eat-whatever-they-want metabolisms and baggy clothes.

I'm sitting in the third row of Mr. Flanagan's first-period Calc class, eyeing the clock as I drum my fingers across the shiny black desk.

Situations like this—sitting in class and wondering if Logan has decided to hate me after all—is why we never should have tried the whole friends-with-benefits thing. Because even though it only lasted for two months over the summer, and started and ended mutually (mostly), I still find myself wondering if things have changed. If Logan's sarcastically biting comments are actually sarcastic, or if he means it now when he says, "You're a cold bitch sometimes, Vee." Because he's said that to me jokingly a hundred times before, but suddenly it feels personal. I feel weird mentioning other guys. *Is it cruel? Does he even care?* He never seemed to before, but now I don't know. Being paranoid sucks. Two months of make-out sessions were totally not worth the stress and second-guessing that have followed.

When I called things off, I told him I didn't want a relationship. Which is sort of true. My parents were high school sweethearts. Mom followed Dad to college, and they couldn't afford law school *and* nursing school, so Mom worked while Dad finished. She supported him. When he was done it was supposed to be her turn, but by then I'd come around. Now Dad's a big-shot lawyer in the city and Mom's working a job with shitty hours. She finished nursing school last year after Dad moved. On her own. Mom's told me their epic love story over the years, but I've read between the lines, and had front-row seats to the live production version. *You put your dreams on hold for him and look what it got you.* But when I told Logan I didn't want a relationship, mostly I just panicked. I didn't want a relationship with *him* and didn't know how to say it.

It's three minutes until the bell signals the start of my senior year, and I'm still donut-less and down a friend. For the record, I would never voluntarily show up last minute on the first day of school. I love camping out in the hallway, catching up on summer gossip, checking out the carefully chosen outfits. The hallways squeak with new shoes and the classrooms smell like fresh denim. If it were up to Logan, we'd always slide in just as the bell rang. He and I are opposites in almost every way. And it's not that he's this super-popular jock-musician and I'm some kind of social zero. He is—but I'm not. I'm not a cheerleader or a star athlete, but I'm nice to everybody.

When I was a kid, I had all my birthday parties on our private beach—back when we had a private beach—and I invited *everyone* in my class. Not because my parents made me—I just wanted them to like me. I'm easy to get along with and I think—even though I don't have a beach house anymore—most people still like me. I don't trash-talk and I'm not about drama. You'd be surprised how far that gets you in a small town. It helps that most of my friends are guys.

So Logan and I are on pretty even footing socially. We're just different in every other imaginable way. With his sarcastic comments and sometimes painful brand of honesty, Logan's one of those "love him or hate him" kind of people.

The thing about Logan is that when he does let you in—when he *chooses* you—it feels amazing. Like one of those bumping electronic songs that makes your chest feel like it might explode, as the pitch goes higher and higher, threatening to shatter your car windows. We were sharing a bus seat in third grade when Logan chose me. And I'm sitting in first-period Calc, at 7:54 on the first day of my senior year, when he walks in. Finally, my nerves begin to settle—until I notice the giant box of donuts he's holding in one hand.

On a scale of one to ten, I'd rate my anger a very respectable seven. The usual first day of school chatter is white noise around me. All I can focus on is the burning heat behind my eyes as I stare imaginary laser beams through the back of Logan's head. I'd like to mentally decapitate him, because Donut Day is supposed to be *our* thing, and he promised me nothing would change.

With only seventy students in the entire senior class, the upper-level classes are always tiny, and Mr. Flanagan doesn't even bother with a roll call. There are twelve of us, and after checking down the list of names and visually surveying each of us, he says just one name.

"Cameron Fuller?" He's looking toward the back of the room, locating the one face that doesn't belong, and we all do the same.

It might be Cameron Fuller's first day at Riverton High School, but it isn't the first time I've seen him. I worked at the beach over the summer and saw this guy every single day for the last few weeks. Always carrying his surfboard, always by himself. Most of the day he would float on his board, never even trying to stand; just floating, drifting. He never even approached any of the girls constantly surrounding his towel who—let's be honest—pretty much had signs positioned over their blankets that said "willing and available."

Clearly he was a terrorist.

Terrorist is our pet name for the thousands of tourists who flood into Riverton each summer, overrunning the restaurants, filling the beach, and terrorizing the locals with their NASCAR-like driving. Anyone local knows the surf shop downtown is a total *terrorist* trap. Waves only get big enough to actually surf during storms, and who wants to be out on the water in the middle of that? Death by lightning while half naked? No, thank you.

But here he is, in my first hour, clearly *not* a terrorist.

Every head turns to look at him in the back of the room. My eyes are on him too, and he looks sad, even though he's now smiling, one hand raised in an awkward half wave. His dark, sun-kissed skin has gone almost as pale as his blond hair. He seems like the kind of guy who should be confident. He's fun to look at, like the guys on all of my college brochures: with their broad shoulders, well-fit clothes and wind-blown hair, walking from the library to the cafeteria.

"Here." His hands are crossed on the desk, and the smile fades quickly when everyone turns away. Everyone except me. I'm still staring at him, but I whip around quickly when his dazzling green eyes meet mine. He has the saddest eyes I've ever seen.

Mr. Flanagan waves his hands in front of him like a conductor. "Everyone?"

"Hi, Cameron," the whole class chants in a lifeless monotone.

New students come to RHS so infrequently, they're basically treated like visiting celebrities. By lunch Cameron will be claimed by one of our class's most eligible bachelorettes and, by the looks of him, will probably be welcomed onto one of Riverton's illustrious sports teams. He's muscular but not bulky, and he doesn't seem like he's suffering from multiple head injuries, so my guess would be basketball or soccer. Teachers all but roll out the red carpet, and I have to say "Hi, Cameron" in three more classes. Each time he looks like he might puke as all eyes turn on him, and then there's this look of immense relief as the stares of classmates drift away.

I may be slightly fascinated by Riverton High's newest student. Cameron Fuller, it turns out, is a real-life high school anomaly: a new student who makes absolutely no attempt to fit in. He doesn't talk to anyone, or make an effort to claim his spot in an established social group. In every class he sits in the back, sometimes several seats from the nearest person, always silent but also seeming to be engrossed in everything around him. He's quiet, but he's watching. I can tell by the way his eyes dart from person to person as they speak. He's listening, observing, soaking it all in. *Maybe he's just sizing things up; weighing his options.* That's what I'd do.

After a curious scan of the cafeteria at lunch Cameron is nowhere to be found. I haven't heard him say one word throughout the day aside from mandatory introductions, didn't see him talk to a single person. Except when I pass him in the hallway on the way to Chem and he's standing next to Jenna Mills. She's holding a clipboard at the crossway of the junior and senior hallways, collecting signatures for . . . something. I don't know what, because no one has actually stopped to talk to her. Except him. The guy who hasn't talked to *anyone* without teacher instruction. I wonder what makes her special, even though at first glance it's pretty obvious.

Jenna has short, spiky black hair with big chunks of blue that you can only see from a certain angle under the fluorescent lights. She's always wearing something black. Today it's a ruffled skirt with red leggings, and her eyelids are caked with red glitter. She reminds me of a deranged Tinkerbell. Seeing him leaning against the orange lockers in his white button-down shirt and light blue linen shorts, it's hard not to notice the contrast between the two. As I pass, he pulls a Melon Ballers' poster off the bulletin board behind Jenna, shoving it into his backpack. *Will I see him at a show?* With a quick nod, he walks away, still looking as sad as before. Maybe someone stole his donuts too.

CAMERON

It's painful. Like someone-taking-a-key-to-the-side-of-my-beautiful-new-car painful. Every class is another new start, a fresh introduction, a new sea of staring eyes. By the time I reach English after lunch, my nerves are shot and, hand to the holy mother, I say an actual prayer that my classmates will be mute. Or that my teacher will take pity on me and saddle us with a five-hundred-word in-class essay or something. Anything to distract them from the most interesting thing about the first day of school, which seems to be me. *It's definitely me.*

I have three hours left and all I really want to do is go back to the apartment. *My* apartment. Two months ago—the week after I turned eighteen—I spent an entire weekend visiting houses and condos in Riverton. When I finally walked into an apartment down the street from the beach and felt like I wanted to sit on the ratty old chair and just stay there, I knew I had found a winner. The rooms are all furnished seventies-garage-sale style. It feels comfortable.

Every room is painted a different shade of blue. The living room looks like the midday ocean—alarmingly bright and strangely calming at the same time. It feels like being surrounded by walls of water; like living in a fish tank. The strips that run above and below the white kitchen cabinets are a dark, almost black blue, and the two bedrooms are a pale powdery shade that belongs in a little boy's room. I told myself I'd paint those, but I still haven't. Something about the blue-ness of it all just seemed right when I saw it. It didn't feel anything like my home, or the house where I had lived with my aunt and uncle. The apartment feels completely . . . other. It reminds me of the ocean—of that part of home, without bringing with it all of the more real parts that I had to get away from.

The landlord had looked me over like maybe I was going to turn the place into a meth lab or a grow house, but I guess three open apartments in the building and a wad of cash must have made his mind up.

"Keep out of your neighbors' hair, son," he said. And then

he was gone, cash in hand, pushing the shiny keys into my palm.
They practically screamed at me.

We're your ticket out, Cameron!

Let us lead you to the pity-free promised land of Anonymity!

Now here I am, in fourth-hour English, living the dream.
After the obligatory introduction (where I'm once again paraded
in front of a classroom of students that I've already met) Ms.
Willard, a tall, skeletal woman, begins to pace around the room.
Her long black hair is so shiny it looks wet, and she's holding a
beat-up cardboard box, pulling out little black notepads and lay-
ing one on each desk. They're small, like something you'd imagine a child detective carrying around, jotting down notes on the
most recent grocery store caper.

"These," she says, in a raspy smoker's voice, "are your
journals."

The class lets out a cumulative moan of disgust, to which Ms.
Willard replies with a giant smile. "I've been an educator for
twenty years." She rolls her eyes as she continues pacing. "You
can't faze me with your sullen teenage ways." She wags her finger in the air. "For the next week you'll work on a character
study. Pick someone you can observe on a regular basis. A friend
or family member, someone who works at a local store. A coach or
family friend. You get the idea . . ." She's pacing across the room
in a figure eight formation, lightly tapping her palms together.
"You'll record everything you can. Their mannerisms and habits, their beliefs, their physical characteristics. Aspirations and
internal conflicts . . . No detail is too small, no fact too trivial.
Obviously this will be easiest with someone you have frequent
access to. Someone you know or would like to get to know."

Then, she winks at us. And I'm pretty sure at least one person
gasps. If there isn't a law against teachers winking at students,
there definitely should be. It's creepy. Like guy-in-a-trench-coat-
handing-out-candy-on-the-playground creepy.

"Gentlemen, perhaps this is a good time to learn more about one of the young ladies you're interested in."

Is she actually encouraging *stalking?* A few girls are looking around themselves nervously. I'm still laughing over the wink. *What kind of school* is *this?*

At the chalkboard, Ms. Willard writes the definition in a scrawled script:

A WRITTEN DESCRIPTION OF A PERSON'S QUALITIES.

This is my kind of thing. After close to a year of being watched like a mental patient, I'm ready to be the observer. For once, my life won't be an open book, thumbed through by every teacher and student, earmarked to one climactic page where my whole life changed. They won't know that my parents are dead, or that I'm a year behind. They'll only know what I tell them. They won't have the chance to see me as a less-perfect version of the old me. I flip open the pad. While Ms. Willard continues to rattle off the books and assignments we can look forward to, I scribble everything I know about Ginny.

Physical Description: Skinny with "tree trunk" legs. Colorful hair?
Habits & Mannerisms: Sarcastic. Spunky. Confident.
Skills: Scaring her grandmother. Being upbeat even in a nursing home. Music.
Conflicts: ?

VIRGINIA

I'm sitting in the corner of Logan's room after school, like I do every day. We don't have much homework the first day of school, but I brought all my books anyway. I need an available distraction if things get awkward. Logan comes down the stairs to his bedroom with an armful of snacks, setting the bowls and cans in front of me. My psychology textbook is open on my lap and I flip through the pages, watching words fly by—*Pavlov, Rorschach, cognition, Freud*—I'm not actually reading them. Logan drops to the floor. He's wedged right up next to me—born without any sense of personal space—and his long arms wrap around his knees. I'm not sure if I should leave my leg where it's at, or move it. We never used to have this weirdness, but now I question everything I do around him.

Logan bumps me with his shoulder. "Wanna make out?"

"Not funny." I throw a pretzel at him. He's laughing, but I'm still not sure if he's joking.

Three weeks ago we would have already been making out. Two weeks ago I told him we couldn't do it anymore. Things were getting weird. In the back of my mind I had always wondered about Logan and me. If he ever thought about me that way (*I still don't know*), if we could be more (*I don't think so*), if I wanted that (*I had thought I might*). No matter which way I rolled it all around in my brain, I think I always knew that Logan and I could never work long-term. We'd kill each other. But this spring when I broke up with Toby Mendon—boyfriend of ten months, first (*of many things*), and King of the Assholes—I vowed I was done with high school boyfriends. I'd wait for college guys. Guys who didn't think making out in the backseat of their mom's minivan was sexy, or that I was supposed to be a seventeen-year-old virgin *and* an aspiring porn star.

A few months ago, when Logan jokingly asked, "Wanna make out?" for the nine hundredth time, I figured why not? For a while it was great. It was casual and fun and comfortable. Until it wasn't. There were no lines, no rules to follow. Sometimes he'd grab my hand in public, or try to kiss me when people were around. And other times he ignored me, and that bothered me too. Even though being Logan's girlfriend was not what I wanted. I think about things too much to do the whole friends-with-benefits thing. I knew it had to end. To preserve my sanity and our friendship.

Push me, pull me, take me or leave me . . . the way I am, can't be like them . . . the words buzz in my head, and I begin to hum a soft melody as I grab my notebook. Music takes over my mind the same way a fever takes over a body: in a hot, unexpected rush. One minute it's quiet and the next there are words and notes and magic swirling around in me.

Logan looks at me like maybe I just changed my mind about the make-out session. "Song?"

I nod. I haven't written a new song in months. Not one I could share, anyway. My thoughts have been wrapped up in the weirdness of our situation, the lyrics much too literal to put in front of the band—friends or not. Logan retrieves his guitar, sitting back down on a stool in front of me while I scribble. I pass him the first verse, and he starts plucking strings and putting it to music as I continue to let my feelings bleed out onto the paper, line after line. We write and hum and play, and hours later we have the beginnings of a song. I'll let Logan finish it, but when I get home—in the privacy of my room—I'll put the words to my own music. Just for me.

CHAPTER THREE

NOW

CAMERON

When Vee finally pries Logan's arms off, she paces to the back of the sleeping area, throwing her bag on the bunk across from mine. The bunk farthest from the one I was sitting on when she arrived. I know why she did it. I can't imagine she'll be thrilled when she realizes *that* bunk wasn't mine. She'll be sleeping less than three feet away from me. For three months. This is either amazing news or the worst idea ever. I can't decide, because my brain isn't really processing anything beyond the fact that she's actually here. And she looks like a different version of the girl I used to know. Her hair is still long, but wilder than it used to be, and a lot more blond than brown. But it's not just the way she looks, it's the way she feels. Like she's off limits.

Logan is standing next to his bunk, across from Anders's. "You going to bunk all the way back there, Vee?"

"I'll see you guys all the time. A little space might be good." Vee never looks at me as she speaks, but she sounds exactly like I remember. Like the recording on loop in my head. As I slowly approach the back of the bus, I wonder if she'll completely flip when she realizes who her new bunk neighbor is. I duck my head and drop onto my bed, waiting for the shit storm to begin. Maybe I'm an idiot, but I'm strangely eager to get this over with. The sooner she yells and tells me how much she hates me, the sooner we can move on. To what, I'm not sure. I don't even know if she hates me, like I suspect she does, or if she doesn't think anything of me at all. *Is there a chance we could actually be friends?* Tucking my hands behind my head, I brace for her reaction. Maybe she'll make one of the guys switch with her. Or insist that I move.

Instead, she unzips her bag and begins to pull out small stacks of books and journals, setting them in the tiny ledge that lines her bunk wall. When she's finished she gives me a forced smile, pulls the blue curtain closed, and walks away without a word.

When Logan tracked me down six months ago at UCLA and invited me to join Your Future X, I knew I'd hear about Vee once in a while. Maybe I'd have to sing lyrics she wrote. I told myself I could do it—convinced myself it was just a stupid high school romance. That it felt so intense because it was first love, and it was new and exciting. It was nothing special; I was over her. I never expected I'd actually have to see her again. Let alone be on the same bus for twelve weeks. I know I shouldn't be, but I'm surprised by how unsettling it's been seeing her again. How confusing. I spent months thinking about how I could get her back, and another year dating girl after girl to convince myself she wasn't that special. *Why isn't she in Chicago?* I could ask her, but no matter what we're doing or where we go, Vee has managed to avoid me, while still being right there.

I've endured two nights sleeping four feet away from her. Trying not to think about what it used to be like to kiss her. To touch her warm skin, sleep in the same bed. What she looked like lying on the beach at midnight in soaking wet clothes. *Shit.*

This is going to be the longest twelve weeks of my life. Of course, twelve weeks is the dream. We don't just have to beat eleven other bands to get to the finale, we have to pray the show doesn't get cancelled between now and then. I overheard our tour bus driver on the phone with his wife, saying what a stupid idea this was. He figured he'd be home in a few weeks. God, I hope he's wrong. Even just making it through a few rounds would take us to a whole new level. We'd be able to play bigger clubs, maybe go on our own tour. Not in a bus like this—hell, probably not in a bus at all—but even a van tour would be cool.

Vee has gone out of her way to greet every new band member—excuse me, every new *guy*—who has loaded onto this bus in the last two days. Everyone is nice to her. Of course they are. Everyone always loves Vee—that's the norm. Whether she realizes it or not—which she doesn't—something about Vee makes people comfortable. She's like the human version of an anti-anxiety pill or something. We're three days into the tour, making our way to Houston, and the only person she hasn't gone out of her way to talk to is me. I've always pictured us hashing out our past in private, but Vee seems opposed to us having even ten seconds alone.

At a pit stop in Fort Worth, I finally decide that I may never get her alone. I just have to go for it. One way or another, we need to push past this, so I can focus on what I came here for. I'm sitting two seats down from her, squeezed between Logan and a red tiled wall. We're in a tiny truck stop diner grabbing dinner at ten o'clock. It turns out that music tours have very little regard for normal meal times. We're all getting used to stocking up on food at rest stops and gas stations, cooking half-assed "meals" in the bus's tiny kitchenette, and grabbing real food when the buses stop once a day. Thankfully bus drivers have to eat too.

Across from me, Anders is wedged between Reese and our bus mate Pax, the lead singer of Caustic Underground. A folded gas station map is laid out in front of them and Pax is using a thick red Sharpie to trace the path of the tour. Through the South, then up to Nashville, looping through New York before traversing the Midwest, and finally landing back on the West Coast. Twelve cities in twelve weeks.

"So Vee, what tour stop are you most excited about?" *Light and easy small talk. Nothing sticky there.*

Silence.

I feel Logan shift next to me as he nudges her.

"Oh. Probably Nashville." Three words. "Pass me the salt, please." Her voice is small. I'm pretty sure she was talking to Logan, but I'm not letting her off the hook that easily. I scoop up the glass globe before anyone has a chance to touch it, and hold it out to her. She makes zero effort to get it, waiting until Logan plucks it from my hand, passing it over to her. "Thanks," she says casually, to no one in particular.

"You have to make it through Houston, New Orleans, *and* Atlanta to get to Nashville," Pax says casually, dragging his finger along the red route on the map. "No offense."

"None taken," Reese says, flicking Pax in the head with his finger. "We'll give you a shout-out from Nashville while your ass is back on your couch."

Vee laughs, and it irritates me that she seems amused by Reese, of all people.

"So what are our cheesy tourist stops in Nashville?" I lean forward so I can see Vee around Logan.

She's shuffling eggs around with her fork. "I didn't really have anything in mind."

Anders's head pops up. "Bullshit. Like you don't have an itemized list of where you want to go in each city."

I laugh. Vee had The Plan mapped out since the day I met her. Where she would go to college (Michigan State), what she would do (become a publicist).

Vee scrunches her nose up as she shakes her head at Anders, like he's an idiot. "I'm spontaneous now," she says. And she's looking at Anders but I think she's talking to me. "You probably didn't know that about me, did you?"

Logan stabs one of the sausages on Vee's plate. "I heard the top bands get to go backstage at the Ryman."

Vee's eyes light up. "No way. I've always wanted . . ."

Logan throws his hand up and Anders high-fives him over the table. "Predictable," Logan says, giving Vee an exaggerated grin as she pokes him in the shoulder.

Reese reaches across the table and grabs a piece of bacon from Vee's plate. "Hey," she says, slapping his hand. She pouts when the greasy meat lands on the speckled green tabletop. "Now neither of us gets it."

Reese plucks the brown strip off the table, tips his head back, and lowers the drippy meat into his mouth.

"You disgust me."

"I heard a rumor you two dated." Reese's eyes dart to me, before settling on Vee again. "Maybe you'd like *my* bacon better than his." He melodramatically chews his bacon.

"Oh my"—Vee picks an orange wedge off her plate like she's going to throw it at his head—"gross."

"She liked my bacon just fine," I say. She turns shocked eyes my way. Finally! And as the orange flies in *my* direction, she's smiling. It only lasts a second, before she's squinting her eyes at me again. It's so quick I'm not sure I didn't imagine it, but it's something.

"You guys are weird," Pax mutters.

Vee points her fork at him, "You'll regret that comment when I'm the one prepping you for your big interviews," she teases.

I keep forgetting that Vee actually came on tour to work. "When do you start working with the publicist?" I ask. "It's Jenn, right?"

"Probably tomorrow, when production starts, right?" She's looking to Logan like he's got all the answers. Logan who secretly invited her onto the bus. My friend, Logan. At least I thought we were friends, before he turned my life upside down again.

"Is it weird that I haven't gotten details yet?" Vee nudges him when he doesn't say anything.

"Right," Logan's eyes are fixed on the pile of eggs he's poking at, like he's digging for buried treasure. "I'm sure they'll give you all the details tomorrow." He sounds nervous. I think deep down, we're *all* feeling the pressure of what happens tomorrow.

By the end of dinner, everyone is talking about the cities they're looking forward to. Anders wants to see whale sharks at the Georgia Aquarium in Atlanta, and Logan wants to swim in the Atlantic Ocean for the first time in North Carolina. Pax is happy to be in any city where he can get out of the bus, away from his newly paired-up bandmates, Sid and Jaclyn. Reese is holding out for—no surprise—Sin City; the semifinals. Now all we have to do is actually stay in the game long enough to make it all happen.

It's after midnight and, like most nights, I'm lying wide awake in my bunk. Tomorrow it all starts. The cameras roll and we begin rehearsing at the first venue, in Houston. Pulling back my curtain, ready to head back to the bathroom, I stop when I see the soft glow coming from Vee's bunk. She's lying on her bed, her face illuminated by her Kindle. And for the first time in days she isn't wearing earbuds or surrounded by other people. The bus is moving and she's in her pajamas. She can't run. I lie back down, crossing my hands behind my neck and focusing on the bunk above me. I have to keep this casual.

VIRGINIA

"I got a tattoo." His voice startles me out of the silence, and before I can stop myself, I'm looking at him. He's lying on his bed in a pair of blue pajama pants and a thin gray T-shirt that clings to him everywhere. Everything about him is bigger than I remember. *Why am I even thinking about this?* Thankfully, he's fully dressed. Most of the guys sleep on the warm bus in nearly nothing, and I've seen more than my fair share of guy parts. Having to mill about in close quarters with ten guys who have just woken up—it's a constant game of divert-your-eyes. I pity the editing crew who will have to ensure the American public doesn't catch a glimpse of any of the private parts of the tour bus—or the band members.

Cam pulls up his sleeve to reveal an intricate black tattoo that wraps around his defined bicep. It looks like twisted lines of musical notes. It's a blur in the darkness. "A couple, actually," he says.

"Um, congratulations?"

"I bought a new guitar." He nods toward the case lying in the lounge of the bus, leaning against the black leather couch.

I turn and finally look right at him, maybe for the first time since I boarded this bus. "Cameron, just stop." No one else is awake, and this is the last chance I'll have to stop pretending. I don't want to do this thing where we pretend like we're two old friends catching up on the last year of our lives. *But when it comes down to it, isn't friends all that we were, really?* I just need to get that through my head, and this will all get easier.

"I tried fish."

"Excuse me, what?"

"I tried fish." He shrugs his shoulders. "And for the record, I hated it. Just like I knew I would."

"Great." I let my eyes wander around the bus, looking into

the sleeping cubbies that line the walls, out the windows, at the floor; anywhere but his face, or the tiny black curls of ink that I can see peeking out of the back of his shirt, creeping up his neck. Another tattoo. *God, I'm curious.*

"Your turn."

My eyes are still fixed on the tiny curls of ink. *Stop looking!* "For what?"

"Three things since I saw you last."

Three Things. *Hell, no.* He thinks we're actually going to go back to playing this flirty little game? I don't think so.

"I'm tired, and we have a big day tomorrow." I grab hold of the curtain next to me and give him a tight smile, reminding myself that soon the cameras will start rolling. And once my internship starts, I'll need to put on this show 24/7. "Goodnight, Cam." I try to keep my voice even as I say the words, even though the familiarity of it hurts my heart. "Congrats on the tattoo . . . and the fish."

CHAPTER FOUR

THEN

CAMERON

The first day of school goes exactly like I knew it would. Lots of staring, plenty of curious questions to dodge. Thankfully most of my teachers are talkative, leaving little time for anyone to get past the basics of "Where are you from?" *Wisconsin.* And "Why did you move?" *To be closer to family.*

The family part isn't a total lie. I do live less than a mile from Gram. And nobody gives a shit about Wisconsin, so no one even asks me what city. Which is good, because I panicked when I said it. I've been to Wisconsin once and it was for my cousin's wedding. I was ten. Lying about where I'm from wasn't the plan, but I had this horrible vision of every kid in my class Googling my name. Right after they looked me up on social media and came up empty. "Cameron Fuller California" would be a gold mine of info. But "Cameron Fuller Wisconsin"? Sorry about your luck.

A few people made it as far as asking me if I was pissed that my parents up and moved me my senior year. *Nah*, I said, casually. *It's cool being close to the beach.* Most of them just nod and smile. I know they're all looking for something interesting—a juicy piece of gossip or a flicker of scandal. They want to hear that I was expelled, or got a girl pregnant. Maybe I'm fresh out of rehab. Anything to spice up their small town. I don't give them anything to work with, but by the end of the week I'm sure I'll be pegged as a former gang member or recovering meth addict. People love a good story—I know I do—but unfortunately for them, my life and story are no longer public domain.

As soon as school lets out Friday I show up at Gram's. By 4:30 I've filled her in on the entire week, and by 5:30 she's dozed off. When 6:00 rolls around I know I should just leave, but I just can't get myself to do it. *Fifteen more minutes, Cameron.* The suspense is wearing on my nerves as every tiny sound has me holding my breath, waiting for her to come back. Like she promised. It's been a really long week, and I've been looking forward to this visit way more than I should have. While Gram sleeps I work on my homework, the tiny black detective's notebook already flipped open beside my textbook, ready to be filled. I'm using the metal food cart as a desk, scribbling out my World History notes, when I hear the door swing open and click closed.

"Happy Tuesday, Nonni! It's VA Day!"

VA Day? Is this some sort of weird holiday? For veterans? How do I not know this?

Her voice is so bouncy and light. Is she just one of those people who gets peppy and loud around old people? The nursing home makes me whisper, like there's a sleeping person around every corner. Which is sort of true.

The poster I found at school today is lying on the food-cart-turned-desk. MELON BALLERS is written across the top and a black-and-white picture of a band is stretched across the center. I don't recognize anyone in the grainy photo, despite having paid extra-careful attention throughout the day. It was wishful thinking, really—it's hard to tell if there's even a girl in the picture. The poster says:

WE NEED YOU!

IN OUR BAND

GUITAR PLAYER NEEDED ASAP!

At the bottom there's an email address, phone number, and a name: Anders.

The room is quiet, and then the squeal of a metal chair being dragged along the stone floor cuts through the silence. Something bumps into the dividing curtain, sending it fluttering toward my knees. My heart sinks in my chest. *She's going to find me.* The fabric brushes against my legs.

Then nothing. Silence.

I think maybe she left, until I hear the unmistakable twang of fingertips on metal and chords begin to fill the room. *Her guitar.* My own guitar had been sitting in my closet—untouched for months—until last night. I pulled it out to learn the song she played. Then I just kept going, for hours. I actually have two guitars—an acoustic Fender Dad gave me for my tenth birthday and a red Gibson that I bought right after I moved to Riverton. *With my blood money.* The same money that pays for my apartment. For everything.

The sound filling the room is rich and comforting. Every note is precise as her voice joins in with the music. It's nothing but a whisper at first, then grows louder and stronger as the song goes on. It's beautiful. Strong but gentle; and somehow her voice conveys so much more emotion than the lyrics alone ever could.

Push me, pull me,
take me or leave me . . .
the way I am, can't be like them.

Under the lens, out of the box,
waiting to explode
tick tick tock boom.
Push me, pull me,
it's over once you hold me.
Tick tick tock boom.

Her voice trails off and the last note hangs in the air. It feels thick and heavy, like the words are still trapped in the small room with us. If I felt guilty before, it's nothing compared to how I feel after hearing her sing. It's so personal. I might as well have opened her diary and flipped through the damn pages. I didn't deserve to hear that song and I feel more than a little guilty now. *I'm a creep.*

"You should play it," Evelyn says.

I wonder if it's one of her band's songs. If she'll play it at their bar gig next weekend.

"I just did." She pauses. "For you."

"Not for me. You should play it for someone else. Anyone else."

"I can't, Nonni. Someday . . . maybe."

"Someday will be here before you know it, Ginny. Eventually we all run out of tomorrows."

True story, Nonni.

"I know. I'm just not ready. It's not ready, it needs more work." Her voice is so soft, I wonder if she's crying. "The second verse is still shaky."

The second verse was tight.

"And there's something off with the bridge."

It was perfect.

The mood has changed drastically, her raucous, bouncing laughter from earlier gone now. The girl who was here yesterday was electric. Fierce. The girl I picture now is fragile and soft around the edges. I want the ringing laughter that cleared my head and made me forget.

Playing my guitar has always made me feel free. Playing hers seems to be making her crazy. That song was perfection—what could possibly stop her from playing it for someone? It can be fixed, whatever it is. People underestimate how many things are capable of being fixed. There are so few things in life that are actually final. Just death. And I'm pretty sure she isn't dying.

Conflicts: Stage fright?

"It will never be perfect," Nonni says. "You just need to get out there. Take some risks. It's your senior year, Ginny. Have fun."

"Nonni—"

"Shush. I know you think you'll have time for everything later. And you will. But I want you to do things now. I want you to put yourself out there." There's a long moment of silence. I can hear everyone breathing and I swear they must be able to hear me, too. Every muscle in my body is tensed. I'm afraid to make the slightest movement.

"I want that too. I—I wish I could, but—"

Evelyn doesn't let her finish. "I want you to do something for me." Her voice is pleading. "Will you?"

"Of course. What is it?"

"I want you to promise me." Evelyn's voice is firm, determined.

"Sure. Yes, of course I will." She sounds nervous, filled with anticipation.

"I want you to say yes."

I have no idea what she means, and it seems that Ginny is just as confused, because the room is silent.

"Say yes to what exactly?" Ginny asks.

"To everything. To anything."

Silence.

"Unless you'll end up dead or on a MISSING poster, I want you to say yes." There's another long silence, and I hold my breath, waiting. "You're a smart girl, you'll know the right choice. The world won't fall apart if you make a mistake."

"Nonni—"

"I want you to do this for me." Ginny doesn't say anything. I wish I were one of those people who could swim the length of a pool underwater. All I can hear is my breathing. "Do it for your old, dying grandmother."

Boom. Just like that Evelyn goes nuclear. Old people love to play the I-won't-be-around-forever card. It trumps everything. There's a long silence and I'm starting to think maybe Ginny left.

"Fine." Her voice is strained, like she's been asked to put her hand in a blender, but is still trying to sound happy about it.

Habits/Mannerisms: Puts up a good front. Brave in the face of blendered hands.

"But I'm not even missing out like you think I am." She's calmer now, her voice gaining some confidence.

"Well, I certainly hope I'm wrong, honey. But you've made me very happy. I look forward to hearing about your adventures . . . big and small."

Ginny stays for another hour, making small talk and playing one more song. There's still no laughter or teasing—none of the brightness she arrived with. When she finally leaves, this overwhelming feeling fills me; the desire to run after her and see who she is. To know her name, her story, ask her why she won't play that amazing song for anyone. Why she doesn't want to play it out in the hallway or on the goddamn street corner, so everyone can hear it. But that's impossibly complicated, of course. What would I even say? *"Oh, hey, I've been hanging out in your grandma's room for hours, listening to you. I just thought I'd say hi. Maybe you could fill me in on the details of your life? Oh, and I'm also writing about you."* If I was lucky it would get me pepper-sprayed. Worst case, I'm labeled a stalker and watched by all three hundred students at Riverton High, who would no doubt hear of my treachery by morning bell.

I stay for a while, giving Evelyn some time to fall asleep before I make my exit. There has to be an easier way to satisfy my curiosity. I pull the poster out of my bag and dial the ten-digit number scribbled at the bottom.

I've been sitting on the edge of my bed for the last hour, letting my fingers run over the cold strings of Betty, my long-neglected Fender. Each strum and pluck chases away another piece of the nervous energy that's been rushing through me, setting me on edge. A sort of panic had rushed over me the second I sent that text. I expected some time to think things over. To talk myself out of it. Convince myself it's a horrible fucking idea to meet her. The guy, Anders, was so excited he insisted I come to their practice tonight to try out. I've played in bands since middle school—I think the spot could be mine if I want it.

Do I actually want it?

At nine o'clock, I pull up to the house, set deep in the corn-filled farmland that lies beyond the beaches and downtown shops of Riverton. The driveway is full of cars, and the pumping rhythm of bass filters out of the house. I try the knob and when it gives way I let myself in, following the music to a set of stairs that leads into a walk-out basement. The first person I see is someone I recognize.

"Cameron?" His hand shoots out toward me. "Hey, man. I'm

Anders." He's severely skinny and in my World History class. Logan, a guy with a black Fender slung over his shoulder, nods up at me when Anders runs off his name. He never moves from his place behind the microphone stand. *Donut Guy.* The bassist is a junior named Steve and one of the few people in Riverton I feel like I haven't seen before.

Disappointment sets in when the introductions end. *Where the hell is she?* I scan the large space, hoping I've missed someone. "This is everybody?"

Anders is sitting behind his drum set, a black stick in each hand, twisting one around the tips of his fingers. "Yup."

"Who sings?"

"We all do. A little." Anders is only half paying attention to me as he taps one of the brassy cymbals. "Mostly Logan, but he could use help. Our old guitarist, Phil, sang most of the backup. He was crazy good, too. Dad got transferred to Minneapolis a few months ago." His voice holds the same distress as the guys on the national news who deliver hurricane death tolls. *"In Florida, three people were killed today in a tropical storm that swept off the west shore. In other news, a Michigan band has lost their beloved guitarist after a devastating job relocation. Details at ten . . ."*

"I sing." The words spew out before I can think it through. *Shit.* I don't even want to stay. *She's not even here!* "A little. I mean . . . depends on the style." This may be the most words I've voluntarily said to anyone in the two months since I moved here. *And look how well it's going.*

Anders continues tapping the cymbal. "Okay, let's play. See how it feels." Logan and Steve are tuning up as I plug in.

This is a stupid idea.

I spend most of the first song—a punky-pop cover I know well—wondering what I'm still doing here. I should just leave. I came to satisfy my curiosity about Ginny, and apparently she isn't even coming. I make a mental note:

Personality Traits: Pathological liar. Temptress. Not in a fucking band.

By the second song I've drifted out of myself, letting my nerves slip away. By the third, I feel like someone else, and also more like myself than I have in months. I've forgotten about everything around me and everything behind me. Each time a song ends, Anders yells out, "Hell, yes!" or "Fuck yeah!" from behind his set. *I guess he's into it.* I close my eyes and feel the vibration of the music run through me, the bass drum pounding in my chest like a second heartbeat, the heat in my fingers against the cold strings. The bass tingles in my toes.

I'm not sure exactly when it happens, because of my music-induced mind-buzz. During a chorus—when Anders's shout pulls me out of my thoughts again—I see her. She's leaning against the doorway, a white binder in her hands and a purple messenger bag hanging from her shoulder. My stomach bottoms out at the thought that it might be her. *I recognize this girl.* She's in a couple of my classes.

As the song ends, Logan waves the girl over. "This is VA. She's our official manager. And unofficial groupie."

VA Day.

"You know I hate that word, Logan." Her hands go to her hips and she's glaring at him, but her voice is still friendly. "It makes it sound like I'm here to have sex with everybody."

"Well . . ." A giant smile spreads across Logan's face and he's ducking away from her before she even moves.

They move in sync like stuntmen. She aims low, anticipating him, landing a smack across his shoulder. "Logan Samuel Hart."

Logan throws his hands up in the air. "I'm kidding, I'm kidding. Settle down."

"He"—her pointed finger is aimed at me—"doesn't know that."

Logan turns to me with a serious face. "Listen." His voice is deadpan. "She's not here to have sex with all of us." He turns back to her with a mocking grin. "There, now he knows. It's official." He puts two fingers to his forehead in a tiny salute. She's shaking her head and smacking her fist into her palm, but a smile is already starting to play at the corners of her mouth. *Obviously, they're friends—or siblings.*

"I'm Vee." She finally sticks her hand out to me, shaking her head and smiling. "Only Logan calls me VA."

"Cameron. I'm in your math class, actually."

"Right." She nods, lazily, and I have to remind myself that she doesn't know me. And she's blissfully unaware of just how much I know about her. "Hey, Cam."

Cam? Huh. Interesting. Everyone has always called me Cameron. All three syllables, every time. My mom used to say that if she wanted people to call me Cam, she would have named me that.

Am I a "Cam" now? I guess I can roll with it. "What's the VA stand for?" *Friends can ask that sort of thing. We're friends now, right? You already "Cam"-ed me, after all.*

"Virginia."

"Like the state."

"The nineties song," Anders says, smiling. " 'Meet Virginia'?"

I shake my head. I don't know it.

Anders starts humming and Logan sings, "Meet Virginia, I can't wait to meet Virginia—"

She rolls her eyes. "No one calls me that, though. Just Vee. Or VA, if you want to be like Logan." The way she says it makes me think I don't.

Vee. VA. Virginia . . . Ginny. Definitely her.

She's nothing like I imagined. She isn't ridiculously thin. No giant tree trunk legs. Her hair is long, in waves over her shoulders, a million shades of brown and blond. Still, seeing her now it all fits together in my mind. Even in her faded jeans, I can imagine her in the leather pants of my mental picture; the tattered T-shirt hanging off her shoulder, the crazy hair. Maybe it's in there somewhere.

Vee opens her binder, pulling out small squares of yellow paper. "Parking passes for the gig at Carnivale this weekend."

The bar gig.

"Put them in your windshield and we can park in the reserved spaces to unload." She hands one to each of the guys, stopping in front of me and looking over to Logan and Anders.

"You in, Cam?" Anders makes a show of crossing his fingers in front of him and looking up to the sky as if he's praying.

"I'm in." The words escape so quickly, I almost don't have time to second-guess them. *Almost.*

A huge smile fills Vee's face as she begins slowly chanting, "Cam! Cam! Cam!" Everyone joins in, clapping and shouting. Anders beats on his drum. Logan plays a crazy riff on his guitar. Looking at Vee—cheeks red against her light hair—it feels like a fifty-pound weight has dropped from around my neck, as I realize that this is my chance to start over. To be a new version of me.

Cam.

Cam has zero baggage—no complicated past. People don't look at him like he's going to break. There are no expectations for Cam.

Cam is freedom.

My fresh start.

VIRGINIA

I'm sitting in my usual corner, across from the band, scribbling down the last of my Calc exercises. The guys are herding up the stairs to the kitchen, like it's filled with naked girls. Or beer . . . I imagine the reactions are similar. Usually everyone has at least one can under their belt by now, but I don't see any empties lying around. Either Cam's appearance distracted them, or Logan's older brother Drew hasn't been home from college to replenish the stash they keep in the garage. Tucking my book into my bag, I'm ready to head upstairs to grab a snack, when I see that Cam's still sitting on a stool next to the equipment, guitar in hand. Just a few feet away. He's playing softly, unplugged, and the song becomes familiar as it grows louder.

" 'Yellow Shirt'?" I ask.

"Yeah." His eyes are on me, but he keeps playing.

"I've never met anyone who actually knows The Icarus Account. They're one of my favorites." I'm trying to keep my excitement in check, but I love this song. I played it for Nonni a few days ago—it's basically my personal anthem. Except you won't catch me in a yellow shirt. For me, it's purple.

He nods. His eyes drift from me to the guitar, then around the room. The only sound that fills the space is the melody of my favorite song, drifting from his fingertips, as we both stare at the dingy gray carpet.

"The guys are probably upstairs grabbing beers if you want one." I wonder if he drinks. The guys getting drunk at practice is one of my pet peeves. I'm not opposed to drinking—I'm not looking to be a nun, or anything—it's just that half of the time I end up having to drive one of them home when things get sloppy. Which is often. Logan's dad is gone on business a lot and his mom lives in Florida with her new husband, Tomas. Even when Logan's dad *is* around, he's not interested in what goes on downstairs. *Boys will be boys.* I sometimes wonder if the guys can even play sober anymore. "They're probably slamming them to catch up."

"I'm good. It'll be hard enough, trying to get home in this corn maze." He's still playing, softly humming along. I could hug him right now, but I just smile instead.

"Is there not a lot of corn in Wisconsin?" His eyes stay on the guitar strings. I'm not sure if he's shaking his head or swaying along to the song, but I don't care about corn. I'm just trying to fill silence.

"Do you ever play with them?" Cam drops a note, catching up again clumsily. "I mean, do you play? Guitar . . . or anything?" He suddenly seems nervous, his eyes drifting between me and his stumbling hands.

"I do, actually. But just for fun. Playing in public isn't really my thing." Playing my guitar makes me feel whole, and powerful. I feel honest when I play, like I can say anything. I can share my hurt and my anger, and let it all out, because no one hates you when you share your feelings in a song. Lyrics are full of gray area and room for interpretation. But the thought of playing in front of people makes me want to cry and puke and scream, all at the same time. It's a great visual.

"Plus, it's sort of a boys' club. I doubt Logan would be interested in me playing with them." I have no idea, because I've never asked. Logan hasn't heard me play in five years. I'm not sure he even knows I still play. For the last few years, I've become the unofficial songwriter for the band. Most of the time that feels like enough.

"I guess it's a girlfriend thing," Cam says. There's this apologetic smile plastered to his face that makes me a little nauseous, because Cam isn't the first person to mistakenly peg us for a couple. Especially up until last year, before my best friend Cort graduated. With her and Anders dating, and Logan and me spending so much time with them, the four of us looked like a permanent double date. I've always suspected it's the reason I've only had one serious boyfriend. *Who turned out to be* seriously *disappointing.* "You can blame Yoko Ono," he adds.

"Oh." I shake my head. "No. Logan and I aren't . . . together."

His lip twitches, like he wants to smile, and it makes me smile.

I can't help but stare at his twitchy lips, while he plays my favorite song. "Logan's one of my best friends. Anders, too. We've been friends forever."

"Well, if you ever want to get together, just let me know. I'd love to play with you." He shakes his head gently, his long hair falling in his eyes. "I mean I'm not weird about playing with girls." His eyes are darting around the room again, looking anywhere but at me and I can't help but laugh. "I just mean . . . I can do that . . . if you want someone to play with you . . ."

I think he just muttered "fuck," and I burst into laughter.

". . . and I realize how that sounds, and it's not how I meant it." He finally shuts up and smiles, showing off his perfect white teeth.

Everything about Cam feels polished and crisp, unlike the other guys, who are wearing hoodies and wrinkled T-shirts. Cam feels like a perfectly styled photo shoot, every prop in its place, every angle checked and rechecked. He doesn't belong in Riverton any more than I belong in a band. As weird as it sounds, he doesn't even belong in Logan's dimly lit basement. He belongs on that surfboard, out in the sun.

CHAPTER FIVE

NOW

VIRGINIA

Nothing good can ever come after the words "There's something I have to tell you." Especially when Logan is looking at me like he knows he's in trouble. He hasn't looked this guilty since he convinced me to be in the basketball team's date auction our junior year—and then forgot to bid on me. I had to go bowling with Jason Fetner, a brace-faced ninth-grade kid whose one redeeming quality was that Hampton (his pet hamster) had his own YouTube channel. It was adorable—still is.

We're all squished in the front lounge of the bus, waiting for our tour briefing, now that the production crew has all flown in and boarded their matching bus. I'm sitting on one end of the leather couch, wedged between the upholstered wall and Logan. "What?"

Across from us, Anders has gone back to playing a beat on his bongo drum, while Cam hums to himself, scribbling in his notebook. All he's been doing lately is writing. When he's not holding his guitar he's carrying around that damn notebook. And it really grinds me, because since the moment I stepped onto this bus the one thing I can't do is write. Not anything

I want to write, at least. Everything that does want to come out of me feels like dredging up ancient history. I refuse to put *that* down on paper. I won't memorialize this feeling—I've already done it once. If you listen carefully to half of the band's songs, it's all right there. The story of *my* life—*my* pain—set to Logan's music.

Logan shifts on the couch. "It probably isn't even that big of a deal. You should probably know, though." Anders snickers under his breath.

I twist on the couch to face Logan. "Spill it, Hart."

"It's about your internship."

Not what I was expecting. I've been anxious to find out more about my internship.

He rubs a hand over his head. "The whole internship—well, it's a little different than what I had told you . . ." There's a long pause and his eyes seem to be fixed on the car driving by, outside our window. "So, well—there isn't actually an *official* internship with the tour." His head is dipped down and he looks at me like he's not sure he should make eye contact. *He shouldn't. This is* such *a Logan thing to do.* No wonder I got such a weird look from the bus driver—I don't even belong on his bus!

"What?" I launch myself into the aisle so I'm standing in front of him. I've been on this bus for less than a week. I haven't seen a single city—we're not even close to Nashville—and I haven't even seen them perform yet. "Logan, that's the whole reason I'm here!" Before I can get away, he has me by the wrist.

"Whoa, whoa. Settle down, Little Miss Temper." He pulls me back onto the couch. "You can still help us—do all the stuff you used to do. You'll be *our* intern. It's practically the same thing."

Except it's not anything close to the same thing. Now I really am just tagging along, like some kind of glorified groupie, showing up at every show, acting like I'm a member of the inner circle.

"This isn't a big deal, Vee—"

The sound of the air lock interrupts us, as the door folds open. A man in his forties in gray dress pants and a bright white shirt steps in, followed by a tall woman in her late twenties. Her hair is bright blond and twisted behind her head. She has a silver tablet in one hand, and a black stylus in the other. Behind them, two guys stand at the bottom of the stairs with cameras hanging at their waists.

The man pulls off a pair of expensive-looking sunglasses before speaking, "I'm Jared, the production manager"—he points to the woman next to him—"this is Jenn, head of tour publicity. I wanted to take a quick moment to introduce myself, welcome you all to the tour." He pulls his phone out of his pocket. "Go through the lists," he says, tapping the tablet in Jenn's hand.

"Sure, I can do that." Her tone is the same one my mom used with my dad when he asked her to do something that he clearly could have done for himself. She reads through everyone's names, confirming spelling, asking for ages and what instruments everyone plays. Jared is still running his finger across the screen of his phone, and I swear he's just fake-busy. It's been nothing but swipe, swipe, swipe.

Jenn's eyes settle on me. "And you are?" She looks down at her tablet, like maybe she's missed something.

Oh, God. "I'm Vee. Virginia. I thought I was—"

"She's with us," Logan interrupts, and Jenn's eyebrow twitches. "I mean, we just figured—since we have an extra bunk and all."

Jared's head snaps up from his phone. "You don't get to just bring whoever you want on the bus."

"She's our songwriter, too—" Cam tries to interject.

"This is our bus—not yours," Jared says.

It's over. And I'm surprised by how disappointed I am, because three days ago, I wanted to run.

Jenn glances at Cam and then Logan, before looking at me. "Are you together?"

"Yes," Logan says, as I shake my head no. *What is he doing?*

"What the fu—" Cam mutters.

Jenn's shrewd eyes dart around again, from me to Logan to Cam before landing on me again. "You can stay."

"Really?" *Why would they want me here?*

"Don't argue, Vee," Anders mutters, shaking his head, like I'm an idiot.

Jared looks at Jenn, who nods. He shoves his phone back in his pocket and makes his way out of the bus. The two cameramen waiting outside take his place next to Jenn, who is now, officially, my favorite person on this bus.

"Like Logan said, you guys have an extra bunk." The way Jenn is tapping her stylus on her tablet so quickly, it sounds like a drum cadence. "It won't hurt anything." She points her stylus at me. "You'll have to sign all the same releases as the bands."

"Of course." I'm nodding like a crazy person, relieved—and surprised—I'm not getting booted off this bus on day three. *But am I really staying?* Maybe, if I just give it some time—even a city or two—I can fix this. Make it worth it. Figuring out how to turn "unofficial groupie" into something resume-worthy seems easier than calling my mother and asking for a plane ticket. *That* would mean admitting how gullible I had been. How desperate I was to not go home for the summer.

Jenn introduces us to our camera guys, Tad and Dave, and goes over the itinerary for the first week, telling the guys how they'll have to tape at least one "confessional" interview each day, answering questions from production crew or her assistants, Kaley and Priya.

Ten minutes later, Jenn leaves us in the bus lounge.

Jenn gave us a lot of information, but all I have is questions. "So where are all the other girlfriends, if they're allowed?"

Reese grunts in amusement. "Mine's in storage."

"There's Jaclyn," Logan says.

"Jaclyn's in the band."

Anders has gone back to lightly tapping his drum. "This is a music tour, Vee. Who wants to bring a girlfriend along?" Then he turns apologetic. "No offense."

"I'm not a *real* girlfriend, you can't offend me." But he's right. *God, does this mean I'm on a bus with* ten *single guys?* I look at Logan, still holding on to my arm. *Nine.* I let out a deep breath and force myself not to obsess over this. I should be relieved. "I'm not leaving." And I think I'm telling myself, more than them.

The real madness starts in the afternoon, when the crew starts filing off of their bus. There are twelve full-time camera guys—two assigned to each bus—and all day they've been pulling the guys away to do interviews. When they aren't getting ready for their first show, they're talking into thin air, responding to questions and trying to act natural. They're pretty much nailing it, except for one overly anxious drummer. Anders is the absolute worst at acting natural. He's one of the biggest attention-whores I've ever met, but once he gets in front of a camera his body goes rigid. Every sentence that comes out of his mouth sounds like it's been mixed in a blender. Maybe I'm not part of the actual publicity team, but I know I can fix this. *He's going to be my pet project; my pièce de résistance as an aspiring publicist.*

CAM

It's hard to breathe when the camera is pointed at me like a firing squad rifle.

"You all went to high school together, right?" Priya prompts me.

"Right, well, except—"

Priya cuts me off. "Don't tell me"—she points to where Tad is standing beside her—"talk to the camera," she says, for probably the nineteenth time. "And be sure to include the question in your answer."

Like a freaking Miss America contestant. I nod. "Me, Logan, and Anders were in a high school band together."

Priya is waving her hand, encouraging me to keep talking, but I don't know what else to say.

"What do you think about Logan bringing his girlfriend on tour? Is that uncomfortable?"

"Why would it be uncomfortable?"

She points to the camera.

"It's not weird at all that Vee's on tour—Vee's always been part of the band. We all love Vee."

Priya turns to Tad. "Time?"

Tad looks at his screen and quickly replies, "7:42:06."

Priya makes a note on her tablet.

"What's the time for?"

Priya shrugs, "We just like to note places we may want to come back to for editing." She smiles and continues. "So let's talk about Logan. He said he's fine with being considered co-frontmen. How do you feel about it?"

When the interview finally ends, it feels like I've been in the little makeshift room for an hour, but it's been more like twenty minutes. Vee is waiting outside, and Priya waves her in as I leave.

VIRGINIA

They talk to the guys one-on-one, in pairs—as a group. Jenn didn't make it seem like I would be in front of the cameras much, so when I'm included in the one-on-one interviews, it's strange and unexpected. It's even stranger when I start getting questions about being Logan's girlfriend. *Ugh. Girlfriend.* Whenever I think the word, I cringe. *Logan's* girlfriend—a title I once actively avoided. My interview is mostly about my involvement with the band. My experience as their high school manager, what I did during their time in LA, and when I met them. Specifically, when I met Logan, and how long we've been *together.* It feels like a slippery slope to lie, and the truth—we've been *together* one day—isn't an option. I stick to the details of our friendship and don't veer too far from the truth. Still, every time I hear that word—"girlfriend"—I get this ache in my gut. I may not have the courage to be an actual musician, but I'm not a glorified assistant anymore. I've been feeding Logan songs for the last year. In the fall, I'll be interning at a PR firm in Chicago. That's a huge deal for a sophomore. But for now, I'm nothing but an accessory standing in the wings again. A glorified groupie along for the ride. Maybe hopping on a bus based on a too-good-to-be-true job offer from Logan wasn't my best choice ever. *Who knew, right?*

CAM

The cameras are a serious adjustment. At first, I notice them everywhere. They're outside our bunks when we wake up, sitting in the lounge while we talk through new songs. It feels like they see everything. Like they are literally everywhere, even though there are only two cameras to follow all twelve of the people on our bus. There's this one cameraman in particular—a tatted-up guy named Tad—who seems to be with our band constantly. The other cameraman hops between Caustic Underground and The Phillips. I can't help but wonder what makes us so damn interesting. Then I remind myself that the coverage is good—it's what we need. It's weird to even think of us as a "we" again. In a lot of ways, we're still all getting to know each other again. And now we need viewers to get to know us too.

Starting next week, the American public doesn't just get to see our performances on TV, they'll see footage of us behind the scenes, too. I hope they come up with something more interesting than watching me get dressed, microwave food, or write songs, because Your Future X needs to be the band that viewers want to watch. I'm trying not to let my distaste for the cameras show, even though there's something about Tad—and his obvious obsession with Logan and Vee—that feels really off, somehow. His stupid camera catches everything. Every shared joke, each hand placed on the small of her back as she gets onto the bus or into a cab. *I don't know when Logan became such a fucking gentleman.* Every playful kiss to her head and every lingering hug will be forever captured online. I could watch it all over and over, for the rest of my life, if I wanted to. If I wanted to torture myself.

It's bad enough living it. At the same time, the thought that I'll be able to see her in those videos whenever I want, when this is all over—it brings me a certain sense of calm.

VIRGINIA

The first two venues of the tour are small. They remind me of the local bars The Melon Ballers would play. The producers want the whole tour to mimic the reality of a rising band, so they're all starting at mom-and-pop bars and clubs. Each week, the venues will get bigger and the productions more elaborate, with fewer bands playing each week. At the end of the sixteen-week stretch, one band will walk away with a record deal and the hearts of the nation. They actually say that in the show intro— "the hearts of the nation." *Cheesy, but true.* The first two shows will be taped, so there's no pressure of a live performance, and no bands will be cut. They'll basically be elaborate practice runs to generate some buzz before the live tapings begin, and tickets are already sold out.

When we load into the first venue, a graffiti-covered two-story bar on the outskirts of Houston, I can't help but be sucked into the memories of past gigs. *I have missed this.* In the afternoon light, everything looks dark and dirty and old. It feels wrong to be here in the daytime, when all of the imperfections are on display. The light fixtures are dulled—probably by years' worth of smoke—and the cement walls are covered in thousands of names scribbled in a rainbow of Sharpie. Thin blue tubes run along the ceiling. I imagine what the walls will look like glowing under the black lights—a tangled web of graffiti popping off of the walls like neon signs.

The crew brings in case after case, loading in the speaker boxes and instruments, and the backstage area begins to look and feel like a storage locker. Trying to escape the claustrophobic towers of equipment, I hop onto a stool in the bar area and begin to scribble notes. The first pseudo-publicist task I've given myself is to update the band's website. Their bio and FAQ sections are first up, because they're embarrassing. Nothing has been updated in ages. Reese's picture looks like a bad selfie taken in a bar bathroom, and Cam isn't even listed as a band member. I jot down a list of questions I think viewers—hopefully their future fans—will want to know. I have a sheet's worth of questions penned when the familiar hum of tuning guitars distracts me. Up on the stage, in all their glory, is my band—My Future X. I can't help but feel a swell of love for these guys for bringing me along on this journey. Even Reese—who has made it his mission to embarrass me with his dirty jokes and shameless flirting—has assured me he wants me here (even if it's just as entertainment value).

Up on the small wooden stage, Anders clicks off the beginning of the first song. Logan and Cam are seamless as they trade off vocals, switching from lead to backup, coming together in perfect harmonies. They're so in sync—a well-oiled machine—like two voices that started as one and are finally being joined together again. It seems like yesterday—and also a lifetime ago—since I last saw them do this. Each of them is lit up from the inside out, happiness and joy radiating off of them in waves, as they belt out each song.

Maybe it's muscle memory, but my eyes can't help but lock on Cam and his guitar. He always was—and still is—like a magnetic force onstage. I watch his hands, sliding up and down the long fret of his honey gold Fender, strumming and plucking and teasing each string. His muscles tensing and relaxing as he moves around the stage, looking so comfortable. My breathing slows as my eyes trace up from his hands to his arms—the black curls of his tattoo still taunting me from the edge of his T-shirt. I want to read the tiny words penned along those twisting notes, curving up and around his hard bicep. Having his voice fill my ears again is like the moments right before you fall asleep, when it's hard to distinguish dream from reality.

My neck heats as I drag my eyes over his broad chest, let them wander across his face, and up to his eyes. Still so green, still so sad, still so—*looking* at me. *God, Virginia, get a grip.* My chest burns hot as I turn back to my website work, contemplating something embarrassing to secretly include in his bio.

The songs drifting off of the stage are some of my favorites. One that I wrote years ago, another that Logan and I worked on first semester, before he left for LA, and a few from high school. Listening to them is like watching old family movies, like being wrapped up in a memory. When they finish the last song of their practice set, I hop to my feet, clapping and whooping, and I know I must look like a crazy person, but I can't help it. *This is it.* I'm watching their dreams come true right in front of me. At this moment, wrapped in the memories, soaked in the songs, it doesn't feel like it was that long ago that this was *my* dream. *My* someday.

The guys jump off the stage one by one, and Logan grabs me around the waist, pulling me off the ground as he spins around with me. This is Flying High off a Performance Logan; my favorite Logan. He uses his palms to wipe my cheeks. I hadn't even realized the tears had started.

"You're a giant, sappy nerd. You know that, right?"

"I do." I drag my sleeve over my wet eyes. "But you guys were incredible." The tears are coming even heavier now, even though I'm smiling. "This is going to be amazing," I say, and suddenly I'm throwing my arms around Cam, engulfing him in a hug. He just stands there at first, frozen in place. Then his arms wrap around me, his hands barely brushing my back. I can smell the mint of his breath, feel his soft T-shirt under my fingertips, hard muscles just underneath. *What am I doing?* Giving him a tight smile, I extricate myself, before hugging Anders. I give Reese an awkward high-five, which turns into him pulling me into a hug. Then he hoists me over his shoulder, spinning us in circles.

I'm screaming, as the lights of the stage become a twist of blurring red lines. "Down!" There's a new band setting up onstage and I can hear their laughter as their faces blur by me. Stage left, Tad has his camera trained on us, and beside him, Kaley is spinning her finger in the air, egging Reese on.

CAM

It's been almost two years since the last time I was onstage, playing songs that I wrote, feeling the energy of the music moving through me, electrifying me. Being onstage tonight, under the hot lights—the audience a mass of blacked-out faces—it makes me feel alive. I can't see them, but for once, I feel like they see me. They hear me. Without saying the words, I share everything I've ever felt. Everything that I try to keep hidden. By the time we finish our fourth song of the night, and relinquish the stage to Caustic Underground, everything in me is laid out in the open, exposed and raw under the black lights.

Vee is standing in the wings, in the purple Melon Ballers shirt she's always worn when we play. A good-luck shirt. That's what she told Logan, when he asked why she wouldn't wear one of the new Your Future X shirts being sold at the shows. When we met with Jenn to discuss the promo for our band, Vee had suggested the shirts be purple. We all agreed. Not because we care, but because she does and we don't. The shirts are already being sold tonight at our first show, and it's pretty hilarious to see girls in the audience wearing T-shirts that say YOUR FUTURE x. Maybe it's prophetic.

By the time the other two bands finish playing it's nearly midnight. As the last of our equipment is loaded, Vee is standing in the alley. Leaning against the metal door, her face is illuminated by the glow of her phone. The bus is idling, ready to take off for the next stop, when Vee finally makes her way back onto the bus. She lies down on her bed, pulling the curtain closed until the last foot. She never closes it all the way, she always leaves a gap. So I do, too. That way I get to see her face. And when she sleeps, it doesn't feel like we're us. It feels like we're *them*. The people we were back before there was ever a Me and Vee. As she rustles around behind the curtain, I know she's trying to change into her pajamas in the tiny space.

"Everything all right?" I say.

One of her feet slips out of the curtain. "Yes." With a final grunt, she pulls back the curtain. "I'm actually getting pretty good at this."

"I meant the phone call." I give her a half smile. "But you really are getting good at the undercover changing. You know you could use the bathroom."

She snorts. "Totally not worth having to walk through this bus in my PJs, thank you."

"So . . ."

"Oh." She's not saying anything. *Maybe she's gone back to ignoring me.* "I was just calling home, talking to my mom."

"How is she?"

"She's fine." Both of us are lying on our backs, whispering in the dark.

"Then what's the problem?"

"Just some stuff going on at home with my parents. It's a long story." She's lying still, looking up at the ceiling, and I think our conversation—if you can call it that—must be over already. Finally she breaks the silence. "I haven't told her yet—about the internship." She makes air quotes with her fingers.

"Would she care?"

"That I'm spending the summer with a bunch of wannabe rock stars, instead of working, or getting college credit, or living at her house?" She rolls her eyes. "Yes, she'd care."

"It's not like she can make you go home."

"Sure she can."

"You're nineteen, Vee."

"And she's my mom." She rolls onto her back and rubs circles on her temples. "My mom, who pays for college." At the end of the bed, her feet are tapping a hectic rhythm against the wall, and it won't be long before she wakes up Pax in the bunk above her.

This is what Vee looks like right before she starts panicking.

"Relax. She's not going to find out."

"And I just don't tell her? I keep it from her?"

"You can tell her when you get back. It's not a big deal, Vee. It's a tiny lie."

Vee's eyes are cold, and fixed on mine, and I regret my words before I even hear hers.

"Right. Just tiny lies." She shakes her head and turns her back to me, her voice muffled by her pillow. "*Those* never come back to haunt us, do they?"

CHAPTER SIX

THEN

CAM

Two hours into my first Melon Ballers practice, I feel like things are clicking into place. We're meshing, finding our groove.

Vee looks up from her notebook between songs. "Don't forget to bring your clothes to practice Thursday night." She tosses the red notebook onto her bag and turns toward us. "Please." Her voice is dramatically sweet as she gives the guys an exaggerated Cheshire cat smile.

"Creepy, Vee," Logan mutters.

I'm confused. "Our clothes?"

"The clothes you're going to wear for the gig at Carnivale on Satur—"

Anders doesn't let her finish. "Vee likes to make sure we're dressed appropriately." His tone is sarcastic, but a smile spreads across his face. "She just likes to watch us change. We're her man meat." Logan almost chokes on the beer he's drinking.

Vee picks up a random sock lying next to her and chucks it at Anders. "*Gross.* I think you mean 'man *candy*,' because I've never seen your man *meat*. And I don't plan to." Her nose is scrunched up like she's disgusted by the idea. "And if you want a manager who doesn't care about anything, then ask Drew to make some time for you in his busy college schedule. I'm just trying to avoid a repeat of the great farm convention incident."

Logan shakes his head. "You're never going to let that go, are you?"

"You guys played a farm convention?" I'm having a hard time picturing it.

"No." They all say in unison, sounding annoyed.

Vee turns to me. "Last year, we played at Fall Fest. It was one of our biggest gigs ever, and these guys"—Vee stabs a finger at each of them—"all showed up in flannel."

Everyone is laughing, except Vee. And me. I don't even *own* flannel. I think the state of California actually banned the sale of it.

"Oh, yeah, laugh it up. One person wears flannel, okay. Fine. But all of you show up in flannel, and you look like those freaking animatronic bears from Disney World who play banjos and wear suspenders and scare the kids." Anders is hunched over his set, shaking with laughter. Vee looks like she wants to hit him with something much worse than a sock. "So yes, I'm checking your clothes. Because I love you. And because I—not you—get blamed when you show up looking like you should be carrying fiddles and washboards."

"So is there a uniform, then?"

She looks surprised, but come on. She can't be serious with this.

"Anything that makes you look like you *belong* in a band."

I smile at her. "I kind of thought the guitar did that."

"I guess the polo shirt was distracting me from the guitar." She cocks her head to the side and gives me an odd smile.

Maybe I should tell her that I *used* to have a lot of really kick-ass clothes. But moving to Michigan meant a fresh start—in every way. And pulling my guitar out of storage doesn't mean I have to go back. "I'll see what I can find."

"And you'll bring it Thursday?"

"If I remember, yeah."

She's trying to look annoyed, but the tiny turn of her lip is giving her away. "Do your best to remember, okay? I'd hate to see anything happen to your beloved polo collection."

"What are *you* wearing?"

She blushes, and all I can do is smile.

Personality Traits: Sadistic fashion cop. Control issues. ~~*A little tightly wound?*~~ *Very tightly wound.*

We don't wrap up our last song until close to midnight. I'm hunched over my guitar case, clicking the locks into place, when I see her eyes. Vee has beautiful eyes—deep brown rings that bleed into green centers—but right now they look like giant white marbles. Before I can ask her what's wrong, I hear footsteps behind me. A bony set of ribs jabs into my back, lurching me forward. Vee lunges, pushing my guitar case out of the way. Under the weight of the monkey on my back, I slam into Vee. I try to land my hands to either side of her, but one of my elbows jabs into her ribs.

"Shit," she yells. She's pinned under me, the bottom of a three-person pileup.

I shake Anders off of me, pushing myself up to kneel beside her. "Shit. Are you okay?"

"What about me?" Anders is lying on the floor next to me, his eyes closed, laughing hysterically. He smells like beer and sweat—which he's drenched in. Drumming is a full-body, cardio event for Anders.

"You've got to be kidding me!" Vee's voice is shrill.

"I'm so sorry. I didn't—" I just look at Anders and shake my head.

She pushes herself onto her knees. "Steve, get your stuff. I'm taking you home."

"No way are you driving my car again." Steve shakes his head maniacally, his eyes half closed. *Also drunk.* "My transmission can't handle it, Vee."

"Should have thought of that before you got trashed here . . . *again*," Vee says.

"I'll drive it." I basically just assaulted a girl I barely know, with my elbow. A girl I've sort-of, kind-of, but-not-really, been stalking. I have to do something to redeem myself. "I can drive a stick. Vee can follow me and bring me back to get my car?" I look to her for confirmation.

"Or I can just drive your car, and *you* can pick me up for school in the morning?" She's asking me, but she's glaring at Logan. *I don't mind the sound of that.*

"No way are you driving his car," Logan says.

Vee is on her feet, one arm still wrapped around her ribs. "Why the hell not?"

I agree. Who made Logan in charge of anything? This idea is brilliant.

"I don't let you drive *my* car, and it's a total piece of junk compared to his."

"It's cool, she can drive. I'll drop off Steve, then I'll drop her off at home." I turn to Vee. "You good with that?"

She nods and without a word she's headed toward the steps.

As soon as she's out of earshot, Logan is next to me. "Seriously, your car's sweet. You'll have to let *me* take it out sometime." Logan smacks my back, like we're friends. *Maybe we are.* "Parents?"

I freeze, glancing to where Vee just escaped. "Drug money."

Another nervous answer. *I'm Cam, a Cheesehead drug dealer. Nice to meet you.*

"Ha. Nice, man." Does he know I'm joking? *I'm joking, Logan.* "Glad you're here."

When I get outside, Vee is standing next to my car. Both of them are almost invisible in the unlit darkness of the driveway. Steve gets into the passenger side of his car.

I cross the driveway and hold the keys out in front of Vee. "Here."

"I can't drive this."

I shake the keys at her again. "You'll be fine, it's an automatic."

Vee still looks skeptical, her eyes glancing down toward the gleaming chrome of the handle.

"It's just a car." It's actually a BMW 4 Series Coupe with leather racing interior, custom rims, Italian tires, and a bunch of touch-screen controls I still haven't learned how to use in the last two months. I could have bought a small house in Riverton for what it cost, but I didn't care about that. I got it, because I could. *And it didn't cross my mind that it would stand out like a sore thumb in this town.* I want to tell her not to stress—that most of the time I fucking loathe the thing. *This* is what having dead parents looks like: a fancy car, a poorly decorated apartment, and an autographed guitar that I'm too guilty to play. And of course, the stupid surfboard. Grand total: $74,752.

I've barely made a dent in the blood money. My dad was an engineer for an alternative energy startup, and my mom was VP of a telecom. We didn't live what I would have considered flashy lives, because my parents didn't grow up like that. But we could have. And I could have moved to somewhere tropical off my portion of their insurance and stock portfolio. Instead, I'm standing in the middle of Cornfield, USA, arguing about letting a cute girl drive my stupid car. *Is this all to get out of riding to school with me in the morning?* I push the keys into her palm, and walk back to Steve's boxy red Buick.

"I won't even tell if you bump it over the speed limit once or twice." I wink at her and duck into the driver's side of Steve's car before she has a chance to argue.

In the rearview mirror, I watch as she hesitantly gets into my car, carefully adjusting all three mirrors. Steve is slumped against the window and I'm reaching over to pull the seat belt across him when a tap against the glass echoes through the silent car. Vee's face is just an inch away and I roll it down, ready for the fight over my car to continue. "What's wrong?"

She holds out her phone. "In case we get separated. I don't want you driving aimlessly through the country with Drunkie McDrunkerson over there." She nods toward Steve, who is motionless against the window, his breath creating moist circles on the glass.

I type in my number, press send, and a second later my own phone is vibrating in my hand. "Cam's Taxi Service. Providing rides to underage drinkers and middle-aged alcoholics since 2016."

By the time I dump Steve at his front door, Vee has moved to the passenger seat of my car. I make my way around to the driver's side, sliding behind the wheel.

She fidgets in her seat when I sit down, like she's trying to put space between us. Her voice is quiet. "My house is in town, by the school." She tips her head back and closes her eyes. All I can hear is her breathing and mine. It reminds me of the nursing home, and listening to her through the curtain, sure she'd find me eavesdropping.

"Start playlist four." I say each word slowly, hoping the system picks it up and I don't have to repeat it four times, like an idiot.

She doesn't open her eyes but smiles in the darkness as the music begins. "Show-off."

We drive for miles in silence before she says anything. "Sometimes it's nice just to be quiet."

I want to agree with her, but then I'd be talking. If I don't say anything, will she think I'm ignoring her? Or that I didn't hear her? *Deep breath, Cam. Get a grip.*

"You know, like sometimes—with certain people—if you don't talk, it just feels uncomfortable?" Her eyes are still closed, her head tipped back against the headrest. "Like your whole relationship is based on the things you say to each other." She looks over at me and I take it as permission.

"Talking can be exhausting. People think it's a contest. Like how much they talk to you—or how much they *know* about you—has some sort of correlation to how much they actually *care* about you."

"And you don't think it does?" She turns to look at me, her cheek pressed against the headrest. "You don't think that's basically the definition of caring about someone? I mean, if your best friend isn't the person who knows the most about you, how else would you define it?"

If she had heard all the people who talked to me nonstop for the last ten months, their words piling up meaninglessly like their frozen meals—words for the sake of words—she would never ask me this. "I don't think you have to know someone's life story to care about them." Even with the music, I swear I can hear my own breathing, acutely aware of how loud it is. *Why does she make me so goddamn nervous?* Maybe I've become completely socially inept over the last few months. "What you don't say means more, sometimes."

Vee sits with her head back until we pass the school, but her eyes are open now. Something feels different. The air around us feels full, heavier, like the last moments before a rainstorm.

"It's just a few more blocks. Sycamore. Fifth house on the right."

Her house is small, just off the main street that runs through downtown. It's yellow, with navy blue shutters, and the lights are all off. Putting the car in park, I turn the music down. *Is she out past curfew?* It's already after midnight, but she doesn't seem to be in a rush.

"Why don't you play in front of anyone?" As soon as the words come out, I regret them. I'm asking questions. *Why am I talking?*

"I'm just terrified." She's twisting a silver ring around her little finger. "I don't even know what of." There's a long stretch of silence. I don't know if she's going to speak again, and I don't want to break it. She finally does. "Terrified they'll hate me, maybe." She sighs.

My stomach is twisting under my ribs like the first time *I* went out onstage with my guitar, wondering if the crowd would like me.

She's taken her ring off completely, fingering it in her palm. "I started playing when I was eight. I was always writing these poems and making up little songs. So Nonni"—she turns to look at me—"that's my grandma. She bought me this pink kids' guitar for my birthday, and I taught myself to play watching online videos. Then Logan and I became friends, and a few years later he talked me into playing at the school talent show. We practiced this stupid song for weeks and I loved it. But onstage, I just froze." She shrugs. "And I know this sounds completely cliché and stupid, and not a good reason at all." She looks at me and rolls her eyes. "But I just sat there. Logan played that entire song by himself and he was amazing. People were floored by him."

"And he was a jerk about it, or what?"

"Not at all. He felt horrible. And that made *me* feel horrible." She pushes the ring back onto her finger. "I didn't want him to feel bad about something he was so good at. That's messed up." She's picking at her fingernails, scraping at the purple polish. "So I acted like it wasn't a big deal. Said I didn't even want to play anymore. And as far as most people know, I don't. It's still this annoying 'remember that time' story for a lot of people. Like that's the one stupid thing people can remember about me. 'Remember when you were ten and totally froze onstage?' It's hard to break out of that, to feel like you're not that person."

"That's crazy." I stare at her, wondering how she could be so confident about every detail concerning the band, and so completely unsure of herself.

"It is what it is." Her voice is rough and quiet. And resigned.

I want to tell her that she's crazy, and she *has* played for someone else. And *he* thinks she's amazing. But I can't say any of that. I have zero clue what to say right now. I should probably just let it go, but I can't. I know all about reinventing yourself, and that's exactly what she needs. "But what if it's not 'what it is'? What if I could fix you?" I regret the words the second they fall out of my mouth.

"*Fix* me?" Vee's giving me the same look Logan got for saying she shouldn't drive my car.

"Not—I just mean—sorry. I just—I think I know how to get you over it. If you want to try. I promise no talent shows will be involved." I paint an "X" over my heart with my finger. "And no one else has to know if you don't want them to."

She doesn't say anything, but finally she nods.

"What you need is an alter ego." Her head swings toward me and I have her attention. "You need a completely different persona. Someone who isn't afraid. No baggage with playing." I give her my most serious face. "It won't be easy. But it will definitely be fun."

She finally smiles and the tension starts to dissipate. We sit in the dark, both of us silent as we stare out at her navy blue garage door. The paint is peeling. I'm counting the squares when she finally speaks again.

"This is good timing." She's nodding like she wants to convince herself of something. "It's time to change things up, right? Say yes to new things."

I know exactly what you mean. "It's a great time to say yes," I say, holding back a smile and keeping my voice even. "Say yes to everything." I can't help myself. It feels like I'm standing backward on the edge of a cliff, just waiting to be pushed off. Her eyes meet mine. And I swear to myself I've sat behind that curtain for the last time, because my heart is about to explode as I wonder if she's about to call me out.

"Right." Her eyes seem wild and on fire. A smile slowly pulls at the corners of her mouth. "Could you actually drop me somewhere else?"

I can still feel my heart pounding in my chest. "Sure. Where to?"

"The beach? It's right down the street." She looks away from me, her eyes fixed on the window. "But you already know that."

I can't help but smile. "I do."

"I worked at the beach this summer and I saw you there. A lot. Hard not to notice someone on a stupid surfboard for that long every day." She's saying it like an apology, but I think I love that she remembers me.

"Hey, surfboards aren't stupid. Lucy will be devastated by your lack of respect."

"My apologies to Lucy. It's not her, it's just that trying to surf on a lake is stupid."

I laugh. I figured out how stupid lake surfing was a long time ago. "What's going on at the beach?" It's already after midnight. She doesn't seem like the type to light up in the dunes with the stoners. On really still nights, the sounds of their guitars and bongos float into the open windows of my apartment.

"I actually go there most nights. I guess it's turned into a bad habit; I can't fall asleep anymore without sitting there for a few hours, listening to the waves."

"I totally get that."

15 minutes later . . .

Cam:
How's the beach?

Vee:
The usual. Sand. Water. Someone rocking the bongo.
And crazy waves
You'd probably like that

Cam:
I've been thinking about what you said

Vee:
About? I was sort of ranty tonight
Sorry about that
Is rant-y even a word?

Cam:
Gig clothes
Mine=horrible. You won't approve.

Vee:
Uh oh

Cam:
Road trip tomorrow?

Vee:
Seriously?
Where to?
We have school

Cam:
After school. I'm not a delinquent
Wait. Are you?

Vee:
You're a funny guy, Cam

Cam:
Finally someone notices

Vee:
No one can notice if you don't talk
Really tho, where?

Cam:
I was thinking the mall

Vee:
Supposed to help Anders with his history paper

Cam:
You could be my personal shopper

Vee:
You know exactly what a girl wants to hear

Cam:
You can drive my car

Vee:
Tempting . . .

Cam:
Full music control. Final offer.
Can you really say no?
I thought we were saying yes these days

Vee:
Ok fine. YES
See you in the morning
And after school

CHAPTER SEVEN

NOW

VIRGINIA

Back when I thought I was coming on this tour as an intern—not as a pseudo-girlfriend slash band cheerleader—I decided it didn't make sense to lug my guitar onto a cramped bus. I would be too busy to play much, anyway. Instead, I have no real job to speak of, aside from taking photos, writing band bios, and posting articles about life on the road. In the mornings most of the guys are still dead to the world, busy sleeping off their hangovers from the night before. It's the perfect time to work on my own music. At least until I can figure out how to win Jenn over and get more involved with promoting the band.

Logan's acoustic guitar has become an almost permanent fixture on my lap, and the small leather banquette in the kitchen area has an imprint of my butt. On a bus full of guys, it turns out the kitchen is the easiest place to hide. Stereotypical, but true. There's only seating for two, and it makes a great hiding spot. Not to mention, the female fans who sometimes accumulate on the bus aren't exactly Susie Homemakers, looking to bake their one-night guy a batch of brownies. If they were smart, they would. Last week, I figured out how to make Rice Krispies treats in the microwave, and received several marriage proposals. These guys are all about food that doesn't come in a foil wrapper or paper bag.

The only person who ever infringes on my hiding spot in the kitchen is Tad. He and his camera have become something of my shadow. It doesn't matter what mundane thing I'm doing—burning a bag of popcorn and filling the bus with smoke, working on the band's website, unsuccessfully writing new songs, watching TV with the guys—he's always filming it. Why? I have no idea. Of all of the things happening on this bus, I am far from the most interesting.

For the most part, though, we've all gotten used to the cameras. It actually reminds me of being at the nursing home with Nonni. There are always other residents around—playing games, reading books, lounging in the community spaces—but to Nonni, everyone seems to fade into the background. Everyone has an unspoken understanding that they exist in their own bubble. And the cameras have become the same; I hardly even notice them anymore. I don't usually sing on the bus, but I'm up unusually early, and everyone is still asleep, so I just finished playing one of my favorites. It's a song I wrote a few years ago called "Catastrophic Love."

Tad pulls back the curtain to the kitchen and points his camera at me.

I set my guitar on my lap. "You've got an awful lot of footage of me." I'm hoping Tad will catch on to my unspoken plea for privacy. "I hope you're not making a Best-of-Vee Blooper Reel. I know where you sleep."

Tad sets his video camera—which really just looks like a fancy digital camera—down on the counter. He gives me a lazy smile, running a hand through the wavy hair that frames his round face. "I'm getting bored filming the guys lying around in bed." He's leaning against the wall across from me. His legs are long and thin, but his arms and chest are wide and bulky. His dark skin is paled by his almost-black hair, which brushes his shoulders in waves. "And you seem much more interesting." His eyes sweep up and down me.

"I promise you, I'm not." I close my notebook and turn toward him. I've spent a lot of time looking at Tad. He's like a really interesting collage of mismatched pieces you wouldn't think go together, but work somehow. If I closed my eyes I'd guess that his were brown, because everything about him feels warm, but they're a strange green. Tad's become my go-to distraction, when I'm trying to avoid eye contact with Cam.

"So what made you come on tour? You don't seem like the jealous-girlfriend type, tagging along to babysit." He's smiling at me, like always. Amused seems to be his perpetual state of mind, and I wonder if he just loves his job that much.

"Oh, I'm definitely not." I love how honest I'm finally able to be. "I'm here for moral support, mostly." I strum a few more notes, plucking the strings idly. "These guys are like my family."

His head is cocked to one side like he's examining me. "You write, too?" He crosses his arms and the brightly colored fish wrapping around his forearm seems to move with the flex of his muscles. "I've caught you singing a few times. And you're always jotting things down in that notebook of yours." One of his long fingers taps against the colorful little journal lying on the table in front of me. "The song you just sang was incredible. It's one of yours?"

"Yes. But—"

Cam's voice comes out of the hallway like a ghost. "Her songs are some of our best." I roll my eyes at his attempt at flattery. How long had he been lurking there, just out of sight?

"Really?" Tad seems interested, adjusting his camera slightly on the counter as Cam takes the seat next to me. I hadn't realized he was still recording everything.

But of course he is, that's his job.

Tad looks at me again. "I didn't know you wrote some of the band's songs." He makes it sound like we've been sitting around swapping stories and painting each other's nails.

Cam looks at me and then Tad—and the camera. " 'Push' . . . 'Tangerine Love' . . . all the fan favorites are Vee's." Cam is smiling at me like I'm absolute perfection, and for a moment I forget all about the pain and the hate and the anger. I smile back. And for one moment, I truly feel happy, ignited by the way he's looking at me, like I've cured cancer or written the Great American Novel, not scribbled a couple of stupid songs. I'm seventeen again, sitting at the beach after sunset, playing a concert for two.

Cam's voice breaks into my thoughts. "Let's do it, Vee."

Tad has the camera propped in front of his face again. It's aimed at Cam, who has slid to the end of the bench across from me, his guitar propped on his knee. He starts strumming a steady rhythm. After the opening chords, I can feel my chest tightening. I know the words that will come out of his mouth, and I wish I didn't.

"*There's this girl, yeah this girl, who makes the world seem brighter than it's ever been. There's her smile and her eyes, and I just wanna make her mine. I hear her laugh and I smile, 'cause I know she's laughin' at me—*" He's looking at me the entire time he sings, and it takes me back. To the two of us in his apartment after school, singing and playing. The two of us lying on the beach and talking long after the sun had gone down. "*There's this girl, yeah this girl—*" All of the feelings surging through me are new, but old, and it feels good to remember them again. And fucking painful to know that the last time I felt like this was so long ago. "*This girl. This girl . . .*" Cam's repeating the end of his chorus over and over, and I know it's my turn to join in, but I don't. I can't go back to that place and let myself feel what I'm feeling; remember the things that I've been able to forget for so long. Every note of this song feels like it's slicing into me, opening old wounds, taking me back to a different version of me.

I set my guitar on the table, turning to look at Cam, so I'm not staring directly into the camera that's pointed at me. "I'm actually not feeling all that great. Headache." I put two fingers to my temple. I expect Tad to try talking me into continuing, but he doesn't say a word. I give him a smile, thankful this was easier than I thought it would be.

I'm two steps from the curtain—two steps from escaping— when Cam's body steps into my path. I pause, thinking he's going to go around me, but he's still and his eyes are locked on mine. We're inches apart, and then we're touching, as his hands come up to gently cup my cheeks. *Move, Virginia.* Long, warm fingers drift back and gently cup my head. His thumbs begin moving in slow circles at my temples, his fingers laced in my hair now. Someone has hit my pause button—I'm motionless. *Move, Virginia.* My eyelids, heavy with emotion and numbed by the shock of his touch, flutter shut.

Cam's voice is soft and cautious. "Better?"

I nod, I think. Cam lets one hand drift down to the side of my neck, his fingers curling softly around it while his other continues its lazy temple circles. All that registers is Cam's smell. His soap and his minty shampoo fill my nose, and I might as well be seventeen. His hand falls away and is replaced by his warm skin—rough like sandpaper against my check, his breath warm in my ear. "I missed you." The words drift past my ear, so soft they're more like a sigh. The old feelings—the bright hot burning that's bubbling up in my stomach and spreading through my limbs—is overtaking me, and I want to lean forward. I want to bridge this tiny gap between us, fill that space with our lips.

Then a door slams, and his fingers are lead weights on my skin.

As my eyes snap open I pull myself out of the grip of Cam's hands. One is still resting on my temple while the other rests on my collarbone, his thumb grazing back and forth there. I twist my shoulders and let them both fall away. I look behind me, where Tad's camera is still rolling, the red light blinking ominously. *What had that looked like?* I know what it had felt like, and now it's been permanently copied somewhere other than in my mind.

I take a step around Cam. "I'm going to go lie down." I'm trying to keep my tone as casual as possible, like we're just two friends. But really, I'm not sure that we were ever friends.

CHAPTER EIGHT

THEN

VIRGINIA

Step One: Say Goodbye to Virginia Miller
A few text messages last night. That's all it took for this guy—practically a stranger—to lure me into his car. *At least I'm not in the trunk.* We're sitting in his car, on the way to the nearest mall, which is a thirty-five-minute drive.

"Tell me about her," Cam says.

Tell you about my imaginary persona? My alter ego. God, this is weird.

"Start with something easy. What's her name?" When I don't say anything, he looks over at me with a smile. "Mine's going to be Parker Sunset."

I laugh. I can't help it. "Does Parker Sunset also work the pole?"

"Only because these band gigs don't pay the bills yet." He gives me a playful smile. "You just combine your first pet and the street you grew up on. Boom."

"I really don't want my alter ego to be Fish Dunewood."

"You had a fish named Fish? How meta."

"It was a cat named Fish, and I was seven. I thought it was funny. And I've already decided I'm going to be Dakota Gray. I get to keep a state name, and Gray sounds . . . edgy." I fidget with the dashboard touchscreen, trying to turn on the satellite radio, while Cam asks me questions about Dakota.

It's actually fun, once I let myself play along. I tell Cam all about her: how she loves racy clothes and her hair is black and straight—the opposite of mine. She's wild and a little reckless; okay with losing control. She doesn't panic and jump to conclusions, and she doesn't have it all figured out. Dakota doesn't care what people think—about her clothes or her voice or anything. She loves to dance. Dakota's a seriously kick-ass guitar player and her voice is mesmerizing. And she knows it. She knows it, and she rocks it. Because Dakota Gray is fearless and badass, bold and unapologetic. Dakota Gray is everything Virginia Miller is not.

Step Two: Become Dakota Gray
Easier said than done. I'm standing outside Carnivale with my arms wrapped around my waist, like I can somehow squeeze myself out of this situation.

Shit. Shit. Shit.

Maybe I can force myself to implode. Even after hours of talking about her, I obviously haven't mastered this whole "become Dakota Gray" thing, because I'm still feeling very much like Vee Miller, Queen of Panic.

This will be the unfortunate moment I get kidnapped. They'll shove me in the trunk of some nondescript, black four-door sedan. I won't even be able to kick out a tail light because of these ridiculous heels. And after they drive me three states away, and dump me in a ditch somewhere, no one will even know it's me. They probably won't even try to identify me, because I'll look like a runaway hooker or something. Oh, God. I'm at the climactic midpoint of one of those dramatized late-night news specials, "Virginia Miller: An Honor Student Fallen from Grace."

Dammit, Nonni. This is all her fault.

Somewhere between cursing my angel of a grandmother, and walking a continuous loop between Logan's car and the door, I break into a sweat. *I'm having a panic attack.* The skin across my chest is burning hot and prickled with sweat, while my cold hands shake at my sides. I have no idea what a panic attack actually feels like, but I want to die, and I think I've earned the right to overreact a little.

I can't go in there. I look ridiculous.

The other day, when Cam had talked me into letting him pick out an outfit for me—*for Dakota*—I knew I couldn't say no. I *literally* couldn't say no, without lying to my eighty-year-old grandmother. And I really wanted to say no. I wanted to say *hell, no.* Instead, I picked out clothes for Cam and he picked out an outfit for me. Well, for Dakota Gray. That was our deal. It was simple enough, fun even. Each of us shopped separately, ringing up our purchases and handing them over, still in their bags. We swore not to look at them until this evening. It had seemed like an okay idea, back when I thought Cam was a nice guy. The kind of guy who lets you drive his super-nice car, even though he barely knows you, and everyone has warned him you'll mangle it. A guy who has late-night conversations in the dark, letting you ramble on about your childish fears. But *nice guys* aren't dead set on making you look ridiculous. Cam isn't a nice guy.

Deep breath, Virginia.

Someone honks and I jump as I stand pressed up against the door, my hand wrapped around the cold metal handle. I rest my forehead against the rough wood. *Son of a bitch.* I take one last breath and slowly open the door, squinting as I step out of the early evening sunlight and into the dark bar.

I can do this. *No, you can't.* But maybe Dakota Gray can.

Everyone is staring, and it isn't just in my head. I know now that I've never actually been stared at before. Because I can actually feel it, the presence of their eyes on me. The white-haired old guy sitting at the long wooden bar. Anders, who looks like his eyebrows are about to declare war on his hairline. And Cam, whose eyes haven't left me for a split second, since I stepped inside. The path that Cam's eyes are traveling feels physical. From my purple velvet peep toes, up to the slick black leather leggings that look like each of my legs has been dipped in black ink, to the sequined top that hangs off one shoulder, draping delicately across my chest and down my sides. I feel his eyes burn my skin as they survey every ridiculous inch of me.

I can't even bring myself to look at Logan, who said two words after I got into his car. He practically sprinted to get inside when we arrived. It's always been ritual for Logan to pick me up for gigs—since we only get a few parking passes—but if I had known I'd be getting in his car looking like *this*? No way.

While Logan avoids eye contact, Anders is gawking at me like the perverted old men who hang out at the beach, checking out girls half their age. "Wow, Vee, that's some—"

I hold my hand up. "Not one word. I swear on your drum set I will smother you in your sleep."

"Will you wear that?" He's biting his lip, and trying not to smile. "That's how I'd like to die." One more word and I'm texting Cort to come kick his ass. It was so much easier to keep him in line when she was down the street, and not in another state. The two of them have been on-again off-again since freshman year, and I swear dating her has completely warped him. He's always been just a little more into her than she was him, and sometimes I think his crazy ego is the only thing that keeps him from being crushed by her. She's created a monster.

As Anders continues to unabashedly stare—grinning like a

fool—the light show taking place in front of me catches my attention. Every bit of light in the dark room dances off of me, tiny specks reflecting onto the floor, flickering around my feet as I walk through the room. I twist to the right and left, twirling once as the shiny facets of my shirt pattern the floor like the night sky.

I had admired this outfit in the store window. It was the sort of thing I could see myself wearing, if I had the perfect body and the attitude to match. Out on the brightly lit street I had felt like a clown; like someone dressed in a costume, playing a part I didn't know the lines for. But in the hazy, dim light of Carnivale, I feel ethereal and otherworldly, like the heroine of a comic book. *I should have a coiled whip or something.* When I finally tear my eyes from the light show I'm creating, Cam is just a few feet in front of me, shopping bag in hand, laughing softly.

"Oh, you think I'm funny?" I snatch the bag out of his hands and shove it into his chest. "Because Dakota Gray isn't afraid to make a scene. She'll kick your ass," I say with a smile. "Just wait until you see what you're wearing, Mr. Polo Shirt." I'm giving him my most devious smirk, hoping that it holds a sort of ominous warning. Even though the clothes I chose for him are far from controversial. "Then we'll see who's funny."

His hands clutch at the bag, grabbing one of mine in the process. "I don't think you're funny." His voice is almost a whisper, raspy and deeper than usual. My breath catches in my throat at the feeling of his warm skin against me, his fingers wrapped around my wrist, face just inches from mine.

"I think you look perfect . . . Dakota." He winks.

Anders clears his throat, shaking me out of the moment.

When I lock myself in the bathroom, just before the show starts, I don't expect to see myself in the mirror. I'm not sure what I expect. I guess to look like a little girl who tried to put on her mom's wedding dress; completely out of place. But I still fit into the picture I see reflected back at me. It's just a new version of me. I don't look like I'm playing dress-up at all. *You look perfect.* The words are caught in my head, like the hook of a song.

The bathroom is dimly lit, with just one buzzing bulb overhead that's covered in a thin film of gray smoke. It makes everything look soft around the edges, like smudged charcoal. Standing in front of the mirror, my shoulders arched back, stomach sucked in, I examine myself from every possible angle. My small chest, my round butt and hips, my long, muscular legs; it all seems to fall into place, seems to work together. *You look perfect.*

Nonni was right. This ridiculously amazing outfit—this night—it's not a worst-case scenario. It's like one of those thrill rides where the bottom falls out underneath you. Once the panic wears off—once you survive—you feel unstoppable. And if I steer clear of the creepier guys, this night probably won't even land me on a MISSING poster, or dead in someone's trunk. As I leave the tiny room, with the buzz of the lightbulb and Cam's words in my brain, I feel like I could do anything. The band plays song after song, Dakota spins and jumps on the dance floor, and the entire night, Cam never takes his eyes off of me, as three words loop in my head on repeat: *You look perfect.*

CAM

As we drive down the dark streets of Riverton, the music of Carnivale is still in my ears. Everything around us seems unbearably loud in its quietness. The click of seat belts, the ding of the blinker, the gentle swish of breath past lips—it all feels like it's being projected through a megaphone, filling my car with deafening sound.

Pulling into her driveway, I finally break the silence. "I'm sorry. If you really hated the outfit, I mean." Her seat belt clicks open, scraping the metallic sequins of her top as it wraps around her. I'm trying not to smile, to show even an ounce of remorse, but I'm not sorry at all. "I swear I thought you'd like it." She sits still, our breathing once again the only sound that fills the quiet space. Pulling her lip between her teeth, she swivels toward me, one leg folding under the other until she's facing me.

"I didn't hate it." She starts picking at the sequins of her shirt, pressing each one flat. She rolls her eyes and the tiniest smile plays on her lips. "The outfit's actually pretty amazing." She looks down at herself, letting out a rush of air that is somewhere between a sigh and a laugh. "I just had to get used to it." The shy smile spreads across her face and I swear she must be able to hear my heart pounding right now. "Vee felt a little out of place, but Dakota likes it. She really does."

"Okay then."

"Okay then." She's smiling as she steps out of the car. "Goodnight, Cam."

"Goodnight, Vee."

Vee turns to face me in the dark. "You looked perfect too, you know." I look down at my new jeans and simple black T-shirt as she shuts the door and walks away.

A block from Vee's house, I stop at the gas station to fill my tank. Swiping my card, a glint of silver catches my eye. Out on the sidewalk, like a disco ball rolling under the street lamps, is Vee. She's striding down the pavement, a little black sweater draped over her shoulders, her heels swapped for a pair of purple shoes. And I know exactly where she's headed so late.

I drop my body down onto the ground next to her and her shoulders flinch for just a second. Leaning back on my hands in the cool sand, I'm glad it's only me surprising her. "Starting a new beachwear trend?" I can't help but grin, seeing the sand sticking to her leather leggings. "I like what you've done with the outfit. I think it's even better than before." I bump my foot against her shoe.

"Stalk much?" Her voice is nothing but sarcasm and tease as her eyes remain fixed on the water in front of us. She's right, I probably shouldn't have come. But then I couldn't get the thought of her alone at the beach out of my head. There's no staff here at night, but who knows who *is* here at night. I sat in the parking lot for fifteen minutes but I just couldn't fight the pull.

"Only on Fridays." I try to keep my face serious as I say it, but I can't help but smile as I catch hers out of the corner of my eye. "Sorry." She gives me a look that says she knows I'm not. "I saw you walking and didn't like the idea of you down here by yourself this late. I can hang out in my car and just give you a ride home when you're done, if you want to be alone." *But please don't ask me to do that.*

"You really are like a personal taxi service, huh? Rides in the morning, rides at night. You're going to spoil me and give me inflated expectations of your awesomeness, Cam Fuller."

"In that case." I push myself up in the sand, wiping my hands together dramatically and rising to my feet. "The last thing I want is you thinking I'm going to be awesome 24/7. Good luck with the serial killers." I dust sand off my pants, stopping when I feel a hand on mine.

She tugs it once, before dropping it. "Shut up and sit down."

"It's nice out here. Quie—"

She cuts me off with a soft "shhhh" that sounds like a sigh. We're sitting just a few feet from the water, far from the lights of the boardwalk. If the wind really picked up, the surf would reach up and grab us. Vee lies back on the sand again, her arms at her sides, and I copy her. Our bodies are just inches apart. The sound of bongos and acoustic guitar drifts down from the dunes; the only noise as we lie in complete silence. It's easy to understand why she loves it here. Staring up at the dark, inky sky, the light breeze sends goose bumps across my skin. The gentle sound of the waves and the drums fills my ears. Eventually, the music stops and I suspect that what had felt like minutes has actually been hours. Time seems to pass more quickly with Vee, like at a concert or on vacation.

"Tomorrow? Same place, same time?" she asks, when I finally drop her in front of her house just after 2 A.M.

I just nod, watching as she slams the car door and walks away.

CHAPTER NINE

NOW

CAM

Aside from the superfans that have started showing up city after city, every week we see a new group of fans at each venue. Where normal shows are about entertaining—and that means playing the same tried-and-true fan favorites over and over, and plenty of covers—when you're playing for a television audience week after week, you're always playing new sets. But it turns out, if you replace your singer six months before you end up on a reality TV show, you can forget using any songs he wrote. Logan got the call yesterday—their jerk of a former singer swearing he'd see us all in court if we played any of the songs he helped Logan write. We're not risking it. If we don't do something, we'll run out of songs eventually.

"I'm tapped," Logan says.

We're all sitting in the bus lounge, going over set lists for upcoming shows while Vee sits in the back of the bus, answering fan mail and managing our social media. She spends hours each day posting photos online, sharing funny things that happen from day to day and engaging the fans in conversations about what they like. It's a huge part of our success so far, because people like us. Vee makes us seem accessible, when really we are so far from it. When we aren't playing or sleeping, we're in no mood to answer emails or post funny comments. She does it all for us.

Logan has his head in his hands, his elbows propped on his knees. "We've played most of our stuff. We can repeat a song or two each night, but we need at least two new songs to get through the next few weeks."

"What about Vee?" I ask.

Logan glances toward the back of the bus, then shakes his head. "She's not writing for us right now."

I pull my notebook out of my bag and throw it over to Logan and Anders, who are sitting on the sofa across from me. "I've got a whole notebook of songs. Lots of them need work, but at least two or three are good to go, if you want to check them out."

"What am I"—Reese is scowling at the two of them— "invisible over here?" He drops down onto the couch next to Logan, and the three of them flip through the notebook, nodding and mumbling, page after page.

Logan rips a page out, and I flinch. "This one." Then another. "And this one. 'Girl in the Purple Shirt.' Play a little for us?" This is the first time we'll play anything I wrote, and I'm trying to push down the little voice in my head saying I should have just kept these to myself.

I grab my guitar and start strumming the melody. Logan joins in with the lyrics, the two of us switching back and forth between verses. Anders taps out a rhythm on the table.

We're in a full-on jam session when Vee walks in. "What's this?"

Logan finishes up the verse. "New song," he says, a giant smile on his face. "You like it?"

"I love it. And the fans are going to eat it up. T-shirt sales will go through the roof."

When I wrote the song—about Vee and her lucky shirt—I

hadn't even considered the fact that our merch shirts would be purple. They've always been purple—since back when we were The Melon Ballers. But when *I* think of the Girl in the Purple Shirt, it's Vee I imagine. In that ratty shirt, standing offstage as we play. Not a fan in an overpriced T-shirt.

I fight the urge to correct her. I won't like her reaction if I say the song is about her. We'll be singing it in front of hundreds of people soon—thousands, if you count everyone watching on television and online. I'm not allowed to tell Vee how I feel about her, so I'm ninety-nine percent sure she wouldn't be on board with me telling the world.

VIRGINIA

Priya, one of Jenn's marketing minions, gathers us all in one of the small backstage rooms of the club we've arrived at in New Orleans. Logan is sitting in a red velvet wingback chair in the corner of the room, and Anders is straddling a brown metal folding chair. The rest of us are standing around, propping ourselves against the counters and old dingy walls of the tiny room. I'm looking at my phone, scrolling through comments on the band's Instagram, when Jenn and her assistant Kaley come in.

"We're busy, so this won't take long," Jenn says. "Logan. Cam." She nods at the two of them and then glances over the rest of us. "I really just needed the two of you, but I'm glad everyone could join us."

"Whatever we can do," Reese says in a serious voice I've never heard before.

"Just a heads up, as things move forward—as *you* move forward—we'll be asking more of you. Meet-and-greets, radio interviews. You'll need to stick around for photo ops. And down the road we have some other ideas in mind for you."

"If we make it," Cam says.

"When you make it." Jenn sounds confident. "Listen, 'Girl in the Purple Shirt' is huge right now. We'll set up some promotions geared around that, play off the idea of rock stars falling in love with someone out in the crowd. Fans love that." Jenn smacks her tablet. "I know—we'll run a contest to win dates with Logan and Cam."

Cam crosses his arms over his chest. "That's not really what the song is about."

"Doesn't matter," Jenn says. "That's what the fans are responding to."

I'm trying to get Logan's attention, because, hello, I'm his girlfriend? As far as they know, at least. Isn't it sort of tacky to send him out on dates with random girls? I clear my throat loudly but Logan is still fixated on what Jenn is saying.

Jenn turns to me slowly. "Virginia—" There's annoyance in her voice.

What the hell am I supposed to say? I'm not even a part of this band.

While I'm panicking, Cam speaks up. "Logan has a girlfriend." He glances over at me but doesn't meet my eyes. "As you know. And I'm not interested in going on dates with strangers. But thanks."

"It's not a request," Jenn says, still smiling. "It's also not necessary to keep up the false pretenses—" Her eyes land on Logan. "Not with me, at least."

"But I thought—" Logan says.

"We've already aired footage of the two of you together"— she's looking at me—"so you'll just keep up the girlfriend act until it's time for the breakup." She doesn't say it like this is some sudden revelation she had. No, this is what it's been about all along. We're just another means to her creating good TV.

"Soon?" I give Logan an apologetic smile and mouth, "No offense."

He gives me a playful wink.

"Soon," Jenn says.

Cam pushes himself off the wall. "And then she'll have to leave?" His voice is laced with concern, and for once I don't roll my eyes at his interest in me. I'm thinking the same thing.

"Of course not," Jenn says calmly, and she seems strangely happy that Cam has joined the conversation. "Virginia can stay. She'll work with us and help with publicity."

Jenn is looking right at me, but I don't say anything. I'm not convinced this isn't a joke. And it's not a question.

Jenn looks to me, her brows raised like she's confused. "That's what you want to do eventually, right?"

"Oh. Yes, actually. I mean, that would be amazing. Thank you." I've been trying to talk to Jenn—to plead my case as an intern—since I got on this bus. She was always conveniently too busy, so why is this all happening so easily now?

"Talk to your college," Jenn says. "Maybe you can set it up for credit." She shoves her tablet into her large bag and turns for the door, then stops and turns back to me. "Let me know if there's paperwork to fill out. Kaley will get you a schedule, so you can join us at the weekly planning meetings." Kaley looks at me just long enough to roll her eyes, and part of me wants to join her.

Before leaving, Jenn tells us to "act normal," until we get the okay to break up. I'm not sure that Logan and I are actually capable of pulling off a convincing breakup scene. Will we even have to, or will it all happen off-camera, and they'll just leak it to the media? It doesn't seem like there's enough interest in us to warrant any kind of announcement. Who would even care?

CHAPTER TEN

THEN

VIRGINIA

Something strange happens after midnight. It's like this invisible flip is switched, and everything that happens automatically feels heavier and more emotional. Like the walls that we spend so much time holding up during the day are just too heavy to bother with at night. And there's something about being at the beach— alone with Cam—that makes me feel brave, when I decide I want to know more about him. After two weeks of sitting in near silence, I want to know *everything* about him, but I don't know how to ask. Aside from the beach, we're always surrounded by people—the band, kids in our classes. And Cam is still quiet. He doesn't offer up any details at school. Or at band practice. And the curiosity—the feeling that I *need* to know him—it's eating away at me. Almost as much as the ache for him to kiss me.

Which he hasn't.

I'm starting to think he doesn't want to, because he's had a lot of opportunities, lying on the beach with me. And I've come to the realization that maybe it's better this way. I'll be leaving for college in less than a year, and I don't even know where Cam is planning to go. Maybe he's heading back to Wisconsin. He probably has tons of friends back there, though he never mentions any. He doesn't talk about much of anything, until you ask him.

"Leaving for school." I hold up one finger. "Living in Chicago." Two. "And performing in front of people." I wiggle three fingers in the chilly night air, raising my brows and giving Cam a look that I hope says, *Now you,* but he just sits there, with a questioning look on his face.

"Oh, we're talking now? I didn't get that memo," he says teasingly, and I smack his shoulder. Cam and I have a comfort with each other that took years for me to gain even a bit of with Logan. I never felt *any* of it with my ex, Toby, even when we had sex at his parents' cabin the week before we broke up. Even when I told him I loved him. *Because I should have, right?* I didn't care what Toby's favorite song was in elementary school, or if I knew his childhood pet's name. Or who he thought was the most overrated band of all time.

I want to know *everything* about Cam. "Three things that scare the crap out of you. Your turn."

"Are you going to college in Chicago?"

"What? No," I say, confused.

"Then why are you scared to live there? It doesn't sound like you have to."

"No, but I want to. The *idea* just scares me. Catching cabs, figuring out train schedules . . . knowing when to pull that weird rope on buses to make them stop. I mean, what happens if I step onto the bus and that stupid little card is out of money? Do they just kick me off? And what if I get on a train going in the wrong direction and I don't even realize it? Until I end up in some sketchy neighborhood, where someone turns me into an unsuspecting drug mule or something." I pick up two handfuls of sand and let them drain out of my palms slowly. "The Plan is to go to State. But Chicago is the end goal. Someday."

"Well, it sounds like you're scared of public transportation, not Chicago."

I pull my hand out of the sand and smack Cam's leg—a move that isn't much more than a twitch of my wrist since we're lying side by side just inches apart. Cam laughs before grabbing my hand and holding it casually in his, nestled in the sandy gap between us. My skin feels tingly and electric, like every single nerve ending I have is aware of him.

"So why not go for college?" He keeps holding my hand as he talks, like we do this all the time. Like we're those people whose hands drift into each other's without even thinking.

"We've always said we were going to MSU. That's The Plan," I say.

"The Plan, huh?"

"Three things." We have spent too much of our time together talking about how neurotic I am. And it feels weird to bring up the fact that Logan and I always said we'd go to State together. Especially when Cam and I are holding hands in the sand like we're—well, *something*. Like we *could* be. I'm still not sure if *something* is what I want or not.

"Okay, let's see." His thumb is rubbing up and down along mine, and it's hard to think about anything else. "Leaving for college. Playing music professionally." He takes a deep, dramatic breath. "And holding your hand."

It had taken me about two hours—the first night we were together on the beach—to figure out that Cam has a varsity letter in deflecting questions. I bump his shoulder with mine. "You're doing that now, and you don't seem scared to me."

"Oh, I am. You just can't tell, because I'm dying on the inside." He rubs his hand over his chest. "My fear's internalized— I'll need therapy down the road."

"Holding my hand is going to force you into therapy?" I try to pull my hand away, but he holds it in place, and I laugh.

"It probably won't be the first thing."

"Thank God you haven't kissed me. I'd hate to see you institutionalized." *What is wrong with me?* Maybe I'm willing it to happen, even though I know it's better if it doesn't. Still, I regret the words instantly, because his face looks pained, like he's not sure if he actually does want to kiss me.

"Oh, I'll definitely be kissing you." There's a huge, cocky grin on his face, and it holds a promise. "Do you need to change your three things now?"

I smack him again but he has a great point, because suddenly getting hit by a taxi or throwing up onstage doesn't seem so terrifying.

CAM

Once she gets started, Vee doesn't shut up. Not in a bad way. More of a surprising way. Over the last few weeks, we've spent almost every night at the beach. And while some of it was spent in quiet silence like our first night, most of it has been spent sharing facts and stories and favorites. I have my own Virginia Miller biography in the works. Born and raised in Riverton, daughter to Ted and Millie.

"Really? Millie Miller?" I asked.

"Technically, it's Millicent Miller," she said, warning me not to bring it up because it was a sore subject. Implying that I *would* be meeting her mother one day. It had seemed weird that I hadn't crossed paths with her mom, until she explained that she worked nights during the week. It made me wonder if Vee thought the same thing about my parents. *You won't be meeting them.*

She told me all about her plans of studying marketing, so she could be a *real* band manager or publicist someday. What she should really be studying is music marketing, but the college she's planning on going to doesn't even have a program for it. Only a few colleges in the country do, according to her. She talked about Nonni, which I liked, because I finally felt like I didn't have to be so careful about mentioning her.

"What do you talk about?" I asked.

"All sorts of stuff. I play her songs sometimes, actually. She's the only one who's heard me play. And she likes to give me life advice."

"Like?"

"You know, 'Get out of your shell. Don't be afraid to live life. Come up with an alter ego and run wild.'" She shrugged and smiled. "That sort of stuff."

I like hearing about her visits with Nonni. I've stopped my behind-the-curtain visits, like I promised myself I would. I'm trying to assume the role of legitimate friend over stalker, because knowing everything about someone is dangerous. You can't unlearn some things. Like the stuff about Logan and Vee and their "more than friends" relationship over the summer. Vee reluctantly shared that little detail last week. I got the feeling she felt like she was supposed to. Really, I wish I didn't know. It's hard for me to look at Logan now without wondering what would have happened if she hadn't called it off. How could he not have feelings for her? I've been swearing up and down to myself that I'm going to keep things platonic with Vee, but every time I see her it gets a little harder. It's pathetic, how beyond-walking-away-from-her I am. I've only known her for a few weeks, and he's had years to get sucked in.

And I've learned that Vee doesn't like to come right out and ask questions. She always offers something first. A fact about herself or a little game to play along with. I like that there's a certain give-and-take with her—she never asks for anything she can't or won't return. And she never presses. Whenever she asks about my family, or why we came to Riverton, the silence never lasts long. She just trudges right along, changing the subject and picking a new line of questioning as if nothing has happened. The fact that she looks past those glaring holes is what keeps me coming back.

"Five years from now, I'm going to be backstage at some crazy music festival," Vee says. "I'll be doing interview prep with a coked-out but adorable guitarist with a heart of gold, who will eventually clean up his act and ask me to marry him." We're lying on the beach on a particularly cold September night, and I love that she's holding my hand even while telling me about her imaginary future husband.

"I'm glad to hear I'll finally kick the habit one day." I squeeze her hand, bumping her shoulder gently with mine. "Please tell me I at least get to go to one of those fancy celebrity rehabs—in Malibu or something?"

I know she's trying to get me to share my plans for the future—for college, probably—but I don't have any. Vee has The Plan, and probably a Plan B, and C, and F, and when I think about the future I don't really see anything. The furthest I think ahead is looking forward to lying on the beach with her night after night. It has quickly become the only constant thing in my life. And *finally*, I don't feel like I'm running. It's fun to imagine a future filled with normal things like getting married someday. Even if I do have questionable habits in this particular scenario.

"Where's the wedding?" I ask.

"Oh, we'll probably do something nontraditional. You know, get married in the redwood forests, or in a field, or something."

"I'm not getting married in a field." *And forests are filled with ticks. Why would we not get married on a beach, or at a golf club, like normal people?*

"It's not going to be a cow pasture. It'll be a wildflower field or something."

"Not happening."

"Excuse me?" She slams our joined hands into my hip. "You're the one who invited yourself into *my* imaginary scenario. You'll get married wherever I say."

I laugh, thinking of Bridezilla Vee, barking orders at caterers and florists and bringing me nineteen different flavors of cake to try, before she finds the One. My sister used to love those shows about crazy, screaming brides, and the thought of her stops my laughter in its tracks. "Nontraditional in a field. Got it. Do I at least get to pick out our song or something?"

"As long as it doesn't suck. I'm not dancing to anything cheesy and overplayed, like Frank Sinatra or Louis Armstrong."

"I'd write you an original song. Obviously." I say it as though I've had this plan for months. Years maybe. As if I've ever thought about any of this before this very strange, exact moment. "And a symphony would play with me. It would be like rock meets classical. Very nontraditional, very rock royalty." I lay my cheek against the blanket we're lying on, so I can look at her. "We *are* rock royalty in this scenario, right?"

She nods and rolls her eyes. "I don't think my parents are splurging for a symphony."

"Hey, I'm a big-shot, formerly coked-out rock star. I'm sure I saved for my wedding."

She giggles. "What formerly coked-out rock star wouldn't?"

"Exactly. Anyway, your parents won't like me much when they find out about my little problem." I tap my nose dramatically.

"*Former* problem," she corrects in a very serious voice. A chunk of hair falls onto my forehead and Vee pushes it away with a warm hand.

I'm never getting another haircut. "Right. I'm sure they'll hate our rock-meets-symphony field-wedding so much they won't pay for it, anyway."

"I want Rice Krispies treats!" Vee shouts.

"Right now?"

"No, for our wedding. I want a cake made out of Rice Krispies treats."

I love the way she's playing along so easily, and I love that with Vee I can actually joke about an imaginary wedding—*my* imaginary wedding—without feeling like I may lose my dinner on this beach. If my ex had brought up our wedding—hell, if she'd brought up *going* to a wedding—I probably would have broken out in hives. And I sure as hell wouldn't be playing along. But there's something about Vee that's different. And it's not that marrying her is so unimaginable that I can just joke about it. Vee is just . . . easy. Easy to be with, and easy to talk to, and completely, one hundred percent genuine, in a way that I know I don't deserve. I can't give her the same thing. It's reason number 192 I should stick with my plan of keeping this platonic.

"I'm not eating Rice Krispies treats at my wedding," I say. "They're like slimy rubber chunks."

"But they're my favorite," she whines.

"Not happening, sweetheart. I draw the line at marshmallow anything at our wedding."

"You're totally unreasonable."

"Do we get to have a bar? Or am I a recovering drunk, too? Do we have to have a hot chocolate bar or something lame like that?"

"God, hot chocolate sounds good," she says.

"For our wedding?"

"No, for now. It's cold tonight." She leans over, resting her head on my shoulder, and wiggling closer so her chest is pressed up against my side. For the hundredth time since I met her, I have to talk myself out of kissing her. I don't deserve it. Or her. And this isn't even what I came here for.

"You want to leave?" I ask, slipping my hand out of hers and looping it under her neck, pulling her tighter to me. "We can stop at the gas station and get your hot chocolate."

She nods against my arm but she doesn't move. We lie in the darkness for hours, listening to the music drift down from the dunes, as her heart beats in rhythm against my shoulder. This isn't what I came here for, but it's what makes me stay. It's what helps me forget.

VIRGINIA

Step Three: Exit Your Comfort Zone

I'm sitting in Cam's car, in the leather pants he bought me and a vintage concert tee I found at a thrift shop. I cut open the neck and stitched it into a wide scoop, so it hangs over one shoulder. My guitar is in the backseat with Cam's, and we're pulling onto the dimly lit streets of a small beach town thirty minutes north of Riverton. We drive down the brick streets, past the gift shops and restaurants, until the road dumps us out onto a small beach.

"Dakota Gray and Parker Sunset are going out tonight." My whole body had tensed when Cam said it this afternoon. I knew "going out" was code for singing. At first glance this beach is empty, but as we leave the car—pulling our guitars out behind us—I can hear the familiar sound of bongos. *Do they give you a bongo the first time you buy weed? Or if you show up at a beach after sunset enough nights in a row? Is it part of a starter kit or something?*

"God bless the stoners," Cam says. "I came here once this summer thinking maybe the waves would be better."

I give him a mocking look. I love harassing him about Lucy the surfboard.

"Yeah, yeah, I'm stupid. Whatever." He's waving his hands in front of him like he's heard it a million times. Which he has. "What I did find here are more beach musicians."

"So you brought me to get my first joint. That's so sweet." I know that's not why we're here, but it actually feels like the lesser of two evils at this point.

"You're not as cute as you think you are." He grabs my hand and starts to lead me toward the wooden stairs that stretch up into the dunes. "We're here to play."

"In front of people?" I plant my feet on the concrete, bringing us to a stop.

"*For* people. Baby steps."

Before I can protest, Cam's face is in front of mine and he's tugging on the ends of the long black wig I'm wearing. *I'm fully embracing Dakota Gray.*

"No one knows you here. We'll start out playing by ourselves, okay?" He's giving me these pleading puppy dog eyes he's so good at. "I really want to play with you. Will you let me play with you?" He's smirking and I can't stop the smile that's creeping onto my face as he teases me.

"You can play with me," I tease.

We make our way up the steep steps and take a seat on one of the wooden observation decks. We're two levels up from where a group of dirty-looking guys—*and maybe a girl?*—are gathered with bongos and guitars. I can still hear the soft beat of their music, but we're above them now and I can't see them. *They can't see me.*

Cam takes his guitar out first, and starts strumming a rhythm he's been working on for weeks, playing in his living room while I sit on the couch doing homework or watching movies. He hums along as I do the same. My guitar is sitting on my lap, but I can't bring myself to join him yet. I've known this song almost as long as he has. As soon as he had started playing it, I went home and learned it on my own. I've even added to it, and changed it.

"I know you have lyrics in your head," he says over the music. "I can practically see them on your lips. They want out." I get the puppy dog eyes again. "They *need* out, Vee." He gives me a huge smile, and I start to lose my resolve. I don't know if he even realizes it, but Cam doesn't smile much. Not like Logan or Anders, who walk around with perpetual grins on their faces. Cam makes you work for it. Each smile he gives me is like a carefully wrapped present. And he's right; there are absolutely lyrics trapped in me. But in *my* mind, the song he's singing is different.

I take a deep breath and steel myself. "In my mind it's actually a duet," I say. "A two-part call-and-response." Cam is looking at me with so much hope and excitement that I forget I'm supposed to be scared. I forget about that hidden fear, and that I don't play in front of anyone. "Like this." I pick the first few notes. "You keep playing, and I'll add."

Cam plays and I add a new rhythm line, and by the time the sun has fully set, Cam has started to add words and I'm beginning to feel alive. I didn't even know I wasn't, until this moment, when everything inside me began to open up, blossoming into something so much bigger. My heart starts to pound in rhythm to this song. *Our* first song.

There's this girl, yeah this girl,
who makes the world seem
brighter than it's ever been.
There's her smile and her eyes
and I just wanna make her mine—

The lyrics Cam is singing aren't the ones in my head. They're better. I add my own response that mirrors his, and we trade verses back and forth, telling each other all the things we haven't said. With the kind of honesty only lyrics can offer. And it's not Dakota telling Parker how she feels; it's Vee telling Cam. When it's just the two of us and our guitars, there's no room for anyone else.

When we play the final notes we're staring at each other and it suddenly feels too quiet. I can hear the blades of dune grass scratching against each other, and our heavy breathing. The soft rush of the water as it rages toward the shore. I think I hear Cam blink. And then a strange rhythmic sound that doesn't fit. I'm still staring at him. I wonder if this is what falling in love sounds like. Like butterfly wings in my ears and trumpets in my stomach and like the pound of bass in my chest. Until I realize it's the sound of applause. I lean over the railing and the group on the deck below us is clapping and cheering. One of them is shaking a tambourine overhead. Cam gives a dramatic bow and I follow. And I know; this is *exactly* what falling in love sounds like.

CHAPTER ELEVEN

NOW

CAM

Sometimes I forget that the whole reason I'm on tour is to win a competition. To walk away with a recording deal and make an actual living as a musician. The first two shows had felt like every other gig we've played in the last two months. We went onstage, did our thing, and the crowds loved it. By the second show, a few of the girls in the crowd were wearing the purple Future X shirts. But now, for show number three—the first live show—I can tell that something has changed backstage. The air is crackling with a certain amount of aggression. Everyone's on edge. The bands are all focused on the fact that two will be leaving soon. After nothing more than a tallying of public opinion, dreams will be ended. The drunken horseplay that had been filling the back rooms of the previous shows is now just drunken nerves.

As we exit the stage from our performance, I see Pax and Sid—our two bus mates from Caustic Underground—sitting on a ratty couch in one of the club's two back rooms. Two guys from The Phillips sit in metal folding chairs across from them. Between them is a large wooden trunk being used as a table, and it's covered with a colorful assortment of guitar picks. The perimeter is lined with glasses and bottles.

I tap the lead singer of The Phillips on the shoulder. "You're in the pit, man. Jenn wants you up front." He throws back the shot in his hand before sauntering toward the stage, his drummer following behind.

"What's this?" I say, taking a seat in one of the folding chairs while Reese grabs the other.

Pax waves a long arm over the table like a magician. "Sit down and find out."

"I'm in," Reese says, rubbing his hands together. "Whatever it is, I'm in. What are the rules?"

He looks at me expectantly. I have a stage high from our first live performance—the cameras moving all around us, the screaming crowd that was so much bigger than we had expected. Even as we walked into the venue, there were fans. Little clusters of kids and women, men and teens, waiting by the doors, in the parking lot, by the bathrooms. Someone even asked me for an autograph. *Whose life is this?* I would do just about anything right now. I feel invincible. "Sure, I'm in."

"Here's the deal," Pax says, setting down a deck of cards that I hadn't noticed he was holding. "We all start by throwing in a pick." He picks up a red triangle with a black bird on it and drops it back onto the table. I dig one of my Your Future X picks out of my pocket, and Reese throws in a black Playboy pick as I give him a questioning glance.

He shrugs his shoulders. "What?"

"Nothing, I just forget you're twelve years old sometimes," I say.

Reese just rolls his eyes and looks back to Pax, who is shuffling the cards, setting them in piles on the table.

Out in the hallway, bands are being shuffled from one staging area to another. I can hear the overly dramatic voice of the former-rockstar host as he intros The Phillips.

"When it's your turn, you pick a card." Pax flips over the top card on the pile closest to him and sets it down for us all to see. He goes through a list of rules that I'm not completely convinced he isn't making up on the spot. Take a drink for this, give a drink for that. It sounds like a really complicated version of Truth or Dare. Some of the cards require us to find girls to kiss backstage, others let us give out a dare to someone else.

I imagine Reese harassing the entire population of women hanging around backstage. "What is this, a slumber party?" Everyone ignores me.

"What about face cards?" Reese says, leaning forward in his chair, his elbows resting on his knees. He's *really* into this.

Pax is still running through the complicated list of probably-made-up rules. And they all lead to a lot of drinking—it sounds like a hot mess waiting to happen. *Thank God we've already played our set.* "Walk us through as we go?"

Pax has a wicked look in his eye. "Absolutely. Let's do this."

After a few rounds, Pax is the first to pull a kiss card. "Watch and learn," he says, dropping the card to the floor. We all turn to watch as he makes his way to the other side of the room where three girls are huddled together, holding plastic cups. Their eyes are fixed on the row of doors that lead to dressing rooms for the host and the guest performer of the night. The girls—two blondes and a brunette all in their early twenties—straighten when they see Pax approach. The tallest of them is wearing a purple Future X shirt that she's cut at an angle across her stomach, and ripped down the neck, revealing a lot of skin. *It's probably not what Vee had in mind when she picked out the T-shirts.* Pax leans into her ear, and with a teasing smile, she kisses him. Then she scribbles on a piece of paper and tucks it in his pocket. Pax turns to the other two girls, and they each hand him scraps of paper that he shoves into his jeans for extra points. When he returns to the game, it's with the blonde he kissed in tow.

"Guys, this is Bri," he says, as she sits down on the chair next to him.

Her eyes don't meet any of ours. "Hey."

If I hadn't just seen her kiss a stranger, I would think she was shy. Reese draws a king of spades, then lets out an annoyed grunt when Pax tells him to close his eyes and take a pick from the table. He fishes around in the pile and when he opens his eyes and sees the purple pick in his hand, I can't help but laugh at the tortured look on his face. This may be the best thing to happen to me since we came on tour.

Pax gives me a knowing look. "He's all yours. Whatever you want him to do."

"I want you to go talk to Jenn." I nod toward the tour's surly publicist, standing by the exit with her arms crossed. She's not much older than us, but she's scary, with her clipboard-waving and her constant yelling, and the way she's always jabbing her pen at someone. But I swear, Reese has a thing for her. She's one of the few girls I've seen him talk to without any indecent proposals or nausea-inducing innuendo.

A cocky grin spreads across Reese's face. "Nice."

"Tell her you need the bus to make a pit stop at a pharmacy." I stare at him, begging him to ask.

He squints his eyes at me. "Why?"

"You need to refill your prescription. For your—you know—rash."

"Hell, no." Reese throws the card down on the floor like it's dirty. "What's the penalty for not doing it?" He's looking over at Jenn, like *she's* the one who needs the prescription.

"Not an option," Pax says.

I'm not sure I've ever smiled so much. "Better jump on it, buddy."

Reese glares at me before walking toward Jenn. His hands are shoved deep into his pockets, his eyes focused on the floor. He shifts nervously from foot to foot as he speaks to her. I know the exact moment he says it, because I watch her eyes go wide and then she just nods at him as she grimaces. Like she's just smelled something rancid. *This is priceless.*

Reese returns to his seat and tips back his bottle.

"Not needed, man," Pax says.

Reese shakes his head at us. "Trust me, it's needed."

We all burst into laughter. Everyone except Reese, who is flicking beer caps onto the floor.

My third turn, when I have to draw a pick, I breathe a sigh of relief as I grab Sid's. Until Reese leans over and whispers something into his ear, eliciting a confused look from Sid. *I'm in trouble.*

Reese sticks his hand out to Sid. "Trust me." Sid nods and clasps his outstretched hand. "I'm going to go get your dare," Reese says as he walks away.

"You have to play the rest of the game with her here," Sid says. I have no idea what he means. Everything looks fuzzy around the edges and I wonder if Reese is bringing Jenn over here.

"With who?" I'm confused, until I see Reese wandering back, one arm slung over Vee's shoulders. She usually makes her way back onto the bus after we perform. I hadn't even realized she had stuck around.

Reese pulls his chair back and waves Vee to it. "Take my chair." Like he's being a gentleman and not the world's biggest jerk right now.

Vee leans forward in her chair, her elbows on her knees. "Reese said you needed one more person." She's looking at Sid, who is shuffling the cards together again. "What's the game?"

"We'll walk you through it as we go," Sid says. "You need a pick to throw in." Sid fishes in his pocket but comes up empty, and I grab one of my spare black picks and hand it to her. With her eyes fixed on the pile of picks, she gives me a mumbled "thanks." *Is this ever going to get less awkward?*

The answer is yes. Two rounds later, Vee is talking to me in full sentences. An hour later, I'm starting to forget she might hate me.

"Go over there. Right now." She's practically yelling, as she points a finger at Sid, who has a row of empty glasses in front of him. "Tell them"—she laughs before she can finish—"tell them they remind you of your mom." She giggles, and I can't help but laugh at how amused she is with herself. "And invite them back to the bus!" She says it in a dramatically sexy voice, then her face gets serious. She points a finger at Sid. "But don't you *dare* bring them on that bus. I mean, how deranged is someone who actually wants to hook up with a guy who compares them to his mother." Vee's nose is scrunched up and she shakes her head. "Gross." She bounces in her chair. "Go! Go!"

Sid pops out of his seat like he's actually excited about his task. "On it," he shouts as he walks away, red cup still in hand.

I laugh, and Vee meets my eye, clearly amused that I'm amused by her challenge. We're sharing a smile when Tad wanders into the room, his camera hanging at his side for once.

"Time to go." Tad waves his hands toward the exit. "And neither of your bands were eliminated, if you care."

Vee gasps, and her face is serious. She looks from me to Reese with a guilty look on her face, then bursts into laughter. We all join her, way past caring about anything Tad is saying.

By the time I make it to my bunk, everything is spinning.

A string of whiny, mumbled curses drifts out from behind Vee's curtain. She's got to be in bad shape.

"Stick one leg over the edge of the bed. The room will stop spinning," I say, looking over at her bunk as she pulls the curtain open.

One leg slides over the edge and she turns to look at me. "Thanks."

"No problem."

"I still hate you," she says.

"I know. Don't worry, tomorrow you probably won't even remember being nice to me tonight."

She doesn't say anything, but there's the faintest hint of a smile on her lips as we silently race toward unconsciousness.

CHAPTER TWELVE

THEN

CAM

At school, there's an unspoken rule: No touching. Friends only. I don't know when it started, sort of like I don't know when I started thinking of me and Vee as "more than friends," or when seeing her became as necessary as my 7 A.M. coffee. For weeks, I've been barely surviving on four hours of sleep, after leaving the beach. *I don't know how Vee does it.* She's actually cheery in the morning. *I've* resorted to drinking caffeinated mud, just to get through the day. That alone should be proof that I have a serious problem when it comes to Vee. I love my sleep like I love my food: in large quantities, whenever I can get it.

Learning that Vee had subconscious lines that weren't meant to be crossed only required a few shoulder smacks. Figuring out the actual *location* of that line was a lot harder. The same way she never came right out and asked questions, she also didn't come right out and tell me when I was crossing the line. But she always let me know. It took a handful of tumultuous days, a shit-load of trial-and-error, and a few elbow-bruised ribs, but I finally figured out what was, and was not, acceptable at school. Or at band practices. Basically anywhere we were in public together, where it wasn't covered in sand and drenched in darkness.

But like any good rule, I've found loopholes. Standing behind her, chest to back, hasn't earned me a slap or an elbow to the ribs. Any time I feel the urge to touch her—which is becoming more and more often—I find myself sliding in behind her and resting my hands on her shoulders. I do it while I talk to her, or while she talks to someone else. While I wait for her at her locker. Once in a while, if I catch her with her guard down, I can drop my hands to her waist. I usually have two minutes max before she coyly wiggles out of my grasp.

I want to ask her what the problem is, but I think I already know. Because when Vee told me about the drama with her parents, it felt a lot like an explanation. I could practically hear the unspoken words: "I'm not looking for a boyfriend." Sometimes I don't even know if that's what I want. It's not what I deserve. Sometimes you don't know what you want until you just do. It hits you like a wave, knocks you underwater, and when you surface, all you want is this one thing. It's like gasping for air. All I can think about right now is how much I want Vee.

It's ten o'clock on a Friday, pitch dark, and she's slipping on the leaves that are caked onto the sidewalk. She's almost fallen three times and still, she's stayed six feet ahead of me the entire three-block walk from my apartment to Todd Winter's house. Todd is a senior jock and a huge Melon Ballers fan. He invited all of us to his party, and even Vee—respecting Nonni's wishes—said yes. She had sounded like she was chewing on rusty nails while doing it, but she said yes. And she didn't put up a fight when I said we were going together. At least not until we left my apartment and she decided to leave a five-foot gap between us the entire walk. The same walk we make almost every night at two in the morning—hand in hand in the dark—when we walk from the beach back to my car. *After hours of practically spooning on the beach.* "This is dumb, Vee."

"What?" She sounds annoyed.

"You know what," I say, jogging to catch up to her, and grabbing her hand in mine.

She pulls it away in one tiny, sudden movement.

"Seriously. What the hell, Vee?"

Her eyes are fixed in front of her, on the giant house we're approaching. "Just don't, Cam."

"I don't get it. You can't cuddle on the beach with me every night and then ignore me all day."

"Ignore you? I see you all day. And we don't cuddle." She says the last word like she's appalled by it. As if I've accused her of pulling the wings off of butterflies.

Please. We cuddle the shit out of each other. "Oh, we don't," I say.

"No . . . we don't."

"I must be confused. Then I guess we can try out a few of our favorite *'not cuddling'* positions at the party and see what people think. Maybe do some spooning on the couch. That's your favorite, right?"

"You're disgusting," she says.

"And *you're* being *ridiculous!*"

We attract some curious looks from a group of smokers by the garage as we approach the house. Vee falls a few steps behind. She grabs me by the wrist and pulls me into a small clearing of trees along the sidewalk, taking us out of sight.

"You don't want this. If you did, you would have done something weeks ago."

She's panicking, talking herself out of this before it even starts. And I should be doing the same; I should be running.

"And we're graduating in seven months," she says.

"So?" I know exactly what she's implying: seven months until she leaves. Seven months until *I'll* leave. In seven months, she'll be at Michigan State with Logan and Anders and I'll be . . . I don't even know. She sure as hell doesn't. "I'm trying to hold your hand, Vee. I'm not asking you to marry me." I kick at the leaves on the sidewalk, scraping them away with my shoe. "Though we've already talked about our wedding, so this whole 'no holding my hand in public' thing seems sort of ridiculous, don't you think?"

She looks at me pointedly. "That was a joke."

Obviously. "Is this about Logan? About what people will say?"

"I don't care what people say—"

Yes, you totally do.

She looks down at her toe, stabbing it into the concrete next to mine. "But I do care what Logan says. What happens when we make . . . whatever this is . . . official? He'll know I didn't want a relationship with *him*. I just don't want to rub it in his face. Everything's already weird, Cam." She crosses her arms over her chest. "And the band knows what went down with Logan and me. They'll think I'm a hussy for hooking up with you."

"You're overreacting. No one's going to think you're a . . . hussy." I shake my head trying not to smile, but I can't help it. "No one even says the word 'hussy.'" Vee looks like she wants to smack me again. I wouldn't mind her touching me.

"There's this nurse who wears red lipstick and scrubs with black stilettos on them. Nonni calls *her* a hussy." She giggles nervously as she rests her forehead against my chest. Instinctively, my hands go to her back, holding her. She sighs, bumping her forehead against my chest again, like she wishes it was a wall and she could do some real damage.

"Who cares what other people think?"

"I care," she finally admits, her breath hot against my chest. "Sometimes I care a lot."

"Dakota doesn't care." I push a strand of hair behind her ear. "And I think Dakota's pretty amazing."

She sighs.

"We don't owe anyone an explanation. Not even Logan. Our relationship is our business."

She looks up at me. "We have a relationship?" Her face is covered in shadows from the nearby streetlight.

"We don't have to label it, if you don't want to," I say.

She shakes her head. "I don't."

Part of me wants to argue with her. To stake a claim and push for what I'm pretty sure I want. But what does a title matter? What right do I even have asking for one? I can't promise her anything.

I'm frozen on the sidewalk, not sure what to do, until she finally looks up at me again.

"Okay."

"Okay, what?"

"Okay . . . whatever. Dakota's in." Suddenly she can't look at me, her eyes roaming from my chest to her hands, to the street. "Just no making it official, or whatever." She gives me a sly smile. "Whatever, I guess. We'll do this relationship our way."

"Whatever?" I can't help the dopey grin that I know has invaded my face. "That's very romantic. You should write greeting cards. They'd say really poignant things, like 'I think you're better than a stick in the eye' and 'Will you maybe be my valentine if no one else is available?' Forget college or music—*that's* your calling."

"Whatever," she says, pulling away from me and nudging my shoulder with hers. That move, I've learned, is as close to "I'm sorry" as Vee gets. She smacks me when she's mad, nudges when she's sorry, and pokes me in the ribs when I'm embarrassing her.

"Okay then." I take her hand and pull her back onto the

sidewalk, pushing a few loose strands of hair behind her ear before leading her toward the house.

VIRGINIA

This isn't the first party I've been to. It's not even the third, or the seventh. It *is* the first one I've ever felt truly comfortable at. Maybe it's stupid or naive, but I feel like someone is watching out for me now. Cam doesn't just like me—he fought for me. He made me feel wanted. Tonight, my goal is to not think so much—to see what it's like to really let go. I should probably know my limits before I head to college next year. I'm not going to play babysitter to Cort or anyone else. Cam has promised to stay sober so he can make sure no one slips something in my drink or shoves me in a trunk. He's my insurance policy against ending up on a MISSING poster tonight. Tonight, I'm getting tipsy in the name of making Nonni proud. *Not weird at all.*

"Ohhhmigosh." Cort throws herself at me as I enter the marble-covered entryway of the ultra-contemporary condo we've just entered. She wraps her arms around my waist, and tries to pick me up, even though I'm a head taller than her. It's only been a month since the last time she was home, and already she looks different again. Her hair has gone from a shoulder-length bob to a shaggy blond pixie cut, with tiny streaks of green. Her nose has a tiny diamond stud in it that's still pink around the edges. "I can't be-lieeve it! You're actually going to do it!"

Cort sets me back down and almost topples onto me in the process. She's wearing tight jeans, black ankle-breaking heels, and a strapless red top—in October. She looks like she belongs in a dance club, and I wonder if this is how everyone dresses at the college parties she's going to now.

I have lots of experience with Drunk Cort. She's a louder, more emotional (if it's even possible) version of Sober Cort. And she's physical. Sober Vee wakes up with bruises the morning after a party, thanks to Cort's bear hugs and couch tackles. Sometimes being her friend is literally painful.

I put my hands on her shoulders, steadying her. "Whoa, there. Where's Anders?" I'm looking across the crowded room and scanning faces. Every square inch of the house is covered—in people, bottles, cans, or cups.

"Dunno." She shrugs. "He begged me to come to this. Now I'm here and he gets mad and walks off." It annoys me a little that she seems annoyed to be here; I'm letting the conversation end, because Cort plus Anders plus alcohol usually equals tears and screaming in the end. And I don't plan on playing referee tonight.

"Let's get you another drink," I say, throwing my arms around her again. "I've missed you."

"You! You need a drink!" Cort waves her arms in the air, and then gives a questioning look at Cam. He's taking full advantage of our new pro-touching-in-public agreement, with one hand on my waist and the other on my shoulder. "Well, hellooo!" Cort says, as if he just joined us and hasn't been plastered behind me since we got here. "You must be Cam." She's giving me a not-at-all-sneaky sideways glance. *Nice, Cort.*

Cam sticks his hand out to her. "And you must be the infamous Cort." He shakes her hand while his other still rests on my waist.

"Ohhh, infamous. I like it." *Score one for Cam.* "You're going to take care of our girl, right?" Cort looks like she's challenging Cam to a staring contest.

"Yeah, I'll take care of her."

I look up at him over my shoulder.

He winks at me. "Or whatever."

Cort's hands go to her hips and her eyes narrow. "What was that?" Cam probably thought she was too drunk to catch his little move, but he doesn't know Cort. At this point, she's acting a lot more drunk than she actually is. "What was that wink about?" She's looking between me and Cam like she's trying to make a choice. Probably determining the weakest link.

"There was no wink." Cam removes his hands from me and shoves them in his pockets. *Smooth.*

"You winked," Cort says.

Cam keeps his voice serious. "It was a blink."

" 'Whatever'?" Cort throws up air quotes in front of her. "I know a wink when I see one."

"Shots!" I push Cam in the direction of the kitchen and pull my wobbly best friend into a sideways hug as he walks off. Cort is giggling, her flushed cheeks heating even more.

"Have I mentioned how cute he is, Vee?" She gives him a long, exaggeratedly appraising look as he walks away, and I smack her. "And I think he's kind-of sort-of in love with you."

"He's not in love with me. Not kind of *or* sort of. We're friends. Don't be stupid." I don't like lying to my best friend, but Cort can't keep a secret from Anders. And Anders tells Logan when he has an itch. So telling Cort about me and Cam isn't an option right now. I just need a few weeks before I start beating the proverbial drums of change, that's all. And he's *not* in love with me, so I'm not even lying. I'm just not elaborating.

"Friends. Right." Cort waves her hands in surrender. "I'll drop it, because I know you're weird about this stuff. But you're *not* just friends. And yes, he totally *is* in love with you. Kind of *and* sort of." She jabs my shoulder with her finger. "I know these things."

"You know nothing," I say. She's known him for exactly two minutes.

"I. Know. Everything." Her words are slow and dramatic.

"You're staying at Cam's with me, right?" Cam's parents are out of town and he invited the three of us to stay at his apartment, since it's walking distance from the party. It's half the reason I agreed to come.

She nods. "And you're staying at *my* house, right?" She gives me an exaggerated wink. "Did you catch my blink just then?" She sticks her tongue out and I try to grab it like we did when we were little kids. When Cam comes back into the living room I'm grabbing at Cort's lip.

Cam wedges himself between the two of us. "You good?"

I eye the three shot glasses in his hand. "Are you? I thought you weren't drinking."

"I'm not, but I found this idiot in the kitchen." He nods behind him at Anders, whose vintage Ramones shirt is soaked in red liquid. I cringe thinking about what—or more likely, who—ruined one of his prized possessions. *I have twenty bucks on the crazy-eyed blonde standing across from me.*

Cort grabs one of the tiny plastic cups from Cam's fingers. "I'll take that," she says. I do the same, and Cort plucks the last cup from Cam's hand and dangles it in front of me. "This one, too. You need to catch up."

I take the second cup, holding one in each hand, looking at them like they're filled with worms. They smell disgusting.

Cam is behind me, his warm chest against my back. He whispers in my ear. "You good?" I flinch, but fight the urge to pull away. *No more hiding.* I let myself relax against him. His lips are almost touching my ear when he whispers, "Whatever?"

I nudge my shoulder into his side and my hand rests on his hard stomach. "Whatever." My plastic glass clinks against Cort's and the liquid slides down into my already warm, buzzing belly. I'm not sure if the heat is from the alcohol, or Cam's hands.

CAM

"Truth," she says.

We're sitting on an oversized chair in one of the house's three living rooms, playing a two-person game of Truth or Dare. Vee is draped across my lap with her legs dangling off the side of the oversized chair she calls a Snuggler. "Because you're forced to sit really, really close to someone," she says. "Or to sit *on* them, in this case." Her cheeks are red like she's been standing in the cold, and all of her words are becoming soft, one sliding into the next.

She lays her head against my chest while I think about what to ask her. Despite all of the time we've spent together, something about being with her still feels so finite. I want to make the most of every minute, each opportunity to know more.

She drums her fingers on my leg. "Any day now."

"Tell me something no one else knows."

"Counter offer." She thrusts her hand up in front of her, holding up one finger and tapping it in the air. "I'll show you something no one else has *seen*." She pushes herself up, using my chest to propel her, and holds her hand behind her as she begins to walk away from me without a pause. I grab it quickly, following behind. She doesn't turn as she talks to me, she just yells loudly over the crowd. "As long as you're up for a walk!"

"When I was really little, like maybe six or seven, my parents would walk me down to the water with one of them holding each of my hands." Vee's staring down at her feet as they sink into the silt along the edge of the water. Her toes wiggle under the surface. She looks peaceful.

Definitely a little drunk.

"We'd make footprints in the sand." Her head turns, just barely, to face me, her eyebrows raised. "You know what they say about footprints in the sand?"

"My gram has an embroidered pillow that says one set of footprints means God was carrying you."

She smiles, but looks confused. I can't help but laugh.

"If you let the water wash your footprints away, they'll be transported to the other side of the lake." She says this like it's a fact. "That's what my mom would always say, at least . . . It's not on a pillow, or anything official like that, though." She bites her lip, trying not to smile.

And now she's sitting down.

Right in the water, where she stood just seconds ago, Vee is lying back in the surf, letting the water rush up her calves, lapping at her knees and up to her shoulders. With her arms stretched out at her sides, she looks like she's making a snow angel in the wet sand.

Maybe she's drunker than I thought.

"Did you eat anything before I picked you up, Vee?"

She's giggling as the waves pull at her, soaking her clothes. I don't know what to do, so I just sit down in the dry sand behind her, making sure Lake Michigan doesn't decide to rush up and drown her. Or wash her away, like her footprints. It doesn't feel real being here with her. It feels like it's a memory already—like one of those moments you know you'll be looking back on, before it's even over. I pull out my phone and take a picture of her, lit only by the night sky. She looks like a ghost. Her eyes are closed, every piece of her washed out into shades of gray by the moonlight. It's quiet. The light whistling of the wind and the waves clawing at the shore are the only noise. We're too far from the boardwalk to hear the familiar sound of the guitars and drums that usually keep us company.

"I used to come out here when my parents were fighting. Before they sold the house." She stretches an arm over her head and points behind me, to where houses are set back into the dunes, crowded by trees. "We used to live in that little green one. It was my Grandma Miller's house, before I was born." There's a long pause. "Anyways, I'd just lie here and wish the water would wash me away. That it would take me somewhere. Anywhere but here. I couldn't stand the idea of being *here*."

"Because you thought they'd get divorced."

"No." Her voice is barely a whisper. "I worried they'd stay together. That things would never feel normal again if they tried to put the pieces back together. A new version of them seemed like it would be better than a broken, poorly pieced-together one." She closes her eyes and turns away from me before she continues. "They're not together anymore. They won't admit it, but I know it. Dad lives in Chicago, and when he does come home, my mom isn't even around. And he thinks I don't notice, because he gets up so early, but he sleeps on the couch. None of his clothes are even in the house. I used to think things were perfect, but maybe it was always a lie." She's rambling, one softly spoken word slurring into the next. "Still, I was horrible to wish for it. I *am* horrible." She shakes her head, tears running down her cheeks.

"You're not horrible." I lean forward and cover her hand with mine, the cold sand rough between our skin. I stand and pull her to her feet. Her soaked-through clothes hang heavy. Her eyes are glossy and distant, like she isn't actually seeing me, even with her eyes fixed on mine. She looks at me under hooded lids as I hold her face in my palms. The warmth of her tear-stained skin seeps into my cold hands.

I want to kiss her.

Dammit. This is probably one of the most inappropriate times in all of history to want to kiss someone, but I want to. I guess I'm an asshole. Because all I can think about is pressing my lips against hers until she stops looking so sad and broken and barely held together. I want to, but even with her clothes clinging to her skin under the moonlight—her body so close I can feel the warmth—I know I shouldn't.

She's drunk. And sad.

And—probably more important than either of those things—I don't want our first kiss to be associated with her crying. I don't want to train her brain to cry every time I kiss her. Like Pavlov's dog. *Is that even possible?* Or worse yet, she'll forget everything when she finally wakes up tomorrow, hungover and miserable. My thumbs drag across her cheeks, ineffectively trying to dry them as water continues to spill from her eyes. It's hard to tell the tears from the lake water, but maybe I'm just trying to convince myself she wasn't just sobbing.

"You're drunk and emotional, but definitely not horrible. You're one of the least horrible people I know. Not even top ten." When she laughs it feels like a small victory. A tiny battle won against the sadness and guilt that I can tell is buried deep inside of her. Part of me wants to tell her that I'm a soldier in the same war, except that I actually deserve it. My parents are dead and it's my fault.

CHAPTER THIRTEEN

NOW

CAM

I had assumed that musicians on tour didn't actually party every night. That it was just a stereotype perpetrated by the old VH1 rockumentaries Anders and Logan were obsessed with watching before we left for tour. But it turns out most shows actually *do* end with everyone out at the bars. Except for those of us who can't get into bars. No one is letting us drink underage with a bunch of cameras trailing us. So we do our own thing. That usually means talking Pax and some of the other guys into buying for us, and setting up camp in one of the buses, or the backroom of the venue we're rehearsing at. When your workday ends after midnight, and you have nothing waiting for you but a tiny bed in a cramped bus, anywhere else looks pretty good.

"On the cover of the *Rolling Stone*!" Anders sings, with an exaggerated rasp, pounding his hands along the wood-paneled hallway as he walks into the dimly lit room. The Room, as they call it, is a lounge space inside The Tabernacle—a historic church converted into a music venue in the heart of Atlanta. In three days we'll be onstage, tiers of balconies looming over us; but tonight, we're camped out offstage, fresh off of an amazing rehearsal. From top to bottom, the Room is encased in wood. It covers the walls and wraps over the doorways, and across the bars that run along one side of the room. A line of wood booths is across from the couches we're sitting on, and the wood floors are covered in huge red, green, and gold rugs that remind me of something in an old horror movie house.

"*Rolling Stone, Rolling Stone,*" Reese joins in as he drops onto the sofa across from me. Soon, Pax and a few of the other guys have joined in this god-awful eighties monstrosity that our bus driver Hal introduced us to. It's just us and Caustic Underground on the bus now. We lost The Phillips after the third show, but one of the empty spots on the bus was quickly filled by Bri, who became a permanent fixture with Pax after showing up backstage at our last two shows. Hopefully she knows better than to divulge too much in the confessional interviews. I don't think Jenn would hesitate to cast her as the country's most pathetic groupie if it boosted ratings. Vee was adorably excited to have another girl on the bus, even though Bri spends most of her time attached to Pax's face. Bri watches from a stool at the bar as Pax keeps singing this torturous song, but Vee and Logan are the only ones noticeably missing from the festivities.

The room is already crowded with band members, crew, and even some fans, standing around in little clusters, eyeing us from a distance. Fans who don't talk to us make me feel like a zoo animal. Like I'm on this side of the glass, and they're out there— wondering what I eat and how I have enough room to run around. At the entrance, Marcus, one of the tour roadies, is dropping cell phones into a basket. Pictures floating around of bands drinking with fans is the last thing Jenn wants. And trouble with Jenn is the last thing any of us needs.

Sometimes I feel like there's a weird alarm in my head, because Vee has barely made it through the doorway before I notice her. Logan has his hand on her back as he gently pushes her through the crowd toward us, with Tad following close behind. Vee's black dress is lower than anything I've seen her wear on tour. Or ever, maybe. It's the sort of thing she would have hated to wear when we first met. A Dakota Gray outfit. *Does she still think about her?*

In the two weeks since our behind-the-scenes clips started airing with each episode, Logan and Vee have quickly become a talking point. A hometown love story for everyone to drool over. *Spare me.* The comments on social media (which, I'm horrified to admit, I'm addicted to reading) run the gamut. There are those who gush: "They are so cute," "Maybe he'll propose on tour," and "She's so lucky!" Then there are the *other* comments: "She's not good enough for him," "Gold digger," "He can do better." There are ten times more of *those* comments, and I hope like hell Vee doesn't read them like I do. Most of America seems to be waiting for Logan and Vee to crash and burn. And I'm not proud to say it, but I can't help but agree. I'm ready for management to pull the plug. *Will I bring popcorn to the breakup extravaganza?*

Vee takes a seat on the couch across from me, crossing her long, naked legs in what feels like slow motion. I shift in her direction. "Hey—" But as quickly as she came, she's gone, following Bri to the other side of the room, where someone has set up speakers and there's a group of people pressed together on the makeshift dance floor. A thumping, electronic beat saturates the room and vibrates under my feet.

Anders and I are as alone as you can be in a room full of people—and it's nice to have a break from the cameras—to be so boring they don't even bother coming around.

"Cheers to a kick-ass new song," Anders says, holding up his glass. I do the same.

"To the girl in the purple shirt," I say, keeping my eyes on Vee, who is swinging her hips from side to side, dipping up and down, in rhythm to the music.

Anders laughs. "The girl in the purple shirt." He shakes his head, looking at me sympathetically. "Man, you've got it bad." We've never talked about the meaning of the song. It's a sort of unspoken agreement among us that we don't pry when it comes to original songs. It started back when Vee wrote all their songs. If she'd had to talk through each of them, they wouldn't have had a single original to play. Of course, the rule doesn't apply to me.

I set my glass on the table. "Don't start."

"I don't blame you, man, but Vee's stubborn. You've got a long road ahead of you."

"Noted." I give him a look that I hope says, *Shut the hell up and move on.*

Anders has his phone out, absentmindedly typing as I grab a bottle of beer from the cooler Pax filled for us and hold another in front of Anders.

"Beer?" I ask, but Anders doesn't seem to notice. "Anders?" Anders nods idly and continues staring down at the screen. I smack the phone in his hand. "Who is that?"

"Cort."

"Scary ex-girlfriend Cort?"

He grins. "That's the one."

"She telling you what a dick you are?"

"Nah, she's sexting me."

I nearly spit out my beer. "Shit, seriously?" The last time I talked to Anders about Cort before we left LA, he said they hadn't spoken since they broke up the summer after graduation. The fact that Cort is now sending him lewd messages gives me a twisted glimmer of hope that maybe Vee and I can get back even a fraction of what we used to have. Though I really don't expect I'll be getting a "touch me here" text from her any time soon.

My eyes drift over to where Bri and Pax are dancing, their

faces interlocked. I spot Vee in a group of fans, talking and laughing, as she throws back the last of a beer. It's hard to take my eyes off of her, even when she catches me staring, and things start getting uncomfortable.

VIRGINIA

If Cam wants to stare at me, I'm going to give him something to watch. Something to really think about. As much as I hate to admit it, when I put on this little sundress, this is the moment I'd had in mind. Him thinking about what he could have had, what he missed, what he wasted.

Tad is standing at the edge of a pulsing group of people, and it's weird to see him without his camera. I put my hands up in front of my face like my own imaginary camera, and weave through the tangle of bodies toward Tad. He's smiling at me.

"What was your favorite thing about today?" I say, still point-ing my imaginary camera at him, doing my best impression of the confessional interviews we're always doing.

He scrunches his lips up like he's thinking really hard, and my eyes drift to his chest tattoo on full display in his V-neck shirt. "This moment is pretty high up there," he says, and I can feel the heat creep up my neck.

"Wanna dance?"

His sexy grin says yes, so I pull him by his wrist to where there's a crowd dancing. I love this feeling, like my head is half detached, like I'm watching myself being so bold, letting the stress float out of my fingers as I wave them above me. I feel a hand on my waist.

"Babe—" I turn to find Logan sheepishly holding a plastic cup. "You left your drink."

"Did you just call me *babe*?" I shake my head. *What is this life right now?*

Tad looks embarrassed, and I don't know why, because I'm sure he was flirting with me. He's probably embarrassed for Logan—the way he's shyly trying to wedge himself between us like he's a middle school dance chaperone or something. I take the glass from his hand and take a long drink—the tangy liquid biting on its way down my throat.

I smile at Tad again, but he's not looking at me the same.

Logan takes my elbow and wraps my arm around his waist. "Dance with *me*, Vee." It's weird to hear, the way his voice sounds like he wants this but doesn't. I start to pull away and he pulls me closer, his mouth to my ear. "Dance with your *boyfriend*, Vee."

I close my eyes. "I'm an idiot," I mutter.

"You're just a lightweight." Logan pulls me into a hug. "Just lay off the crew, okay?" he jokes.

"Don't leave me alone with Bri again," I say, thinking about the shots she was so excited about when we were getting dressed. Of course Bri doesn't have to worry about a fake boyfriend, or an ex-whatever, or anything, really.

"Deal," Logan says.

CHAPTER FOURTEEN

THEN

VIRGINIA

I thought he was going to kiss me. There was that look—the moment of hesitation just before a guy kisses you, when they're giving you a chance to run away. At least, I think that's what that moment is for. Otherwise, why hesitate? Just go for it. But Cam isn't a creep, and I just spilled my guts and cried. And . . . *Oh, God, did I ugly-cry?* My tears had felt delicate. Sure, there were a lot of them, but I'm not snotty or hyperventilating, or exhibiting any of the other telltale signs of the ugly-cry. Thanks to the ever-present lake breeze, my face is already dry.

Taking my own advice, I don't hesitate. *Just do it.* There is no chance for him to run, as I slam my lips into his, grabbing fistfuls of his shirt to steady myself. His reaction is immediate, as his hands slip around my waist, pulling me tight to him. Warm hands slide under my shirt, landing on the cold skin just above the waist of my soaking wet jeans. It sends a shiver through me as hot meets cold. His tongue brushes along my lips and just as mine part, I feel his body go rigid. Still holding me by my hips, he pushes me back, and suddenly there's a foot of space between us. My hands fall away from his neck at the abrupt movement, landing on his shoulders.

"Shit," he mutters.

Not the reaction I was going for. "Shit? Really?" I twist in his grip, trying to pull myself loose, but he keeps me firmly in place.

"I shouldn't have."

"You shouldn't have?" I shake my head and let out something that sounds like an agitated grunt. *Did I imagine the moment?* I really don't think so. Two minutes ago, this stupid jerk wanted to kiss me. "What happened to 'whatever'? You didn't seem to have a problem feeling me up in Todd's living room, in front of Cort." I place a finger on his chest. "And *I* kissed *you,* genius. In case you didn't notice."

"I noticed." He lifts a hand from my waist and runs it through his hair. "But you're drunk."

Is that all? He doesn't want to kiss me when I'm drunk? Relief washes through me. *Am I drunk?* I don't think so. I just feel fuzzy. My cheeks are sort of numb and my skin is hot everywhere. *Is this what being drunk feels like?* "I don't think I'm drunk."

"The fact that you're not sure, means you probably are." We're still standing together, locked in our middle school dance position, and all I can think about is kissing his twitchy lips; revealing that smile I can see just under the surface.

"Maybe you should test me." I pull away from him and walk backward, using my toe to drag a line through the sand. "I was going to say I should walk along this, but I think the fact that I can walk backward in the sand right now actually says a lot more." I giggle as I hold my arms out to the side, lifting one index finger to my nose and then the other, before walking heel to toe down the sandy line, like people do on cop shows. Like a tightrope walker. The entire time I walk toward him, Cam's grin grows bigger, and as I reach the end of the line, I cross one foot behind the other and curtsy like a princess.

As I hold up the skirt of my imaginary dress, Cam breaks into a fit of laughter. "I'm sure the police would love that little move. Very cute. Definitely use that some day."

"I'm adorable. They'd love it." Cam is still several feet from me, and as we continue to stand apart like this, a tiny twinge of doubt sets in. *Maybe he thinks the kiss was a mistake. A temporary error in judgment. Maybe he was just being nice, trying to avoid this without hurting my feelings. If he wanted to, he could have kissed me weeks ago. Maybe he thinks this is a horrible idea. He has to see me at band practices, after all. At school. Earlier, I basically told him to deny our relationship.* I know this thing between us is something more than an elaborate friendship. Whether I admit it out loud or not, I do know it. I stare down at my toe, drawing loops in the sand as I nervously chew my lip. Sometimes I wish I weren't such an idiot.

"I've wanted to kiss you since the first time I saw you." His voice jerks me out of my thoughts and I meet his stare. Taking a step toward me, he closes the space between us and reaches for me, gripping my wrist and pulling me the last few inches toward him. He stops me short of crashing into him and holds me there, as his other hand brushes away the hair flying across my face. "Just one stipulation."

"There are stipulations to kissing you? Like, you have demands?"

"Just one."

My hands settle on my hips. "I don't negotiate with terrorists." *I don't mean it.*

"Vee."

I look up at the dark sky, so I don't have to look at him. "Fine. What are your demands?"

"If you wake up tomorrow and don't remember any of this"— he's giving me a threatening look, but he's on the verge of smiling—"I'll have to jog your memory by kissing you." In the absence of his voice, the sound of the waves fills my ears. "In the middle of the cafeteria. Monday morning. In front of *every-one*." He tucks another wild strand of hair behind my ear and his hand lingers on my neck, sending a shiver through me. "And there'll be no denying . . . whatever . . . if that happens. So, consider yourself warned."

"No forgetting. I promise to remem—" but before I can finish, his lips are on mine again. They're soft but urgent, warm and wet. I lean into him, our bodies pressing tightly together, and his arms twist around me, trying to pull me even closer. Fingers tangle in my hair and his tongue finds mine. I've never been kissed like this before. We've waited so long to cross this line, and now that we're on the other side, I don't know how to step back. *Why did we wait?* He bites at my lip and runs his hand up my back, and I decide we might stay like this forever. We're never leaving the beach. The wind has picked up, and suddenly the sand is pelting us, but I don't even mind. Until Cam turns his head away and spits, wiping at his mouth.

"Sand is—everywhere." He laughs and so do I. "This is really sexy."

I start wiping at the sand caked to my face, but my hands are covered in it too.

Cam makes a futile effort to brush off my cheeks. "I think it's hopeless." He kisses me on the lips, which are definitely covered in sand as well. When he pulls away, his lips scrunch up and his tongue pokes out just a little, like a lizard, darting in and out. I think he's going to spit again, but he doesn't.

I can't help but laugh, but I'm also not ready to stop. All I can think about is his lips and his tongue, and my lips and my tongue, and his hands and my hands. The possibilities, the combinations. He wipes a hand across his mouth and lets out a little cough.

I brush my thumb across his mouth. "You really want to spit, don't you?"

"I really do. I think it's in my teeth." He turns away from me and I do the same. We spit in opposite directions. Maybe he was right, and I *am* drunk. I'm standing next to the guy who gave me the best kiss of my life, and I just spit. I should be horrified, digging myself a deep hole to crawl into. Instead, I'm looking at Cam, while he looks at me, and we can't stop laughing as we walk along the beach, making the slow trek back to the parking lot, hand in hand.

There's definitely a storm coming—the air has gotten colder and when a shiver ripples through me, Cam lets go of my hand and wraps his around my hip, pulling me toward him and cradling me into his side. I fit perfectly against him, like I always do. The sounds of bongo drums and acoustic guitar float across the air and I know we're getting closer to the beach entrance. Closer to reality.

Cam leans down and kisses my hair. No one's done that before, and somehow, this simple gesture feels like the most intimate thing that has ever happened to me.

CHAPTER FIFTEEN

NOW

CAM

If watching Vee playfully flirt with Tad was like getting a root canal—*which it was*—then watching her wrapped around some random guy is like open-heart surgery minus the anesthesia. I had stopped watching Vee a long time ago, but now my eyes are back on the dance floor. On *her*. Partly because Logan has long since abandoned her, but also because I'm lacking the self-control to stop myself. I've lost count of her drinks, but she's swaying more than dancing. She's been dancing with the same guy for a while now, since all the camera crew left. He's got his arm wrapped around her hip, and they're headed for the door; I can't ignore it any longer. By the time I've pushed through the now very drunk crowd, I basically have to lunge in front of the exit. Vee looks more like a rag doll than a person, like she can barely keep herself on her own feet.

"Come on, Vee." I grab her hand gently, and pull her toward me, while this idiot pulls her back toward him. As though we're going to have an *actual* tug-of-war over her.

I take a step forward. "Don't." I'm a head taller and have

thirty pounds on him. And *I* won't even consider leaving this club without Vee.

She's scowling at me, but her eyes seem playful. "I'm just having fun, *Cameron*." She says my name slowly, like my name is a swear word.

"Really? Because it looks like you're just getting dragged out of here by some creep." I glare at the stranger's hands still resting on Vee's hips. "Hands off, man."

"You're the boyfriend?"

Vee looks up at him and shakes her head like he's crazy. "Oh, no, this isn't my boyfriend. My boyfriend is the *lead* singer."

"We're both lead singers." I don't know why I'm even arguing, and I grab for her hand.

"I want to see the Ferris wheel, *Cameron*." She nods to the window where the massive SkyView is blinking, the covered gondola seats moving across the window and out of sight.

"We can go tomorrow, Vee." I reach for her hand once more and she jerks it away.

"You . . . ve noright." Her words are all blurring together. "I don't wanna go anywhere with you, *Cameron*!" She's getting loud and attracting some attention, and her new friend is looking annoyed. He raises his hands in the air and takes a step back. Vee stumbles as she loses his support, and I grab her arms and pull her toward me. Instead of thanking me for keeping her off a MISSING poster, Vee uses her tiny fists-of-fury to nail me in the shoulder. Over and over. All the while telling me how much she hates me. How she wishes I weren't here. The tour would be perfect if I weren't on it, and why did I have to make her life miserable? *Making her miserable is my life's work, apparently.*

"You have anger management issues," I say. "You know that, right?" This girl will be the death of me—I throw my arm behind her knee, knocking her off her feet as I scoop her up into my arms. As much as I wanted her to finally explode and just let me have it—I'm just annoyed. And this is nowhere near private.

She lets out a squeak of panic. "You coulda cracked my head open."

"Not likely." I smile at her in my arms, just to push her. "Too hard."

Her mouth is scrunched up like she's sucking on a lemon. I could tell her how cute she is when she's mad, and really piss her off, but I don't feel like dealing with her fists again. We're making enough of a scene. As I push through a cluster of people gathered in front of the exit, Vee kicks her legs, clipping people with her flailing limbs, squealing apologies of "Ohmigosh. Sosorry. Isallhisfault. I'msodrunk."

"No shit," I mutter.

"No one asked you to do this." Her voice is acerbic, hateful.

"You never have to ask me to do this." I look down at her body in my arms. "I'm not just standing around while you get dragged half unconscious into the alley by some drunk asshole."

"He was nice," she says matter-of-factly.

I roll my eyes. "He was an asshole."

"How's Sienna?"

I don't answer, I just push the bar on the metal door and step out into the hot Georgia night. We're in the small roadway that runs along The Tabernacle. The huge Ferris wheel spins over us, and we're so close to the bottom of it, I feel like we're miniatures. Vee is staring up at the lights, and I think maybe this is over.

Vee's eyes go back to my face. "How about that girl you kissed backstage, then? How's she?" I hadn't even known she was backstage. Of course that's my luck. *Thank you, Universe.*

"That was a stupid game, and you know it," I say. "I would have made out with *you*, if you weren't busy acting like I was some kind of monster. So that wasn't an option, was it?"

She says nothing, and I can feel the irritation growing inside me, burning alongside the drinks. *Why does she get to ignore me for days at a time, spend the night making me jealous, and then treat me like an asshole when I save her from some guy who actually is an asshole?*

"No snarky comment about how horrible I am?" I ask. "That's an interesting change."

She just stares up at me silently, and I keep my eyes focused on the road ahead of me.

When the bus is in view, Vee starts twisting, trying to stand up on her own. I let her legs go, letting them drop to the ground, my other arm still wrapped around her waist, holding her up. Her chest is pressed up against me, her face so close our noses are almost touching, and there's a feeling between us I don't quite recognize. The sweetness we had before is gone. There are no "I love you"s, no forehead kisses or gentle touches. She takes a deep breath, and I can feel it against me; the air trapped between us.

I turn us toward the building and walk her backward, my eyes locked on hers, until the brick wall of The Tabernacle stops us. Until all I can feel is her body. I feel the weight of her against me as her back hits the wall. My hand goes to her hip, roughly pulling her closer. I'm going to remind her how good we were. I run my hand down her leg, feel her slick dress turn to bare skin, and she gasps. I brace myself for her to tell me I've gone too far. We're not us anymore. "Vee—" My voice is hoarse and tense, as I dare her to look me in the eyes when she tells me she doesn't feel the same way I do. But her wide eyes aren't on me. They're on the blinking red light at the end of the alley, pointed right at us.

CHAPTER SIXTEEN

THEN

CAM

By the time we walk back to the party, Vee looks like she's ready to curl up on the sidewalk and go to sleep. We collect Anders and Cort, who made up sometime while we were on the beach, and if I didn't think Vee would kill me, I'd leave them here. The last thing I need is the two of them going all Discovery Channel on my living room couch. Vee climbs onto my back, and I walk the three blocks to my apartment with her wrapped around me like a half-asleep baby monkey.

By the time I get her to my room, she's dead weight. I sit down, letting her drop onto the bed behind me. She's still wearing her wet clothes, and water is bleeding all over my blue comforter.

"Vee?" She's lying motionless on the bed, her legs still dangling over the edge. I shake her lightly but she doesn't move. *Shit.*

I walk out to the living room, hoping Anders and Cort are still decent. "Hey, Cort, can you come help me?" The two of them are sitting on the edge of the couch.

"You propositioning my girl, Fuller?" He's joking, but his voice doesn't have the same arrogant confidence it usually does.

"Definitely not." I wave Cort over to my room. "I just need

to borrow her for a second, to help Vee." I turn to Cort. "Can you just get her undressed?" I hand her one of my shirts and a pair of boxers. "She's soaking wet."

Her eyes narrow and she tips her head to one side. "*You're not wet.*"

"Long story. Will you please just—" I thrust the clothes at her.

Cort winks at me as she pushes past me. "I'm sure she'd rather you did it."

"I'm not risking getting my ass kicked in the morning."

"Probably a smart choice." Just short of the bed, she turns back to me. "But I'll be the one doing the ass kicking, if you screw this up." Cort is small and dainty—barely five feet—but she seems like the kind of girl who would exact revenge. There's this gleam in her eye that says she'll carve her name into the side of your car if you give her a reason. Or an excuse. I grab a glass of water from the kitchen and fish the Tylenol out of a cabinet.

Cort drops back down onto my couch, which Anders has pulled out into a bed. "All set," she says.

Vee is tucked under the covers and I crawl in, staying as far from her as I can. There's a good chance I'll wake her if I have a nightmare. *I didn't think this through.* As much as I want her in my bed, want her closer to me more than I should, it reminds me of the last time I slept in the same bed with someone. And I'm all the more certain I'll be waking her up when those memories inevitably invade my sleep.

I wake up and I can't figure out why it's foggy. I'm sleeping in the guest bedroom; Sienna is next to me, lying in just her tank top and panties. The covers are pushed down all around her. My vision is hazy. It's so warm, even for March in northern California, and the strangest fog is hanging over us. It drifts toward

the bed, wrapping around me, and as I yawn it invades my lungs.
I cough, harder and harder, until I'm finally awake, finally thinking, and throw the covers off of me. Everything is quiet except
for a soft rushing and clicking sound.

"Sienna!" I push her roughly and she startles, disoriented. I
grab her arm, pulling her off the bed with me as I make my way
to the door.

"Cameron." She pushes me away as she tumbles off the bed.
"What the hell?"

I edge toward the door and touch the knob, hesitantly. I'm
not sure if it's warm or if it's me—heated from sleep—but it
doesn't seem hot. It's not scorching my hand but it's definitely
warm. Do I open it? Sienna is behind me, wrapped around my
arm, her chest pressed up against me as I start to turn the knob,
easing it open slowly. Smoke billows in thickly from the hallway
and I slam the door shut as Sienna screams, pulling at my arm
roughly.

I look at the nightstand, remembering that I left my cell
behind when we left my room. This guest room—my sister Maggie's old room—has a bigger bed than my tiny twin. "Give me
your cell," I say, grabbing her by the arm and pulling us both
toward the window.

"It's—it's—I don't have it." She's digging through her backpack next to the bed. "It's in your room. It must be. Or in the
kitchen?"

"Fuck." I run to the window, unlocking it and shoving it open,
letting in a gust of air. It's windy—really windy—and it feels
amazing against my hot skin.

"Cameron, the door." Smoke is coming in heavy through the
cracks, the air getting thicker and thicker with hazy gray.

Hunched low, I scramble to the door. "Give me the sheet!" I'm
kneeling on the floor, the hot smoke against my bare knees, waving my hand in the air behind me. Sienna pulls at it frantically,

removing the flowery yellow fabric and shoving it in my direction. I cram it under the door, filling the small crack with the soft fabric. Sienna is sobbing, her shoulders heaving up and down as she looks from the door to the window.

"Down," I say, grabbing her hand and pulling her to the floor. She's taking jagged breaths and I don't know if it's her asthma, or if she's panicking. It's freaking me out. I can't remember if I'm supposed to leave the window open or closed. Air feeds fire. But the smoke. We make it back to the window and shove our heads out, feeling the cool night air invade our lungs as we gasp to take in the clean air. We're at the back of the house, and I can see just one tiny light in the distance—the Andersons' porch light. They live in a nearly identical home on the other side of the small river that divides our property from theirs. What time is it? We didn't even go to bed until two.

I grab my white undershirt from the floor and hang it out the window, waving it frantically as I scream at the top of my lungs. I don't know what to do. Do we wait? Stand here in the window until someone sees us? Or sees the fire? Do we have time for that? I lean my head out of the window, trying to get a look at the house and can see that the windows below us are glowing, casting light out onto the patio below. It looks like every light is on in the house, except these lights are dancing and snapping and hissing. The air all around is opaque with smoke.

Fuck.

"Cameron?" Sienna still has her head hanging out the window. "It's getting hotter in here. It's hotter, don't you think?" Her voice is panicked. I crawl over to the door, putting my hand on it again and it's hot to the touch.

"Put your clothes on, Sienna." I'm already pulling my shirt over my head. "Put your shoes on. Quick."

"Cameron?" Her voice is tiny, like a scared little kid, and

I'm trying to keep calm, but I wish my parents were here. I push the wet hair off of her cheeks. We're both drenched in sweat. I'm back in my jeans and shirt from the night before and she's got her flowery sundress on in one quick move. She slips her pink flats on as she hangs her face out the window. "Cameron?"

I look down, surveying what's below us, the hissing and popping of the flames filling the air. It's almost three floors down to the ground. We're on the second floor, but the back of the house has a walkout basement and most of the ground below us is a flagstone patio that bleeds out to the river's edge.

"Fuck," I mutter, waving my shirt in the air again and screaming until my voice breaks. The patio below us is illuminated like the afternoon by the flames. Surely the Andersons will notice soon. *The lights are still off, there's just the one single porch light taunting me. What if they aren't even home? It's a Saturday night.* Mom and Dad have gone to a bed and breakfast for their anniversary and won't be back until tomorrow night. *"Fuck." The heat is almost unbearable now and the smoke is thick around us, choking me even with my head out the window.*

"Get on the edge," I say, grabbing Sienna's waist. "Get your legs out."

"Cameron."

"Do it, Sienna! I'll hold on to you."

She scrambles up into the window frame as I hold onto her. Both of her legs are over the edge and I wrap my arms around her waist as she ducks her head down, swinging her upper body under and out the window. Her body goes rigid and I know what she's thinking.

It's a long fucking drop.

I'm trying not to think about what hitting the stone from twenty-five feet up will feel like. We don't have another choice.

Aside from the Andersons', the nearest house is a half mile away because my parents always dreamed of living in the country.

Some dream.

"Don't think about it. You got this." Sienna's a cheerleader—she was a gymnast when she was a kid. She's small and cat-like. The girl the other cheerleaders all toss in the air and catch with their arms. But there's no group of perky, ponytailed girls in red to catch her now, and we both know it. "Push off with your feet. Roll when you land. On three I'll let go." My head is wedged out the window by her shoulder, and I kiss her sticky skin. It's not something I would normally do, but God, this isn't how our nights normally go.

"Camer—"

"On three." I know I can't give her too much time to think about this. I can't think about this. "One. Two. Three." I release her waist as she pushes off the side of the house. She's on the ground in seconds and I hear a piercing shriek as she makes contact, rolling on the stone in a rigid, unnatural way. She screams again, a shrill sound among the pops and cracks and steady whooshing of the fire.

I hoist myself over the windowsill, gripping the frame as I twist my upper body under and out. Sienna is slightly off to the right, and as I jump I think "roll left, roll left, roll left." The flames have lit up the river, reflecting oranges and yellows, and the Andersons' house is bathed in light. All of the lights are on now and I see a single figure running down the dock, pulling the ropes free from the small speedboat.

Pushing off with my feet, I propel myself away from the house as another shriek of pain cuts through the air. Roll left, roll left, roll left. I think it like a prayer. As my body twists against the hard rock I hear the snap of bones, and in the distance, the soft wail of sirens.

VIRGINIA

Just like I promised Cam I would, I remember everything about last night. Cort's squealing, the drinks, the feel of Cam's hands on my waist. The cool wash of the water against my hot skin. My drunken rambling. Walking a jagged line in the sand, his lips on mine. His hands all over me. Even though it feels like someone is shoving a drumstick in one ear and out the other, every moment of last night—good and bad—is seared into my brain. The only detail that's escaping me is how I ended up in Cam's bed.

I smell him before I see him, because I'm wrapped in a cocoon of Cam. I bring the blue comforter tangled around my waist up to my nose, trying to identify the clean, minty, musk smell. I'd like it to take up permanent residence in my nose.

"Did you just sniff my sheets?"

I want to pretend like it didn't happen, but I'll never get away with it. Using my best sleepy voice I say, "Shh, I'm sleeping."

"Mmhmm."

I roll over slowly, keeping the covers pulled up to my chin. Cam is lying on the bed on top of the comforter facing me.

"I like your bed." I don't know what else to say. What do you say when waking up in the bed of the guy you're dating (but not dating) after crying and then kissing him?

"Mmhmm."

"Is that the only thing you can say in the morning?"

He nods, smiling at me. "Mmhmm."

"Whatever."

At that word, his whole body shakes with laughter. Realizing what he thinks is so funny, I grab my pillow. Launching myself at his face, I attempt to smother him.

"You have anger management issues. You know that, right?" he says, holding me back with one arm.

I laugh. "You have boundary issues."

"I didn't hear you complaining about my boundary issues last night."

"Har har," I say, flopping onto my back and pulling the pillow across my face. The bed dips and the pillow is jerked away.

"Whatever." He smiles and kisses me softly, slowly on the lips, before rolling away from me and hopping to his feet.

I've never seen him this chipper in the morning. When he picks me up for school he's basically a zombie, until he's gone through his coffee and mine.

"I'm going to wake up Anders and Cort." Cam closes the door behind him and I stand up, feeling like a baby deer as I make my way to the bathroom. It's a Jack and Jill bathroom, shared by the two bedrooms, and the door is always closed, so I've assumed Cam doesn't use it, but the door is cracked open. I don't feel like wandering out to the hallway bathroom in the blue boxer shorts I'm wearing. My T-shirt is slung across the shower rod, still damp, but my pants—and more importantly, my bra— are nowhere to be found. I had to have left the party with those two very important pieces. *Right?* I remember leaving the party. I don't specifically remember having my pants on, but I have a feeling *not* having them would be memorable.

I turn on the tap, filling my hands with cool water and splashing it onto my face, before wiping down my neck, chest, shoulders, and arms. I just can't bring myself to get naked in Cam's shower. After drying myself off with the only towel I can find—a tiny white hand towel—I head back into Cam's room. The light is off, and I fumble next to the door, trying to find the switch. When the light clicks on, the room is empty, except for a stack of boxes along one wall. The room is baby blue—an identical twin to Cam's—but it isn't his. This isn't what I had in mind when he said his parents weren't here, and we could stay over. *Are they moving? Why would—*

"Vee?" My train of thought is interrupted by a soft tap on the bathroom door, and Cam's voice. "You okay?"

I lurch back into the bathroom as if the mossy green carpeting in front of me has caught fire. I turn on the faucet, feeling like I've been caught. I probably have. *Maybe his parents travel a lot?* "I'm fine," I say, over the rush of the water. "Do you know where my pants are?"

The bathroom door creaks open far enough for Cam to shove his hand in, with my jeans—completely dry—hanging by a belt loop off his finger. Right next to my white cotton bra. I own *one* sexy bra. It's black lace over purple satin, and it's tucked away in my top drawer. I didn't expect anyone to see my bra last night. Or to be holding it this morning. *Kill me now.* I grab the clothes, shove his arm, and close the door in one swift move.

"You're welcome!" I hear the creak of his mattress as his body slams against it and my whole face flushes at the thought of him on his bed again. Of me in his bed. All the potential that bed might hold for us now. Even though nothing has changed—not really—everything feels different. Life feels full of possibilities. I slip on my bra and jeans, leaving Cam's red-and-white Coachella T-shirt on. It doesn't look like anything else I've seen him wear, but it's threadbare and worn-in, with tiny holes around the hems. Before I open the door, I take a second to smell it, letting the memories of the last twenty-four hours wash over me.

Just like during our nights on the beach, I'm filled with this overwhelming need to know Cam. Not just his favorite movie (an apocalyptic thriller) or song (anything classic rock), or how old he was when he had his first kiss (twelve—which seems old, because I was eight on a swing set). I want to know his secrets. All of the things he's not telling me. I want to know the stories that fill the gaps of silence, when he shuts down and gets quiet. The stories he doesn't tell anyone else. I want him to tell me about that room, and those boxes. Why he drives a car like *that,* and lives in an apartment like *this*—small, with its mismatched furniture and zero decorations and that empty room. I don't just *want* to know everything about Cam, I think I *need* to know. But when I open the door and see him lying on the bed, smiling and shirtless and *mine,* all the questions seem to drift away.

CHAPTER SEVENTEEN

NOW

VIRGINIA

As an official member of the publicity team, one of my new duties is to make sure the bands arrive early to every show and sign autographs for the fans that line up outside the venues. Afterward, they do a meet-and-greet with fans who won that week's contests. I ask fans to post pictures of themselves in their purple shirts, or to tell a story about their worst breakup, or share the lyrics to their favorite Future X song. Each week, the ten or fifteen winners join us backstage to watch the guys rehearse and get autographs. Usually, I'm glued to my phone, responding to online comments, but today all I can do is stare at the screen. My chest burns at the thought of Cam's hands on me, the cold bricks against my back, the feel of us against each other. *Don't ever drink again, Virginia.* I had just enough to give in to the feel of him. Just enough to forget why I should have pushed him away sooner. Before the cameras were pointed at us. Before we had to make stuttered excuses no one believed.

The guys are onstage, finishing up their rehearsal. The contest winners are huddled around the backstage area with me, when I hear the whispers begin.

"I can't believe he let her stay."

"Stupid slut."

I look around the small backstage area, wondering who they could be talking about. It's practically empty back here. There are a few groupies sitting with one of the bands, and Bri is standing by the exit with Pax. Are they talking about her? *Why do they care if she stays?*

"*I* heard the band might break up."

Another one of them whispers behind me. "Do it."

I feel a tap on my shoulder.

The tiny, pigtailed blonde behind me barely comes up to my shoulder. "He's too good for you. And he's going to figure it out pretty soon. So . . . enjoy it while it lasts." It sounds like a threat. A confusing, nonsensical threat. "Bitch."

"Excuse me?" *What is happening right now?*

Another girl chimes in. "You heard her." And another. "Yeah, bitch. You'll be out on the street soon."

"Woah. Hold up." The music has stopped and all I can manage to do is glare at the two girls as a third steps up alongside them. "What the hell is your problem?"

"You're our problem," one says.

The other girl takes a step forward. "You, bitch."

"Stupid skank," the third girl mutters.

What the hell is going on here? I can feel my face burning red as a hand lands on my shoulder and I flinch.

"Everything okay?" Logan steps next to me and the guys gather around. I look at him, unsure of what to say. *Is everything okay?* No. "What's going on, Vee?"

The blonde steps forward. "Logan"—she's using a sugary sweet voice nothing like the way she spoke to me—"we were just setting your *future ex* here"—she nods to me—"straight."

"Bitch," the other girl mutters.

I take a step toward the nasty little pixie waving her mani-cured finger at me as Cam pulls me back by my waist. "Hey, now."

Logan steps between me and the group. "I think it's time for all of you to leave." His arms are spread wide like he's herding the fans.

"You're *defending* her?" The blonde looks at Logan, sound-ing disgusted. "Look what she's doing to you. Right in front of your face."

"Defending her?" Logan keeps pushing them toward the exit. "Paul." He waves the security guard over. "Show these three out?"

"Wait 'til Logan sees the pictures, you stupid slut!" the blonde yells as Paul firmly leads her toward the door.

"What the hell was that?" Reese says, throwing his arm over my shoulder. "You starting chick fights now? When we're not even around to enjoy it?"

"I have no idea. It came out of nowhere." *Did I do something to offend them?* I had welcomed them, and explained they'd be watching rehearsal before getting autographs. That was it.

Kaley walks toward us, her hands flapping in front of her. Like usual, she's squinting her brown eyes at me. "Virginia, they're late for the group waiting outside."

"What photo was she talking about?" I say to Logan, who has already been distracted by the band sound-checking onstage.

"Virginia?" Kaley groans, hand on her hip.

"I'm sorry, Kaley—" I turn for the door and pull my phone out of my pocket, waving a hand behind me. "You guys just go, I'm going to catch up with you."

My phone is buzzing in my hand as all of the guys walk across the stage, toward the exit that is undoubtedly surrounded by anxious fans waiting for the autograph session to begin. I take a deep breath as I step onto the bus and swipe my phone to life. I have fifteen notifications, and ten of them are from Cort.

> Cort:
> *WTF!*
> *Seriously?*
> *What happened to keeping your distance?*
> *I don't see any distance!*
> *I'm going to kill you*
> *It's my duty as your best friend*
> *Call me*
> *Are you there?*
> *Has your mom seen it?*
> *Call me*

> Vee:
> *Hey crazy*
> *Has mom seen what?*

My throat tightens just typing the words. Immediately, my fingers fly over the letters of my name. I never thought I'd have to Google myself to find out something about *myself*.

> Cort:
> *The video, stupid*

A link pops up on my screen, and I click it, landing on a celebrity gossip site. A preview box for the "clip of the day" appears, and I press the PLAY button. My heart waterslides down to my stomach as I watch the pieced-together clip of myself. The first few images are just photos; me pulling Tad out onto the dance floor, Logan holding me close and whispering into my ear. And then, a photo of Cam carrying me outside. My head is

turned away from the camera, and it almost looks like I'm leaning in to kiss him. But if you look closely, you can clearly see
that I'm not. You can see his stupid mouth, free of my stupid
mouth.

Then, the photo of Cam and me morphs into crystal clear
video. *No, no, no.* I had hoped it was all a drunken dream. But
there I am, pushed up against the stone wall of The Tabernacle.
My chest burns thinking about the cold stone up against my hot
skin. And then the video stops. *This is all wrong!*

> Vee:
> *Nothing happened! I pushed him away!*
> *I was drunk*

Cort:
I would hope so

> Vee:
> *This looks horrible*
> *No wonder they were calling me a slut*

Cort:
Don't read online comments
they're jealous
and jerks

Online comments? I pull up my Facebook page and have two
hundred new friend requests. Every one of them has included a
message letting me know I'm a slut. Or a bitch. I'm not good
enough for Logan *or* Cam. *There's a real lack of creativity among
the fans, if you ask me.* The other sites are no better. The breath
seeps out of me as comment after colorful comment tells Logan
how they support him, how sorry they are for him. Yoko Ono
seems to be the go-to nickname, which is ridiculous, because I'm
pretty sure that's not even how Yoko Ono allegedly broke up
the Beatles. I think she was a weirdo, not a home-wrecker. I'm

torn between crying and screaming, because this is absolutely ridiculous. *I'm not even dating anyone!* And while Cam is clearly the one introducing my back to that wall, everyone seems to pity him, too. *Poor Cam; somehow I lured him into my sticky web of sluttiness.*

Dammit!

Sitting at the tiny table in the back of the bus, I stare blankly at my computer screen. Do I comment? Ignore it? I could try to explain, but what would I even say at this point? *"Logan and I were never together, so who cares if it looks like I hooked up with another guy in the band?"* The more I consider the truth of the situation, the more I think maybe I *am* the horrible person the anonymous trolls are describing. I only flirted with Tad to make Cam jealous. Same with the other guy. As I sit in the booth at the back of the bus, head down on my laptop, my phone chirps and buzzes over and over. An endless stream of new love notes from the band's adoring fans, no doubt.

I'm still sitting head-down on the table when Cam's voice enters the kitchen. "You okay?"

After last night, avoiding Cam was today's mission. *Dream on, Virginia.* Sometimes I think he's planted some sort of secret monitoring device on me. Something that registers when I'm in distress, so he can swoop in for the save. "Sure, I'm great," I say. "Don't I *look* great?"

Cam sits in the seat across from me in the booth. "You don't, no."

I flip open the laptop without looking at it, and push it toward him. I can hear the background noise of the Ferris wheel as the video clip starts.

"Fuck."

"Yep."

"So those girls earlier?" he asks.

"Yep." I click the notification symbol that's now showing

"672" and shove the computer back toward him. "Seems I'm everyone's favorite tour slut."

"Vee—"

"Don't, Cam."

"I shouldn't have—" Cam's hand is an inch from mine on the table, and usually I'd make a big show of pulling it away, but I don't even make the effort. He drums his fingers next to mine. "Where'd they even get all that stuff?" he says.

"Someone's phone, obviously. It's not like they were frisking everyone." I focus on the table. "And you know where the video came from."

"Ten seconds *after* this, you were pushing me away." He runs a hand over his head. Cam looks behind me, toward the front of the bus, and suddenly he's out of his seat, striding down the aisle. Tad is standing by the bunks, his camera trained on us.

Crap.

I get to Cam just as he pulls the camera out of Tad's hand.

"What the hell?" Tad's face is twisted in shock as the camera crashes down to the floor.

"You've got some nerve, getting friendly with her." Cam pushes Tad in the chest, not nearly as hard as he could have, but hard enough to make me nervous. "Acting like you give a shit." My hands are on Cam's forearms as I try to calm him down. "You said you wouldn't air it."

Tad picks up the long lens lying by his feet. "I said I wouldn't *mark* it, and bring it to anyone's attention. And I didn't. But you know I don't choose what gets used." Tad pushes his sleeves up, revealing his colorful forearms. "You should be happy they're giving you so much coverage."

"Happy?" I ask. *Why would anyone want this?* "Why would we be happy that we look like some kind of twisted love triangle?"

Tad sets the three pieces of his camera onto the couch. "Whose fault is it that people think you're dating Logan?"

He has a point.

"Listen, when it comes to shows like this—reality contests—
all coverage is good coverage. You guys interest people, and as
long as there's a good story, people are going to keep you around
to see how it ends. And the producers like you, so they're going
to do what they can to sway things your way."

"Sway things?" I ask.

"You honestly think these things are left completely to the
public?" Tad rolls his eyes as he grabs his camera up off the
couch. "You can't be that naive." Tad is still shaking his head in
disbelief as he stomps down the steps of the bus.

Two hours later, the guys are at another rehearsal, and I haven't
stopped thinking about that video or those comments. I'm
standing in front of my bunk, stuffing my clothes into my bags.
The next plane to Chicago will have me on it. This is nothing
like how I pictured my summer going; I'll take my chances with
boring Riverton.

I hear the breathy squeal of the bus door, and Tad steps on,
with our second cameraman, Dave, behind him. When Tad sees
me, he waves Dave away. Dave crosses the parking lot toward
another bus while Tad makes his way down the aisle toward me.
"What are you doing?"

"Packing," I say, as I shove my laptop into my bag.

He sets his camera down, and—surprisingly—it isn't point-
ing at me. It's facing a nondescript wall. "I can see that." He rolls
his eyes. "*Why* are you packing?"

"Didn't you get the memo?" I ask.

He stares at me blankly.

"I've been cast as the tour slut." I pull my notebooks off the
tiny shelf.

He grabs the strap of my bag and pulls it down the bed,

toward him. "The memo *I* got didn't say anything about you leaving," he says.

I pull the bag back to me, and position myself between it and Tad. "Well, I'm not just waiting around for some crazy fan to jump me at the next show."

Tad crosses his arms over his chest and shakes his head. "That's a little dramatic."

It is. I'm feeling very dramatic at the moment. I zip up my bag, and sling it over my shoulder.

Tad steps in front of me, blocking the aisle. "Listen to me. This will blow over. The fans will get over it."

"They won't even let us break up." My voice catches in my throat as I try my best not to cry. "Jenn said *they're* not ready for that yet. Jenn, the producers—*everyone but me*—is obsessed with keeping this thing with me and Logan going. It's sadistic." And I'm over it. If they won't make the call to end it, I'll do it for them. It may be the coward's way out, but at least it's *my* decision."

"This hasn't been about you and Logan for a long time, if you haven't noticed—"

I'm confused, because this is *all* about me and Logan and this stupid lie.

Hands on his hips, he tips his head back, like he's talking to the ceiling and not me. "And apparently you haven't. God, Vee, I know you're not this dumb."

"Excuse me? What do—"

"Why do you think the clips of you and Cam were leaked?" He puts his hands on my shoulders and lowers his face to mine. "The only thing more intriguing than a love story is a *forbidden* love story. And trust me, anyone who has seen the two of you knows there's something there."

"Was," I say.

"Was. Is. *Whatever.* It's my job, not my business. All I'm

saying is don't leave. You're going to want to be here when this happens for them. You're a part of it," he says. "Don't leave. And don't waste this opportunity that *you* have."

Suddenly I'm mad at myself for even considering walking away from this internship. I filled out papers last week. I have actual responsibilities. Maybe I did know right from the start that there were ulterior motives behind keeping me around—and officially bringing me onboard—but now I'm in. I have an *actual* college-official internship on a huge network TV show, and I'm going to milk it for every resume-worthy line I can get. I can't let this drama push me off course. "I'm not leaving."

"That's not what it looks like."

"I just wanted to be ready," I say. "For when I really *do* need to run from a crazed fan." I scowl at him, and punch him softly in the shoulder.

Like usual, there's a smile on his face, and he picks his camera back up. "Get it all out of your system. In two minutes this camera goes back on and I can't have you giving me the Angry Girl death-stare for no reason." He points at my bags. "Get that shit unpacked. Quickly." He taps his camera. "No evidence, please."

I nod, unpacking my bag and shoving it back under my bed.

"I spend my entire day watching you guys," Tad says. He's leaning against Cam's bunk. "I think I've officially spent more time with all of you than I have with my own girlfriends over the years, so trust me when I say this"—he pushes at his sleeves, looking nervous—"the way Cam looks at you? That's not normal. Because you're not even looking back at him, and he's still trying."

I may have promised myself to see this through to the end, but I still feel violated. There's really no other way to describe it; it's like someone published my song lyrics or stole a pair of my underwear, or something. The picture of me and Cam was staring at me from a truck stop magazine rack the other day, and I considered buying all of them. Or knocking the rack over, and letting one of the buses run it over. Then I thought of all of the truck stops, in all of the cities, in every state. The grocery stores. And bookstores. Department stores are probably selling magazines now, just to spite me. Every time I see that video or the pictures they've now made of it, I get a little angrier. A little more hurt and frustrated. At first my anger has no direction, no target. It just radiates around me, blaming *everyone*.

What Tad said keeps replaying in my mind. If it hadn't been obvious that there was a story between Cam and me, no one would have given us a second thought. My face wouldn't be plastered on every celebrity gossip site out there. My parents wouldn't have called me, worried that I must be on drugs or something, because "That's so unlike you Virginia." I know I shouldn't, and I don't even want to, deep down, but all of the anger I've been pushing away is finally focused on the bunk across from me.

I open my laptop to work on the schedule for the next round of preshow meet-and-greets. Kaley and Priya are sitting across from me in the lounge of the production bus, piles of papers stacked on their laps. It must be rough, trying to do office work out of a bus. Jenn stays at a hotel in whatever city we're in, but Kaley and Priya are relegated to the bus, like the camera guys and band members. Priya pushes her dark hair out of her face and tosses a stack of papers into my lap. "He didn't fill out half of it," she says.

Who? I flip over the pile of stapled papers and see Cam's name scribbled across the top. I flip through the pages. He actually filled in *less* than half. There's a page with his personal details: his height and weight, favorite color, food, band, and song. Three whole paragraphs are dedicated to a cute story about his first dog, Parker. *Parker Sunset.* But under most of the sections, all it says is "None of your business," scrawled in black ink.

"Someone should tell him we give them these as a courtesy," Kaley mutters. "We've got Google."

Shit. I know exactly what they found on Google.

"He's the next big story for Your Future X." Priya looks at me. "Once the drama dies down, we'll start producing a special segment on him. You should prepare him for that."

"Can you do that?" Kaley says. She's about my age, and it's been clear from the start that she hasn't appreciated my spontaneous addition to the marketing team. Every word she says to me is laced with disdain.

I nod. "I can do that." *But can I?* Am I willing to throw Cam under the bus to prove that I can do this job? *To prove, once and for all, that I don't care about him anymore.* "You'll let me know when production is actually scheduled, so I can warn him?"

The two girls nod, and as I cross the parking lot to our bus, I pass a small group of fans who have made their way behind the club. It's still three days until the next show, and no one expects us to arrive this early, so the crowds are light. In two days, there will be fans milling everywhere, trying to get a glimpse of the bands. Sometimes they just want to get caught on camera. Two of the girls glare at me as I pass them, and I make a decision. *Yes, I can definitely do this.* No one's secrets are safe anymore. We will all suffer together.

CHAPTER EIGHTEEN

THEN

CAM

"That!" Vee is yelling, pointing her spoon at the TV. Green flecks of ice cream splatter onto the beige carpet of my living room. Wearing a pair of faded jeans, and one of my Rolling Stones T-shirts (that's four sizes too big for her) she's in her usual after-school spot on my couch. *"That* is what I'm talking about!"

I have no idea what the yelling is about. I zoned out a while ago. Sitting at the dining room table, on the other side of the room, I'm scribbling lyrics and chords into my notebook. Vee is sitting cross-legged on my couch, watching a movie. A giant bowl of mint chocolate chip ice cream is settled in her lap. There are at least two cartons of it in my freezer at all times now. One day, scientists will prove that Virginia Miller's veins actually pump the stuff.

I look up to see that there's a marching band prancing across a stadium, while playing a booming rendition of "Can't Take My Eyes off of You." Trombones and trumpets gleam. Stunned students look on in bewilderment, and the band's leader, a shaggy-haired late-'90s Heath Ledger, thrusts his baton while simultaneously singing and weaving through the stadium, evading security guards. *Why are there security guards on the football field?*

"What is it?" I ask.

"It's just the grandest of all grand gestures," she says, sounding annoyed. Her eyes never leave the screen. I'm pretty sure she sighed. "You wouldn't understand. None of you do." She says it angrily, as if I've personally affronted her somehow.

"Excuse me? None of '*us*'?" I'm trying my best to sound offended, but she looks so damn adorable, pouting over her melting ice cream and waving her arms at the TV. It's hard not to laugh at her. I keep the smile that's threatening in check.

"Guys. Boys." Her face twists into a scowl and I almost lose it. "Men," she hisses, jabbing her spoon at me. "None of you."

"Movies like this give you all unreasonable expectations." I idly strum a chord. "As if we can actually commandeer a marching band, or set up a moonlit picnic on the Empire State Building."

"Oh, 'us all'?"

"Yes. Girls." I try to look at her as seriously as she's looking at me. "We can't actually make that shit happen. It's unrealistic."

Another spoonful of ice cream slides into her mouth. "No one expects a guy to re-create this movie stuff, Cam. Grand gestures aren't actually about scale." The silver spoon twists in her fingers like a drumstick. "They're about putting yourself out there and creating a moment."

"A moment?"

"Yes, a *moment*. It's about doing something outside of your comfort zone to show someone what they mean to you." She's looking at me as if this is the most obvious thing ever, and not girl-speak that basically requires a translator.

I give her an "I still don't get it" shoulder shrug. Just to irritate her.

She rewards me with a dramatic eye roll. "Conducting a marching band in front of a football field of students," she says, gesturing at the TV. "Or standing outside her bedroom window with a giant boom box, playing a love song?" *She watched* that one *last week*. Her eyes are fixed on me. She's waiting for an *aha!* moment, but I'm not going to give it to her.

I shrug again.

"Ugh. It's about creating a freaking moment." Her spoon drops into her bowl with a loud clang.

I'm trying to play along and keep a straight face, but I can feel my lips betraying me now. "It's unrealistic."

"*You're* unrealistic," she says with mock anger, sticking her tongue out at me as I shake my head.

I finally give up a laugh.

The spoon is sticking out of her mouth and she's facing the TV again, but I can tell she's smiling. "Shut up and write your song."

I've had plenty of girlfriends. A lot of the middle school, movie-date-with-your-parents kind, and just one of the sort of serious, I'll-show-you-mine-if-you-show-me-yours kind. I know all about remembering birthdays and favorite foods, and buying flowers on Valentine's Day and presents at Christmas. Still, I've never considered myself a particularly romantic guy. Not like Anders. That guy's always sending Cort flowers, or driving three hours after school to meet her at her college. He takes her out to the kind of restaurants that require reservations and clothes nicer than most of what he owns. That all seems forced and fake to me. I don't want to do anything for Vee just because I feel like I'm supposed to.

This is definitely something I have to do, though. Before she finds out, I have to tell her. And when I found the light on in my spare room the morning after she slept over, I knew it was a matter of time. Weeks have already passed, and it's felt like a bomb in my back pocket, just waiting to blow my legs off. I've put this off long enough, and I'm hoping if I make the moment semi-romantic, I can distract her from what a big deal it is. Vee is always swooning over romantic, grand gestures, but this is more of a romantic diversion.

The whole apartment smells like pepperoni pizza. I turn off the movie Vee's playing—another one of her chick flicks—and flip to one of the music stations. I yell into the kitchen. "How long?"

"Ten minutes." She's standing in the archway between the living room and dining area.

"Come in here."

She's smiling as she walks toward me. "I'm not making out with you again." She pretends to think about it. *She's adorable.* "Well, I will, but I can't stay late tonight." Vee falls asleep here some nights, waking up before the sun's up, to get home before her mom does. I sleep strangely well with her next to me. I haven't had a nightmare with her beside me, since that first night. For the most part, we've swapped our nights lying on the beach talking, for nights lying on my bed talking.

"I don't want to make out."

Her expression falls as I say it, and I can't help but laugh at her pouty face. I grab her hand and pull her over to me. "Not now, I mean." I keep her hand in mine, placing the other on my shoulder. I wrap my arm around her waist and pull her obscenely close to me.

One corner of her mouth turns up in amusement. "We're not going to make out, huh?"

I kiss her forehead and leave my lips there, brushing her skin as I speak. "There's something I need to tell you." I feel her tense for just a second as I say it, a moment of hesitation in her step. "Don't panic."

"I'm not," she says, as if the idea of her jumping to the worst-case scenario was absurd, rather than expected.

I can tell, just from the tone of those two words, that she is. "I need you to know I don't really want to talk about it . . . or get into details . . . but I do want you to know."

"Okay . . ."

We continue to sway back and forth. *Maybe I don't have to say anything. She'll forget the empty bedroom eventually, or maybe she won't even ask about it. That's ridiculous, though, because she's not an idiot. I know it's only a matter of time before she starts to ask questions.* And my hesitation is just making this all worse. "My parents . . ."

She looks up at me, a question on her lips that I'm not going to answer.

"You've probably noticed they're not around."

She nods.

"They . . . don't actually live here." I don't say anything else and she nods again, then rests her head on my shoulder. It's not what I needed to say, but it's all I can say.

"I just wanted you to know." *Liar.* If she'd never gone into that room, I never would have had to tell her.

VIRGINIA

With Cam's arms wrapped around me, I feel safe. I want him to know that he's safe too—he can tell me anything. "Can I be Dakota? Just for a minute?" We're still swaying, still pressed up against each other.

"Always," he says. "For as long as you need."

"Do you still want to know something no one else knows?"
He nods, urging me to go on.

"Sometimes I hate my mother."

In truth, I hate my father, too, but he's never around. It's harder, somehow, to hate him. But my mom—even though she isn't physically there most of the time, she still is. Her voice sits in that house. In the living room, where she told me we moved because of money issues. In the kitchen, where she makes my breakfast every morning. We tell pretty lies, talking about upcoming family vacations and weekend outings that won't ever happen.

"I found a key last week." I pull it from my pocket and dangle it from my finger.

Cam wraps his hand back around mine, crushing the cold metal in my palm.

"What does it open?"

"My old house." It's my mother's old key ring, a silver music note charm I gave her for Mother's Day when I was nine or ten. I found it in a drawer in the kitchen. "It made me think about the house, so I went by there. Mostly, I just wanted to see if it looked any different."

"Did it?" Cam asks.

"Not really," I say. "I walked around, looked in the windows, like some sort of burglar. I was curious what it looked like now, with another family's things." I try to swallow down the emotion that's rising up out of my chest, choking me. "I didn't expect it to be empty." My eyes are fixed on the poster hanging on the wall behind Cam. I'm staring it down, like I'm waiting for it to leap off the wall. "Except there was one room full of stuff."

Cam kisses my forehead, his breath hot against my skin. "What kind of stuff?"

"Her old comforter, Nonni's old vintage dresser," I say. "It's my parents' old room, and it's still full of her stuff."

"I thought your parents sold that house."

"She's a liar. I hate her." It feels good when Dakota says it. When I say it, I feel guilty. "How can someone who's supposed to love me more than anything think it's okay to lie to me like that?" Cam tightens his arms around me, and I lay my face against his chest. My silent tears soak through his shirt, and I feel like I'm marking him with my pain. Like we're sharing this secret now. I should have told him last week, when I found the key, because I feel better now that I've told him.

I *don't* tell him I used the key to go into the house. Or that I curled up on the floor of my empty bedroom. And I don't tell him that before I left, I sat in the three seasons room, looking out at the lake, until the sun finally set and I had to go to band practice. I don't tell him that I'm questioning everything now.

There have been countless times over the years when Logan and I have gone for days without talking. It's always Logan's fault. Usually it's over summer break, or when he gets a new girlfriend. Or if his brother is in town for the holidays. When something occupies Logan, it isn't uncommon for him to forget to call. And if he doesn't call me, I refuse to call him. Until we inevitably cross paths. He acts hurt for not hearing from me, I act like I don't know what he's talking about, and things go back to normal. It's a familiar, choreographed routine. It's another reason the two of us would never work as an actual couple. We'd be the worst kind of dysfunctional.

So this little stint of radio silence between me and Logan? It's not a first. And it's not like we never see each other. We're at band practice twice a week, in calculus class together, and we eat lunch at the same table five days a week. Logan sees me more than my mom does, and one hundred times more than my dad does, but we haven't actually been alone together in months. I don't think we've really talked in weeks. My life feels fuller than ever. I've been pleasantly wrapped up in my "whatever" with Cam, and I've kept busy setting up gigs for the band. I'm actively avoiding thoughts of college and what I plan to do. Because The Plan—it's been teetering on the edge for a while now, and I think it's about to fall off a tall building and splatter all over the sidewalk. The Plan feels like it's in a million unrecognizable pieces lately, and I'm not even sure why. Maybe because *I* feel like I'm in a million unrecognizable pieces.

Last night, Cam and I played at the beach. *Our* beach. It was just the two of us, playing for the waves, but I felt vulnerable and exhilarated and terrified all at once. And as scary as it was, it was also incredible.

"Hey, Vee." Logan is crossing the parking lot toward me as I lean against Cam's car and fiddle with my phone. "How's it going?"

I straighten up and try my best to sound normal. "Good. What's up?"

Logan shoves his hands in his pockets and leans his hip against the car next to me. "Nothing, I just—haven't seen much of you lately."

"I've just been busy." *This is not my fault.*

"Right. It seems like things are good with Cam."

"We're just friends." I don't know why I said it—why I just outright lied. Once the words are out of my mouth, all I can think about is how wrong they sound. "But yeah, things are good."

"Oh." He's looking at me like he wants to say something, but he's not. Logan and I have been friends since third grade, and for the first time since I was ten, I don't know what to say to one of my best friends. Instead, we just mirror each other, leaning against the car, him looking at me, as I look at him, in a verbal stand-off.

"I'm going to visit my brother at State this weekend. You should come." Logan dips his shoulder and lets his backpack slide down his arm. "Check out the campus again?"

Right, The Plan. I shake my head. "I'm still not sure about State."

"Well, you should be. Going to the same college will be awesome. Anders is going. And he's working on convincing Cort to transfer. We'll all go."

"Seriously? He'll never convince her to go to State. She loves it in Chicago and she has a scholarship. Plus, there are about a million colleges out there that I want to check out."

"Since when?"

Since I'm thinking about music again, feeling like maybe I could actually do it. Since I realized State wasn't the only option. I shrug my shoulders.

"Think about it, Vee, if we don't go to college together, when would we see each other? I've hated not seeing you the last couple months." I feel a twinge of guilt as I look him in the eyes and see that he means it.

"We'd see each other," I say.

"When? Holidays? I'll get tired of coming home for those, eventually. Holidays are depressing." Logan doesn't talk about his parents much anymore, but I saw the Logan most people never did. The first day of third grade, I walked onto the bus with an apple cinnamon donut from my mom. My favorite. Going down the aisle, I looked at all of the names posted above the seats, looking for the spot I'd spend the rest of the school year. Logan was sunk down in his seat, his knees wedged up against the seat in front of us. Even at nine, I could tell he was upset. He didn't talk to me that whole ride, but before we got off the bus, I gave him half of my donut. And the next morning, we talked about our favorite TV shows. It was three weeks before he told me his mom had disappeared two days before school started. At Christmas, he still hadn't heard from her. By the end of the year, we were inseparable.

"We'll visit." *Won't we?*

The look on Logan's face answers my question. He doubts it.

"Just think about it. State would be amazing."

It would be amazing at State, and if we don't go to college together, we'll drift apart. It would be amazing at State, and if you don't go, I won't make an effort to see you. It would be amazing at State, and if you go somewhere else, you can plan on our friendship being over.

"And it fits in The Plan. You know it does," Logan says.

I can't keep talking. The hot sting of tears is pricking at my eyes. "Mmhmm."

I pull my eyes away from my feet and see Cam walking toward us. When he gets to the car, Logan slaps him on the back with a "Hey, man," and starts to walk away, shouting, "Think about it!" before he disappears into his car. It's like a strange changing of the guard for my heart, old to new. And that realization alarms me, the fact that Cam holds a piece of my heart now, maybe all of it. *How did that even happen?*

"What does he want you to think about?" Cam asks as he opens my door.

"Nothing. We were just talking about old plans," I say, lacing my fingers together with Cam's on the console between our seats, because it's become habit. We're one of those couples with our hands stitched together now.

CAM

With the wind whipping by us, Vee and I huddle on the frigid sand, a blanket burrito-wrapped around our bodies. We both have our heads under the blanket, our cheeks resting on the warm flannel, against the sand. I can feel her warm breath against my face as she speaks.

"Sand castles, bongo drums"—Vee kisses me on the nose with each word—"and you."

"Three things that are all too cold to be out on the beach right now?" I ask. She smacks me under the blanket for the joke, but I'm serious. "Fuuuuck, it's cold."

"Three things I love about the beach." She rolls her eyes. "It's almost winter." Her voice is soft. "Winter's the worst."

"There are good things about winter."

"Untrue," she says.

"What about Christmas?" This seems like a solid argument, since Vee has told me she "loves Christmas more than ice cream." Which, for her, is really saying something.

"Christmas exists in plenty of places that don't have winter."

"We can do most of the same things in winter we do now."

"Oh, please," she says. Even though it's dark under the blanket and I can't see her very well, I know she's rolling her eyes. "That's not even close to true. We can't come here. Not much longer."

I kiss her on the forehead, because her voice sounds so sad. "I want you to know that I *want* to be one of those guys who says yes to everything, just to make you happy." I kiss her softly and slowly. "But you're right. We can't. It's fucking freezing out here."

She lets out a long breath and snuggles further into my side. "Not surprising. You're a total baby about the cold." She snuggles her face into my chest. "You're like a pineapple, or something." Her voice is muffled by my arm.

"A pineapple?"

She pulls her head out of her hiding spot and smiles at me.

"Yes, a delicate tropical fruit." We both laugh, and the way we're lying—chest to chest with our faces almost touching—I can feel it vibrate through me.

I pull her face to mine, brushing our lips together, softly at first, and then more urgently as she parts her lips. Our tongues move, giving and taking, slow and fast, as my hands search up and down her back, dipping under the waistband of her jeans and resting on her hips, before running up her stomach to her chest, slipping under the soft fabric.

I feel Vee shiver under me as I run my hand over her warm skin.

"You're sure?" I kiss along her neck and work my way down.

"I'm sure." She kisses my forehead like I always do to her. I kiss her back, a smile spreading across my face as my lips meet her warm skin.

The blanket dips into the sand underneath me as I shift around. "We might be smothered under here."

She giggles.

This beach is where I fell in love with her. We had our first kiss here. And our second, better kiss. Last week, this is where she told me she was falling in love with me, though she didn't actually say those three words. And I can deal with this hot blanket if this is what she wants.

I kiss her collarbone. "I love you." I say it because I do. I never thought saying it to a girl would be easy, but it just fell out of my mouth one day. And I've been saying it for weeks now.

Vee presses her forehead against mine. "You're not just saying that because I'm going to have sex with you, are you?" She's trying to sound serious, but she's smiling, teasing me.

"No. That's just one of the many reasons," I say, which gets me smacked in the chest.

She pulls at the buttons of my pants. "Good."

VIRGINIA

I can just barely make out the faint cadence of bongos. It feels like they're beating in rhythm with my heart, playing a song that's just for us, just for tonight. The lake seems more urgent tonight, the waves crashing just a little harder, cresting just a little closer. Cam's hands are under my shirt, on my stomach, over my chest, running down my back. His fingers sear a trail across my skin, as they cover every inch of me, turning cold to hot. I push my shoes off, he pulls at my shirt; we twist and tangle, bend and dip. There's me and him, but mostly there's just us—everywhere. His hand on my hip, my hand on his chest, his lips on mine, each of us like an extension of the other. It's frantic but soft, gentle but powerful.

And finally, we feel together. He feels like mine, and I am nothing but his. Every quick breath and slow sigh feels engrained in me, written on my skin, etched in this memory I'm already holding on to.

CHAPTER NINETEEN

NOW

CAM

Vee's been getting almost daily phone calls from her mom the last two weeks, and every time I try to ask her about it, she shuts me down. She either acts like she didn't hear me, or gives me some two-word answer like "checking in" or "saying hello."

Her phone rings for the third time today. "Hi, Mom . . . just a second." She wanders away from Anders and me in the lounge, walking into the kitchen before she continues.

Instead of giving her space, like I usually do, I follow her. In the kitchen, I open the tiny fridge, pull out a string cheese, and sit down across from her. She dips her head down as she talks, like that's going to stop me from hearing her one-sided conversation.

"They have the measurements, right? . . . Then I'm sure it'll be fine . . . Yes, I'll check it as soon as I'm home . . . I'm sure I did it right . . . Yes . . . Then we'll get it fixed right away . . . I'm sure, Mom . . . No, just me . . . I'll double check, yes . . . I'll see you soon . . . Love you, too."

"Mom again?" I ask.

She nods.

"What's going on? I don't remember her needing daily check-ins."

"Because you knew her so well?" Vee says it casually, like a sarcastic joke, but it stings.

She starts to stand, but I get up first. "No." I hold my hand out in front of her, suddenly pissed off. "Let me."

VIRGINIA

When I walk into the lounge, Logan is giving me his annoying "you're being a bitch" face, which he breaks out every time I talk to Cam. "You need to cut him a break," he says. "Jeez, back off once in a while." Cam just walked off, but I can see him through the bus window, pacing on the concrete with his hands shoved in his pockets.

"*You* back off. You don't know anything about it," I say.

"Vee, come on. I know."

"You know what?"

He looks outside at Cam, and then at me. "I *KNOW.*" And the way he yells it, I know exactly what he means. "And I can't believe you've seriously gone this long without telling me yourself."

He's right. And he has every right to be mad at me, but I'm too pissed to care. Right now, on this bus, Logan is the one who made the bigger mistake.

"And when *exactly* did you start *knowing* this?" I ask. I suppose the more accurate question is, when did Cam decide to share all the gory details with you? With *my* best friend.

Logan rarely gets angry with me. Usually when we fight, we just avoid each other until we cool off, but his face is red now, and his voice is harsh. "When did I know you were in love with him, or when did I know he was in love with you? Because—"

"Stop it." *Why is he being such a jerk about this?*

"—I knew you loved *him* the day I found you huddled on your bed."

"Logan—"

"And I knew he loved *you* at band practice, when he let you drive that stupid fucking car."

"God, you're an asshole."

"Sometimes, yeah. Just like sometimes you can be a real bitch."

I shove his chest, pushing him until he falls back onto the couch. "You're an asshole for bringing me here." Logan grabs my arm and yanks me down next to him on the couch. He still has my wrist, and I jab my elbow into his stomach. Not hard enough to hurt him, but enough to elicit a low moan of annoyance. "You knew and you still brought me here." Tad is coming down the aisle and I stop struggling. As he passes us with the camera, I lean into Logan's shoulder like we're having a private conversation. It will probably look sweet and loving on film, not like we're a pair of ten-year-old siblings fighting. *More lies.*

Logan whispers, "Face him."

I face Cam every single day. Seeing his face is a direct assault on my heart.

"You need to do this, Vee."

"Do what?" I spit, because I truly don't know what I'm supposed to do. *Why do I have to do anything?* "I don't owe him anything, Logan."

"Do whatever you want. Just do *something*."

I'm sitting in the back of the bus, scribbling lyrics, when Cam sits down across from me in the tiny booth. Eyes on my notebook, I tell myself I can just ignore him. This is shared space, so I can't ask him to leave, but I don't have to chitchat with him. *Maybe, for once, he'll get the hint and go away.*

I twist in the aisle to look toward the front of the bus, where Logan and Anders are practicing in the lounge while Tad watches them, camera in hand. For a few more minutes the music fills the air, then I hear the breathy airlock of the bus door, and everyone is gone. Even Tad, and Tad *never* leaves.

"Where did they go?" I ask, before I can remind myself that I'm not talking to him.

Cam crosses his arms over his chest. "Out," he says. "So now we can finally talk."

This isn't a coincidence. I stand, and he mirrors me, blocking the narrow aisle with his body. "Cam, come on." I move to the other side and he does the same.

"I have things to say. So don't talk if you don't want to. Just listen."

I sit back down in the booth, determined to be unaffected by him. "Fine. Talk." I hold my pen to the paper and focus on watching the lines blur together.

"When I came to Riverton, I was messed up, okay? I didn't want anything to do with anyone." He sits down again, leaning toward me, and I can feel his eyes on me, but I refuse to look up. "At some point you made me start to forget—you made me feel like I could be someone different. Even if it was just for a little while. Even though I didn't want it."

"You didn't want *me*." I can't believe I said it out loud. When the words escape my lips they feel like the truth. I think this is what I've feared all along; that Cam meant so much more to me than I meant to him. That I needed him more than he needed me.

"I did—I do. I just couldn't do it, Vee. It was just"—he shakes his head like it hurts to remember—"it was too much."

"It was you, not me? You're kidding, right?" I push myself

up out of the booth—I need to leave. Words can't go back in time and undo it all.

Cam stands up, blocking me again. "It *was*, Vee. It is." He's approaching me with one hand up, like I'm a rabid dog, waiting for a chance to bite a finger off. Which isn't far from how I feel right now.

I focus on the shiny black handle of the refrigerator, so I don't have to look at him. "I don't know what you want me to do, Cam. I'm not slashing your bunk or setting your clothes on fire. I'm being cordial. I'm slapping a smile on my face. I don't know what else you want from me." I'm glad everyone is gone, because the scene playing out right now is the last thing I want on national television.

"Slash my bunk! Admit you fucking care!" The anger in his voice startles me. He has absolutely no right to ask me for anything, but I can hear the pain in his voice.

"You're the one who ended it." I take a deep breath and bite my lip, trying to will away the hot tears that are threatening to spill over. *I will not cry here. Not in front of him.* Not in front of whatever cameras are probably hidden in this kitchen.

Cam steps toward me, his hand reaching for my face, and I slap it away. "I was a kid, Vee."

"So was I. I *needed* you, and you weren't there." My calm, controlled voice is quickly slipping, the words catching in my throat as it collapses in on itself. *Deep breath, Virginia. Deep breath.* "I guess it just wasn't good enough. *We* weren't good enough." I turn away. I don't owe him anything.

Cam's face hardens as I push past him. "Right, just go. Walk away. Run to Logan." He throws the words at me like a knife, and I stop. My hand twitches at my side, eager to grab something. Or hit something. Anything to release the energy surging through me. "That's your thing, right?" Every word is slow and controlled, acerbic.

"You fucking asshole." I turn and close the gap between us in three quick steps. "You want to know what you meant to me? What our time together meant to me? You need me to say it so you can feel good about yourself?" Angry energy is filling me, eager to get out. *If he doesn't like my silence, I'll give him something to listen to.*

He glares at me, his eyes full of passion, and throws his hands in the air. "Just be real with me."

I focus on my bare toes, unsure of where to even start. At the beginning? The end? He was both.

"I'm not going to let you pretend there's not something between us, Vee. That you don't feel it."

I feel his warm fingers rest on my arm, and push them away. "You were *everything* to me." I swallow, almost choking on the words as a loud sob rips out of me. "You were the missing lyrics to a song I didn't even know I was writing." I take a step back, needing as much space between us as I can get. "You made me believe in myself . . . made me want to change. You made me feel strong."

"You *are* strong, Vee." Cam's eyes look the way I remember them—sad and full of heartbreak. His strong shoulders sag and he looks as defeated as I feel.

I let the warm air slowly fill my nostrils and slip out past my lips as I raise my eyes to meet his. "You did everything you could to pry me open. You took everything you could, and then you took it all away. My heart. My hope. My trust." My eyes are burning, my cheeks hot. Everything feels like it's on fire. "And the worst part is that when it was all over, I realized I was in love with someone I didn't even know."

Cam looks shocked. "You knew me."

What a joke. I wipe at my wet cheek with the back of my hand and try to laugh, but it comes out like a strangled squawk. "You don't get it. It doesn't even matter." I take a step back from him, wishing it were a mile. "You want me to feel something? Well, I do. I feel something for you. I just don't know what to call it. There's this strange gray area in my heart—somewhere south of love and north of hate—and that's where you live now. I think it's where you'll always live."

Cam doesn't say anything. He just stands there. His hands are shoved into his pockets, his shoulders slumped, as I slowly back away. I finally get my chance to leave him before he can leave me, and it doesn't feel anything like I'd always hoped it would. I stop in front of the bunks, my voice quiet.

"You're right, though; you were just a kid, and so was I. It was naive to think it would be forever. I can take some of the blame too . . . for not realizing how ridiculous it was to think it could last."

Cam is gone. Probably not for years this time, but I still feel the absence. Everyone is out or at rehearsal, and the entire bus is empty, quiet. Logan's acoustic is lying on his bed, so I take it and sit in the lounge, my notebook beside me. I let my feelings seep onto the paper, and echo off the strings, and ring in my voice. The words I spoke this afternoon were angry, but the words that land on the page aren't. I think that, maybe, I'm finally moving forward. I'm letting it go.

CHAPTER TWENTY

THEN

CAM

Vee is shouting through my closed bedroom door. "Your phone!"

"Who is it?"

She's standing in my doorway. "Sienna." There's an unasked question in her voice. "Want me to answer?" Vee asks.

Translation: Want me to let her know you have a girlfriend?

"No, just leave it." I'm trying my best not to sound as panicked as I feel.

"She's called a couple times this week."

She's been calling *daily*. I keep meaning to call or text her to make it stop, but if I'm awake, I'm with Vee. It seemed like it would be easier to just ignore her until it stopped, but it's only gotten worse. "It's my cousin." I'm not sure why I say it. Why I don't just leave it alone.

Vee gives me an apologetic smile. Shutting my bedroom door behind her, she makes her way across my living room. She's pulling my St. John's Prep sweatshirt over her head, examining the red stitching across the front as she smooths it down over her hips. It's gigantic on her. The sleeves hang over her hands and she clenches the ends in her fists. It's my favorite thing to wear, because she steals it so often that it smells like her. Flowery and sweet and comforting. Everything about Vee is comforting. She'd probably be completely grossed out if she knew I hadn't washed it in months. I'm sitting in *her* usual spot on my couch. She tosses my phone onto my lap as she approaches.

I put my hands on her hips as she stands in front of me. "Don't be mad."

She sighs, and takes a step out of my grip, planting her hands on her hips. "Famous last words." When she rolls her eyes I can't help but laugh, because I know how her brain works. She's already thinking worst-case scenario, and the way she gets worked up is so fucking cute.

"Come here." I pull her wrists until she's sitting across my lap. I reach into the drawer of the table next to my couch, where we've been sitting and watching movies for the last two hours. There are two envelopes inside, and I lay one on her lap, tucking the other under my leg.

Her eyes get comically large. "What is it?" She shakes it dramatically like it's a gift box. She tries to hand it back to me, and I push it back into her hands. "It's really for me?"

"Open it."

"I hate surprises. You know this."

"I do. Open it up, so you can be horribly surprised." I kiss the top of her head. She flips the envelope over and sees the logo in the corner: NORTHWESTERN UNIVERSITY. Her hands go still, her body tensing against me. It's addressed to her, but with my address, and her brows scrunch up when she looks at me in question. I don't give her an answer; I just shake my head. "Just open it, please."

I watch her face, holding my breath and hoping I played this right, as she tears open the envelope and pulls out the papers carefully and calmly, like they might combust at any moment. She reads it to herself, and I glimpse words over her shoulder.

Dear Miss Miller . . .

. . . Congratulations

. . . A wonderful addition to Northwestern

Welcome . . .

She's motionless, holding the papers in her lap. "How did you—but I didn't even—" Her face is scrunched up in confusion, a deep V wrinkling between her eyebrows. "Why?"

Because this *is the school you* should *be going to.*

Pulling the second envelope out from under my leg, I drop it onto her lap. I wait anxiously, as she pulls the papers out of the open envelope.

"Read it," I say, and I kiss her temple, because I'm so nervous that I have to do something.

"Dear Mr. Fuller"—she sounds extremely formal, her voice huskier than usual—"it is with great pleasure that we welcome you to Northwestern University . . ." Her voice trails off and I'm not sure what to do, because I don't understand her reaction, or her lack of one. She shakes her head. "I don't understand."

She turns in my lap, her knees pulled up to her chest, one foot to either side of my hips. I hate that her expression looks torn and not ecstatic.

"I thought we could go to Chicago," I say. "Together." I tuck a piece of hair behind her ear. "I promise to ride the trains with you, and make sure crazy taxis don't run you down in the street, and to refill your Metro card so you don't get kicked off the bus."

"Cam, I don't think—"

"Cort and your mom helped me get everything I needed for the application." Thank God it didn't require an essay. I'm rambling because I'm not sure I want to hear what she has to say, and I can't stand the thought of silence.

When a tear falls down her cheek, I want to jump out of a window and end this torture for myself. And for her.

"Shit." I brush her cheek with my thumb, holding her face between my hands. "I thought you'd be excited. I wasn't trying to make you cry. It was stupid. Forget it, okay?"

She finally breaks her silence as she lets out a long whoosh of air, like she's been holding her breath. "No, it's fine, I just—I mean . . . God, I'm a jerk."

"I didn't want to say it, but you kind of are—" She slaps me playfully on the chest and I pull her tight to me. "I want to go to Chicago with you, Vee. Just think about it, okay?" I feel her nod against my chest and I promise myself I'll never try to surprise her again.

VIRGINIA

"Nonni! It's VA Day!" I place the cappuccino on her bedside table, and she stares longingly at the steaming cup of gas station contraband.

"You've always been my favorite," she says.

I've been so wrapped up in Cam and thinking about my future, I haven't seen Nonni in a few weeks. "Sorry I've been away."

It's easy to put coming here out of my mind when I'm caught up in life. When I'm actually sitting in this room, the guilt catches up to me. Every time I come, I promise myself I'll be better.

Nonni hasn't met Cam yet, but I've told her all about him. Last time I was here, I brought in a few pictures and a shaky video of the two of us playing our guitars at the beach. She teared up when she watched it. "You got some good stories to tell me?" Nonni's eyes light up. "How are things going with that boyfriend of yours?"

"He's not my boyfriend, Nonni." I don't know why I'm even

arguing the point anymore, when Cam and I obviously became a couple so long ago. It's become habit. And it annoys Nonni, so I keep it up. We're old news to everyone else. No one even asks us questions around school anymore.

Nonni waves her hand in the air like I'm being ridiculous. "Well, whatever you call him, how is he?"

"It's good. He's good." I take a sip from my own Styrofoam mug. "He wants to go to college together." It's the first time I've said it out loud to anyone. "In Chicago. He actually applied for me and surprised me with the acceptance letters."

I'm not sure why I haven't already told Cam I'm going with him, because I know I am. I just needed a few days to freak out. Saying the words is hard for some reason. Going to college with the guy I'm dating makes me uncomfortable. Even though Northwestern is the school I really *should* be going to. I've pictured State with Logan and Anders for so long that it's hard to see myself in this new picture; me and Cam, in Chicago. Every time I think about telling Cam I'm going, I start thinking of all of the reasons why I shouldn't do it. I've been telling myself it doesn't matter; I have plenty of time to decide. A lot of people I know haven't even finished their applications yet. It matters to him, though. And I need to start a whole new plan, if I'm moving to Chicago in less than a year.

Nonni is giving me a dreamy look like I just told her I'm getting married. "Well, that's something, isn't it."

"It's something, all right." I smile at her. "Most of the time I'm sure about going . . . but then sometimes . . . I have second thoughts."

"What do you think about?"

"What?"

"When you have second thoughts. What are you thinking about?" she asks.

"I feel like Cam has secrets, I guess. Sometimes I think we

know each other inside and out, because I'm so comfortable with him. But when I really think about it, there are lots of things he hasn't told me." I actively try *not* to think about this.

"Have you asked him?"

"No. I mean, it's not really my business to make him tell me. Not if he doesn't want to."

"He says he loves you?" Her mouth is scrunched up like she just ate something bad and her brows are pinched together. She's ready to get serious with me. It's life-lesson time.

I nod. Cam tells me he loves me all the time.

"And he wants you to move to another state to go to school with him?"

I nod again. I have a pretty good idea of where she's going with this.

"Then I think you've earned the right to pry, dear. Love entitles you to some of that." She winks at me and I take another sip of my steamy drink.

"What if he won't?" I swallow back the lump in my throat. I spent seventeen years without Cam, but now it's hard to picture my day-to-day life without him. I'm not sure how that even happens. How someone is able to permeate your life so quickly, seeping into all the cracks and becoming the glue that holds it together.

"Then he won't tell you," she says. "And *you'll* have to decide if you're okay with that." She grabs my hand from my lap, and pulls it onto the bed next to her. "You're the one who decides what you deserve, Ginny. Not him."

CHAPTER TWENTY-ONE

NOW

CAM

Vee usually disappears for a couple hours before she turns up in bed, so tonight I'm going to find out where she goes. After our fight the other night, and the days of silence that have followed, I have nothing to lose. I climb over the last rung of the ladder and kneel down on the shiny black roof of the bus.

"Still at it, huh?" We're parked for the night in the lot of the auditorium we'll play tomorrow night. Aside from the six buses lined up like dominoes, it's a pavement desert around us.

Vee turns her head to look at me. "Who gave me away?"

I wasn't sure she'd even acknowledge me. I came up here knowing there was a decent chance she'd try to push me off. A red blanket is spread out under her at the center of the bus and she's lying on her back, hands folded over her stomach.

"Tad," I say.

She giggles, a mischievous curl to her lips.

I point to the edge of the blanket. "Can I?"

She gives me a quick nod and I wonder if she's hoping I'll roll *myself* off the roof. "He's afraid of heights," she says.

I slowly make my way toward the blanket, scooting on my knees, and gently lowering myself down.

"And he's not the only one, apparently." She smiles, and I'm glad that for once, it doesn't feel forced. Lying side by side, we look up at the sky. Vee whispers, like someone might hear her. "I wish you could see the stars. There's too much light pollution everywhere we go."

"I didn't realize light was a pollutant."

She shakes her head. "It's not. It's just what they call a bunch of lights that drown out the stars. Because the sky is polluted by light, I guess."

"Hmm."

"Yeah, hmm," she says. I keep waiting for her voice to get harsh with me, but it stays light. It's not the indifferent tone I listened to for the first month of the tour, or the hostility I've gotten used to over the last two weeks. She almost sounds like the old Vee, and I don't know if that's a good sign or a bad one. Maybe this is the calm before the storm.

"I'm sorry about the other night." I've thought of a million ways I could tell her how I messed up. What a jerk I was for making her say all those things to me. In the end, "I'm sorry" is all that comes out.

"Don't apologize." She turns her head against the roof and looks me in the eye. "The way I've felt about you—the hate, the anger—I've been keeping it alive for so long. Feeding it, letting it grow and bloom." She turns her eyes back to the sky. "I had to let it out—and I wouldn't have done it on my own. It needed to happen."

"You used to open up about everything."

"No, I was always like this. I was just different with you. And I was different after you." She's quiet, and the soft hum of the nearby freeway fills the air. "It wasn't all bad."

As we lie in the warm summer air, I'm reminded of all of the nights we spent on the sand, looking up at the same stars. She was like an unlocked diary on those nights, sharing everything. More than I ever deserved. I still don't deserve her secrets, but I can't help myself.

"You told your mom you'd see her soon," I say. "Are you leaving?" I hold my breath, waiting for her answer.

"I'm going home next week." A wave of regret hits me. Why did it take us this long to get to a place where we could talk? "Just for a few days," she says, and it feels like a second chance. "My parents are getting remarried." She says it like a joke, and even though I can't see them, I know she's rolling her eyes.

"Wow." I don't know what to say; I didn't even know her parents were divorced. "So are you the flower girl or something?"

"Very funny." She smacks my leg, and I grab her hand and hold it in mine. Maybe it's muscle memory. Vee flinches, but doesn't pull away. Her hand is rigid inside of mine, tense. "Close, though," she says. "I'm a bridesmaid. Cort, too. As if it's not weird enough that my parents are old and getting married for a *second* time, my best friend is also one of my mom's bridesmaids. Mom's stressed about my dress. I had to order it over the phone."

We stay this way, lying side by side in the silence, her hand in mine, our eyes on the sky, and she never relaxes. I've thought about a moment like this for so long, and now all I can think about is how different this feels from the way it used to be. I always felt like re-creating the past would be like a victory, but this just feels like a bad copy of what we used to have.

She finally breaks the silence. "What would you do differently?" Vee picks at the buttons on her shirt with her free hand, and I realize it's the first time she's ever asked me something without giving her own answer first.

I squeeze her hand. "Besides the obvious?"

"Obviously."

"I would have taken you to Chicago," I say. "We would have set up on some busy corner and busked on the street. We would have made bank—*at least* twenty bucks. You would have made your musical debut, and then we would have walked through Millennium Park and taken one of those cheesy pictures, kissing in front of the Bean."

"I would have liked that." Her voice is soft and sad. "I've been to the Bean."

"Yeah?"

"Yeah," she says.

"I'm going to make it up to you."

Vee doesn't say anything. She gives me a tight smile—a hesitant smile—and turns her eyes back to the polluted sky.

CHAPTER TWENTY-TWO

THEN

CAM

Since we're a high school band, ninety percent of the fans that come to watch The Melon Ballers are from nearby high schools and colleges. A few parents and teachers are mixed in. There's an orange sea of underage wristbands waving through the air when we sit down after our show the following Saturday at Carnivale. We've played here twice a month since the first gig. Vee has gone back to wearing her purple Melon Ballers T-shirt instead of her Dakota Gray outfit. I like the leather pants, but it's hard to argue with tradition. I wear the same pair of boxers for every show, and Anders has a lucky set of drumsticks he keeps in his pocket, even though they're too beat up to actually use.

We're in a booth in a back corner. Vee is next to me, and Logan and Anders are squeezed in across from us. As Logan complains about taking an early break so Steve can run home to get a replacement string, Vee and I hold hands under the table. We're planning a trip to Chicago next month, and hashing out details. I haven't told her yet, but I'm going to take her to busk on the street. It will be Dakota Gray's first public performance, and I think by then she'll be ready. We're also checking out the Northwestern campus while we're in Chicago. Vee hasn't officially told me she's going, but we talk about it a lot. Things seem to be falling into place for it to happen.

"Hey," a voice says from the crowd of people around our table.

"Can I get a Coke?" Logan says, and I ask Vee what she wants before turning to order.

"I'll have—" I stop when I realize it isn't the waitress.

"I'm not the waitress, actually." Sienna gives Logan an apologetic smile.

I'm not sure what you're supposed to say when your ex-girlfriend who lives two thousand miles away is unexpectedly standing next to you. "Hey" is all I come up with.

"Hey," she says. She's standing next to the table awkwardly, looking between me and the other three people at the table. "Um." She raises her hand up in a little wave, and puts on the fake smile I used to call her Cheerleader Face. "I'm Sienna. I'm a friend of Cameron's, actually." Her voice always gets high and squeaky when she's got Cheerleader Face on. I used to think it was cute, but right now it makes me cringe. Vee straightens in her seat and leans forward to get a look at Sienna.

"Cool," Anders says, around a pile of fries in his mouth. "Another chunk o' cheese in the mitten."

Shit.

Sienna looks at Anders, her face scrunched up in confusion. "I'm not sure what you mean."

Anders holds up his hand. "We call Michigan the mitten," he says. "You can probably guess why." He waves his hand in the air. "And *you're* from Wisconsin." He says it slowly, like she's missed something really obvious. "So cheese . . . in the mitten."

Sienna shakes her head. "I appreciate the visual, but I'm from California." Cheerleader Face is back in full force. "Cameron and I went to school together."

Vee's eyes turn on me, along with everyone else's. Act normal, Cam. "Sienna, these are my friends: Logan, Anders, and Vee."

"Cool," Sienna says, cheerily. "How have you been?" She's only talking to me now, ignoring everyone around us. "I've been calling you."

"I'm good, thanks."

Anders taps Sienna on the hand she's resting on the table. "So, why are you here?"

Logan jabs him in the ribs with his elbow.

"Fuck, come on. I mean from California." Anders rubs his ribs dramatically. "Damn, it's a legitimate question. We're not exactly *on the way* to anything."

Sienna is finally starting to fluster, her smile pained. "Your aunt and uncle told me you were here. I'm at Michigan now, and I was driving through to Chicago for break." She shrugs her shoulders, clearly uncomfortable. "It actually *was* on the way. So here I am." Sienna looks around nervously and shifts on her feet, looking uncomfortable standing here.

Shit. She probably is. "You want to sit down?" I get up to grab a chair from a nearby table, praying it isn't the dumbest decision of my life. Vee is drumming her fingers on the table, glaring in confusion as she pieces it all together.

Sienna sits down awkwardly, bending one leg and leaving the other mostly straight. "Thanks." She's visibly relieved. "Still sore sometimes, you know. Three hours in the car doesn't help."

I don't know what to say.

Sienna is quick to fill the silence, looking past me to Vee. "So are you in the band too?"

"She's the manager." I say it quickly, not thinking. In some ways I know I don't owe Sienna a thing. Not an explanation or a diversion. In other ways, I feel like this is my chance to protect her. For once.

Vee's drumming fingers stop suddenly. "Yep," she says tightly, "I'm the manager."

"So, how's Maggs?" Sienna turns to me again.

Shit. "She's fine."

"Have you actually talked to her, Cameron?"

Vee leans to the side to see around me. "Who's Maggs?"

Sienna shifts in her metal chair. "Maggie? His sister? She and I were friends long before we dated."

Vee's wide eyes burn into me. Her voice is casual, controlled. "Right, of course." She smiles and rolls her eyes, as if she must have forgotten. She taps my shoulder. "Excuse me, I'm getting out."

I don't move. "Vee—"

She pokes me hard in the side but doesn't look at me. "Move it, Fuller." I can tell from the way her voice quivers and her cheeks have pinked-up that she's upset. "Please, Cam?"

I move out of the booth, letting Vee slip past me, watching as she makes her way toward the restrooms. Logan is staring at me like he's contemplating murder, then he abruptly gets up and leaves, with Anders in tow.

Sienna looks around at our now-empty table and her lips twist into a questioning pout. "This was bad." She's looking at me for confirmation and I don't even have the energy to lie. For once.

"It was bad," I mumble.

"Sorry." Sienna rests her hand on my shoulder, then pulls it back like I'm electrified.

"It's not your fault."

Sienna dips her head down to meet my eyes, where they're fixed on the wall. "It's not yours either, Cameron." She's not talking about Vee, or tonight, but she's still wrong.

I don't see Vee again until she's silently getting into my car. Every time I try to say something to her she just puts her hand up to stop me, but for some reason she still comes home with me. When she crawls into my bed, I'm not even sure why. Her body vibrates against me, and I can tell she's crying as I hold her, but I still can't say any of the things I know she wants to hear. When her gentle shaking stops, I think she's finally fallen asleep. Then she lets out a long breath and rolls onto her back, her eyes on my ceiling. "You told me you lived in Wisconsin."

I nod against her shoulder. It's a lie I told so long ago it's started to feel like the truth.

"Who's Sienna, Cam? She's not your *cousin*." She says it like it's disgusting, like it's the worst word she's ever had to say. "She drove here from Ann Arbor. And it's not *that* on-the-way."

"We"—God, I don't even know what to call it—"dated."

"Why did you lie?"

I can't answer, because I don't even know.

She's shaking her head back and forth, and in this long silence that hangs between us, I start to hope that maybe this is over. "Where are your parents?" She says it slowly, and it sounds like a threat, not a question.

"Vee—" *Say the words, Cam.* "I just—I can't." I try to hold her hand, and she pulls away. "Please don't ask." *Say the words, Cam.* But even though my heart is breaking with her, I've never actually said those words out loud before. To anyone. She won't look at me, won't take her eyes off of my ceiling. "I love you. This doesn't change anything, and I just—can't."

"Right." She roughly rolls away from me again.

"Vee—"

Her whisper sounds loud in the silence. "I didn't even know you had a sister, Cam. I was ready to let you lead me to Northwestern, and I don't know you at all."

It's the last thing she says to me before she finally does fall asleep, and when I wake up at 6 A.M. she's already gone.

CHAPTER TWENTY-THREE

NOW

VIRGINIA

We're in New Jersey, and the guys are finishing up their set. The venues have gotten bigger, and I like watching from offstage, where I can see the show, but not the crowds. Even though I'm not the one up there playing, seeing the mass of fans gives me the chills. Thanks to multiple rehearsals, each live performance is timed to a tee. So when Logan walks offstage and pulls a stool up to the microphone, I know something is off. Cam, who usually plays lead on the band's few acoustic songs, is already perched on an identical wooden stool at center stage. *They're playing a new song? One they haven't rehearsed?* I've skipped out on some practices to respond to the constant online comments and backlash from the recent video drama, but how could they have learned an entirely new song? *And they didn't even mention it?* When they learned "Purple Shirt," it was all they could talk about.

Logan pulls the stool next to Cam's, positions the second mic in front of it, and then walks to the back of the stage next to Reese, who also seems to be sitting this song out. *What the hell are they doing?* I wave my hands frantically at Logan. He winks at me, with a giant, goofy grin that does absolutely nothing to ease my nerves.

"We're going to try something a little different tonight," Cam says, in his sultry, raspy stage voice, running a hand through his hair. "If you don't mind." He looks out into the crowd of squealing and cheering fans, a sea of purple Future X shirts filling much of the auditorium. "This song is sort of special, so I hope you like it." He strums a few notes and my heart sinks. No, it deep sea dives.

Oh, God, no.

"It's a love song." A few more notes. "The first love song I ever wrote, actually." The crowd is going crazy, and he's glancing toward me, without actually looking at me. "For the first girl I ever loved."

No, no, no.

He gives the crowd his sexy half smile and again squeals and cheers erupt as someone in the back shouts out, "Love *me*, Cam!" during a moment of silence. "The thing is, I can't play this one on my own." His voice is sad and melodramatic and I think about choking him. "It's actually a duet." He strums a few more notes. "Does anyone want to join me onstage?" The crowd is erupting with volunteers.

Hell, no.

"What's happening?" Pax is standing next to me, swaying a little on his feet. "Does he need someone? Should I go out there?" He's about two seconds away from rushing out to join Cam onstage.

"Something like that." I put my hand across his chest to stop him from lunging onto the stage, though part of me thinks I should let him. Let *him* be the one to suffer this humiliation. He's *not the most hated person on the tour—they won't eat* him *alive out there.*

I feel like time is standing still as Cam continues to pluck out the intro to the song, looking from the audience to where I'm standing offstage, in a repetitive loop. The time for their last song is ticking away. What is wrong with all of them? Cam is seriously going to do this to me?

Logan walks over, leaving the stage with his acoustic unstrapped in his hands. "Vee, come on."

I turn away from him, looking backstage. "I don't owe him anything."

"No one said you did. Do this for you. Show yourself you can do it. Cam's not going to let you fall out there." He holds the guitar out to me. "You want this. You've always wanted this."

I can feel the tears welling up in my eyes, and I let the adrenaline push them back. The only thing worse than going out on that stage is letting Cam think I'm weak. I grab the guitar roughly from Logan's hands, slinging it over my neck as I make my way onto the stage. I'd like to think I'm walking with a sort of confidence I've never had before—strutting—but I'm just glad I've made it to center stage without tripping or passing out. And no one has hit me with anything. *They just don't recognize you yet,* a mean little voice in my head whispers. On the opposite side of the stage, Tad gives me a thumbs-up from behind his camera.

Cam is still talking to the crowd as I take my seat on the stool next to him. "Give it up for Virginia Miller," he says.

The loud crowd has fallen silent, but there's still a handful of people letting out small cheers. *Maybe they don't* all *hate me.*

"Hey, now," Cam scolds them, "Vee's our best friend and part of the Future X family. So if you love us, you gotta love her, too."

Logan picks up his own mic, shouting, "Let's hear it, people!" The crowd lets out a hesitant cheer—more like a five-thousand-person golf clap—but I'm thankful no one has pelted me with anything . . . yet. My hands are shaking as I adjust the mic in front of me.

Cam leans into the mic and the crowd goes quiet again. "We

wrote this song a few years ago, back when we were young and stupid," he says, smiling at me, and my racing heart slows just a bit. "I was stupid, at least. Vee was always perfect." And then he begins the song again, strumming each note of the intro, until his deep, perfect voice joins along:

There's this girl, yeah this girl,
who makes the world seem
brighter than it's ever been.
There's her smile and her eyes,
and I just wanna make her mine.
I hear her laugh and I smile
'cause I know she's laughin' at me.
There's this girl, yeah this girl—
I think she's the girl for me.

He's still playing, repeating the last line again, as I join in on the melody, my fingers plucking the strings easily as I finally focus on Cam, and everything around me melts away. It's just me and him, on his bed, under the stars, in our own space.

There's this boy, oh this boy,
who's got me all tied up
in the best kind of knots.
There's this look you've gotta see,
when he's starin' at me;
it's his hands on my hips,
and in the way that we kiss.
I can't help but smile
'cause he's lookin' at me,
oh he's lookin' at me.
There's this boy, oh this boy—
I think he's the boy for me.

My face feels stretched tight as I stare at Cam, wondering how he has possibly gotten me to do this. Thankful that he has. I'm onstage, in front of thousands of people; real, in-the-flesh people. But I can't think about any of that now. I'm playing with Cam again. He's still staring at me when he starts in on the next verse. He's not singing the song to the audience, he's singing it to me. My heart is beating out of my chest watching his hands run along the strings, his lips caress each word he sings. I fight the urge to lean in to him.

> There's this girl, yeah this girl,
> she's the only bright spot in
> my dark, dark world.
> This girl, yeah this girl,
> she sets my world on fire,
> in the best kind of way.
> It's a rush and a thrill
> and I swear that I will—
> I swear that I will.
> There's this girl, yeah this girl,
> she's become the center
> of my whole damn world—
> and I swear that I will—
> I swear that I will—
> call this girl mine.
> Wish she'd be mine.
> Forever she's mine.
> There's this girl, yeah this girl,
> she's the center of my whole damn world.

I'm choked up and staring at him, and I'm supposed to sing my last verse, but the words won't come. Because those weren't the lyrics I had expected. The words both exhilarate and crush me. Cam starts in on the bridge and I take a deep breath before joining in.

> *There's this girl, yeah this girl*
> *There's this boy, oh this boy*
> *I'm gonna make her mine.*
> *I'm gonna make him mine.*

I'm frozen on the stool as Cam leans over and kisses my forehead, the crowd erupting into applause. Real applause this time. They aren't chanting at me to get off the stage or telling me how horrible I sounded. They don't hate me. They are legitimately cheering, as loud as I've ever heard them, and even if maybe it's all for Cam, everything inside of me is lit on fire and glowing. I take a tiny, nervous bow, and run offstage, feeling like I could fly.

CAM

Caustic Underground is playing their first song. Vee is backstage, swaying a little from side to side when I return from our post-performance pep-talk with Jenn. Everything about Vee is relaxed, loose. I walk up behind her, so close there's no way she can't know I'm there. Still high off of our performance, I feel like I could do anything—even face off with Vee. But right now, I just want to be close to her. Bringing her onstage was the only way I could apologize for how much I hurt her. And thank her, for how much she loved me. I wanted to give her something she had always dreamed of, something she didn't believe she could do. I always knew she could.

"If you get any closer we'll be cuddling," she says, looking over her shoulder at me, her brows raised.

"Would that be horrible?"

"It might be." She shrugs with a smirk. "It might not be. You've caught me in a good mood."

I say a silent prayer as I wrap my arms around her shoulders and pull her into me. Slowly, she relaxes against me, letting her head fall back against my shoulder as we both watch the band in front of us.

"I'm sorry," I say, leaning down to her ear. "I don't think I ever said that. Those two words. But I am." I squeeze her a little tighter, feeling like I can't get close enough to her. "No more excuses."

She nods against my shoulder, but doesn't say anything.

I kiss her hair and feel her body tense. "I'm not giving up on us."

CHAPTER TWENTY-FOUR

THEN

VIRGINIA

It's nine days until Christmas, and twelve hours since I snuck out of Cam's bedroom. The house smells like cinnamon and spruce. In the kitchen, Mom stirs a steaming pot of pasta for our Thursday night dinner together. There's nothing on TV but holiday movies—I've been flipping through channels for ten minutes. *And God, love is* everywhere. From what I can tell, not a single song has been written, or movie directed, that doesn't have two idiots falling in love.

Mom shakes salt into the pot. "I saw Logan at the grocery store yesterday. He thinks you're still considering State." She's stating a fact, but there's a question there too.

Mom taps the wooden spoon on the edge of a saucepan. "Why don't you give him a call later and tell him about Northwestern?"

"Don't worry about it, Mom."

"He said he's going to visit State in a few weeks. He wants you to go with."

"Mmhmm." I slam my thumb down, assaulting the remote as I ascend to the premium channels we don't get. I click on *Gold*

Rush, and an obnoxious blue box fills the screen, telling me what I already know: we don't get this channel. "Why can't we get any good channels?" I slam the remote down onto the coffee table. All I'm asking is to see some fat, beardy guys dig in the dirt. Love-free. Why can I not watch the one safe show on all of television?

"Virginia." Mom's face is tipped down and she's staring at me from over her dark rimmed glasses, giving me a squinty look that says, *Shut down the attitude.* "I think you should tell him, now that—"

—*Now that I'm going to Northwestern with Cam.*

"*I* think"—I'm yelling, throwing my arms across my chest as I swivel on the couch to stare at my mother, who is still stirring the steaming pot—"maybe you should consider telling *me* that you and Dad are getting divorced. If we're so concerned about disclosure in this house." Tears are scraping at the corners of my eyes, my throat is tight. "Actually . . . maybe you should have considered it a few years ago, when you started this whole charade." I wave my arms around me, at the house that shows no trace of my father. "Where's his stuff, Mom?" She's stopped stirring, resting the wooden spoon on the edge of the silver pot. "Isn't it strange that he has to come *home* with a bag of clothes?" My eyes are fixed on the window behind her, steamy and opaque, tiny droplets of water dripping down. It's nice not to be able to see all the snow outside for once.

Mom takes a step away from the counter and stops. "We did."

"You did what?"

"We got divorced." I tear my eyes from the window and meet my mother's, which are shiny. "We were waiting to tell you after you graduated. We thought we could work it out with space and a separation. It was finalized over the summer." Her eyes drop to the counter, where she's fidgeting with the spoon. "We didn't want it to overshadow your senior year."

"That's the stupidest thing I've ever heard." My shoulders are shaking, and my breaths are tiny and short—I feel like they're stuck in my lungs. "What a great graduation present *that* would have been."

"That's not the whole story, Virginia—"

I throw the black remote, shocking both of us, and watch as square plastic panels crack off and litter the floor. "I don't want to hear the whole goddamn story. You should have told me."

She's staring intently into the pot like something interesting is happening there. "Yes."

"And the house?" I wonder if she's going to try to lie. "I've been there. Your stuff's still in it."

Her head pops up and she looks surprised. "Your father kept the house. But Virginia—"

I don't let her finish her pointless excuse. I storm into the hallway, and with one hand on my doorknob, I summon my most composed voice. "I'm not going to Northwestern, Mom. Drop it." I turn on my music and let it drown out the sound of my mom at the door. If I want lies, I'll get them from love songs. I don't need them from my mother.

CAM

At seven o'clock, after a day's worth of text messages and voice-mails begging her to come over, Vee is standing in my living room. Her jacket is still on, and she doesn't look like her plans include staying, but she's here.

"We need to stop this." Even as she says the words, I hope she doesn't mean them. She waves her hands between us. "Whatever this is, it has to stop."

I know this is my fault. Between Sienna showing up and my dodging Vee's questions about my family, there's no one to blame but myself. But there's no room for the guilt, because all I can feel right now is anger. I've felt guilty for so long, and finally, I'm mad. At everyone. Because once again, I'm losing everything.

"So you don't want to be *friends* anymore?" I ask her.

Vee narrows her eyes at me, and I've never seen her look like this. "Don't be an asshole. We became more a long time ago, and you know it."

"I guess you'll have to be more specific with me. Exactly what parts were my 'friends with Vee' benefits, and which were my 'more than friends' benefits? I'm just curious what exactly will change. I mean, do I still pick you up for school? Do you pretty much live at my house? What about sleeping in my bed? Do I still get to touch you? Where exactly will you draw the line?" Her face pales as I say the words but I still can't stop. "Hopefully the benefits packages between Logan and me won't get too confusing for you."

There's a moment when I know it's going to happen. It's the second after she bites down on her lower lip, when her face fills with something I've never seen before. Hate, I think. Then she slaps me across my face. There's no flirtation or playfulness. She's out for blood. And when her ring makes contact with my lip, she gets it.

"Shit, Vee." I swipe my thumb across the warm blood seeping from my lower lip as she shakes her hand out in front of her, staring at it.

"Sorry. Cam, I . . ." She reaches out for me, then recoils. "No. You know, I'm not sorry. You don't get to speak to me that way." She slams her hand into my shoulder. "You don't get to act like—like—"

"I didn't mean it, Vee. I just—" I can't even get my thoughts together, because the only thing running through my mind now is Vee walking out of here. And how I deserve it. "I don't know what I'm doing. I'm just so mad." I grab her hand and she lets me take it. "Not at you, though."

"I know." She squeezes my hand. "You need to get shit figured out, Cam. There are things you need to tell me. And until you can, we can't do this anymore." She slowly pulls her hand out of my grip. "I can't do this to *myself* anymore."

"You don't have to know everything about someone to love them, Vee."

"I get that, Cam, but you *do* know everything about me. You know all my secrets, all the things I thought I'd never tell anyone. And we're not talking about knowing each other's favorite ice cream flavor or which boxers are my favorite to sleep in." She stops for a second. "It's the blue ones, by the way. The first ones I wore." She's forcing a smile and trying to lighten the mood. She's as nervous as I am, and I would kiss her right now if I thought she'd actually let me. "This is serious, Cam. You can't tell me the most basic things about you . . . about your family. Where you're *from*. The fact that you can't tell me—that says something."

"It's not that, Vee." When I reach for her this time she flinches; like my touch will physically hurt her. I feel like her touch is the only thing that can fix me.

"Then say something."

But I can't. There isn't anything I can say that will make this better, because the truth is just as ugly as the lie. *I don't deserve you; I don't deserve anyone. I should let you go.*

"You don't have to tell me," she says.

I feel the tiniest bit hopeful, but all I see in her eyes is resignation, defeat.

"If you're not ready, you don't have to. But until you are, this"—she waves her finger between us—"can't happen. I deserve better than this."

"I'm fucked up, Vee." I don't even know how to explain it, but maybe if I can, I could fix this. "That's just who I am now."

"Maybe you are," she says. "But I love you, and nobody ever said you had to be fucked up by yourself." She tucks a piece of hair behind her ear. "But you have to let me in."

"I want to. I can, maybe . . . eventually."

She nods. "I guess we'll worry about it when it eventually happens, then." She's staring at the corner of the room, where I have a picture of us tacked up on the wall. She had made fun of my bare walls, so one day I printed a bunch of photos of us and stuck them to the wall with thumbtacks. She laughed, but then said it was tacky, and took them all down. Except for that one. We're lying on the beach, and the tops of our heads are cut off. We're supposed to be kissing, but we both started laughing, so we look like we're just smiling at each other with our faces pressed together. We look happy.

She has one hand on the doorknob, and before I can think of an explanation, she's leaving. And as the door closes, all I can think is, *This house is burning around me too.* And she said she loved me.

I'm exhausted after Vee leaves, and at the same time, I'm filled with a sort of nervous, anxious energy. I feel like I just ran a race or was punched in the gut. Everything hurts in a way I haven't felt in a long time, and I only know one person who understands this amount of pain.

Cam:
Sorry
For everything

Sienna:
Stop it
I'm sorry for showing up. I shouldn't have
I'm sorry about Vee

Cam:
Not your fault
I haven't told her. I can't talk about it

                                                    Sienna:
                                                I get that

Cam:
I know

                                                    Sienna:
                                        Just breathe, Cam

The words repeat in my mind, over and over: *just breathe, just breathe, just breathe*. As I collapse against my bed, I can feel the heaviness of the day washing over me. Pinning me down.

I'm lying on the stone, a few feet from Sienna, and I'm not sure what's broken. The jump was so much farther than I'd expected. Maybe it's all broken. The pain is radiating down my left side, stabbing through my shoulder, throbbing in my wrist. I gasp for air, and feel another sharp jab to my chest. I can feel the heat of the flames. It's uncomfortable, almost unbearable, like having your legs too close to a campfire, but a thousand times worse. Leaning to my right, I push myself up carefully. My legs feel okay. Bruised, maybe, but nothing broken. I hold my left arm to my side as I make my way to Sienna's crumpled body.

She's slumped to one side, her leg twisted unnaturally. I don't know if a full minute has passed since she jumped. If five have passed since we woke up. Everything feels surreal. I sink to the ground next to her, still cradling my left side. She looks delicate, fragile; broken and unfixable.

"Sienna, we need to move." The heat is rolling off the house in waves, the smoke stinging my eyes. "Can you stand?" I reach my right hand down to her, wincing as I release my grasp on my

left side, but we have to move. She's sobbing, her shoulders and chest heaving, but I can't actually hear her over the noise of the flames and the sirens and the lapping of the river, which is choppy. It's like watching the television on mute. She shakes her head, over and over. I'm hunched down, trying to slip my arm under hers, when I see movement. Mr. Anderson is running from the river, missing the dark-rimmed glasses that usually sit on his plump face. He's older than my parents, with black hair quickly fading to gray, and a round, friendly face. His cheeks are always red, but now they look almost sunburnt.

He waves me toward the water. "Get on the boat, I'll get her!" He's beside me, carefully lifting her up into his arms, as her screams pierce the air. "I know, I know. I'm sorry."

"Maybe—" Sienna fell, and maybe we shouldn't move her. I think about everything I've heard about emergencies—wait for the ambulance, a stretcher. Don't move them. But I don't know what else to do. We can't leave her here, we're too close to the house. There's burning debris and ash falling around us, swirling in the air like toxic snowflakes. A portion of the roof is collapsing in on itself at one corner of the house. Mr. Anderson makes his way to the boat with Sienna shrieking in his arms and I follow behind. I hold the boat steady as he steps on, and carefully deposits her on the bench seat in the back. She cries out again, another strangled sob of pain as her body comes to rest against the cushion. I'm in the bucket seat across from her, stroking her hair and trying to calm her. Sienna used to be friends with my sister Maggie, so I've known her for years, but we've only been dating for a few months. She's a year older, and we don't have much in common, really. It's still new—and casual. I've never had to comfort her; I've never even seen her cry. I don't know what to say to her.

"Shhh. It's okay . . . just breathe. You're okay . . . just breathe.

Just breathe . . . you'll be okay. Just breathe." I mutter the words over and over until they don't sound like words anymore. *Until I start to believe it. Start to believe maybe it will be okay. Maybe she's just panicking, she's not hurt as badly as she seems.* I hear a crash. Another chunk of the roof is falling in on itself. The first-story corner of the house where my room is—*where my room used to be*—is completely engulfed. *If Sienna hadn't come over, I would have been in that room.* The house looks like a giant bonfire, so bright it's hard to look at for long. We're on the opposite side of the river, docked in front of the Andersons' twin house. *This is what mine used to look like,* I think. I can see the spray of water coming from the other side of what used to be my home.

At the river's edge, three firemen are dragging a hose with a piece of machinery attached, and push it into the water. *A pump of some sort.* They run away from us, in their heavy equipment, and two more streams of water join the effort. I'm still idly stroking Sienna's hair. Everything looks fake, like I'm watching a news special. *Maybe it's all just a dream.* Mr. Anderson's voice is faint in the background.

"Yes, I called in a house fire. 2241 Sunset . . . yes . . . yes, I'm on the other side of the river. I have two of the victims with me."

Victims. It takes me a second to register that he's talking about me.

"Yes . . . two teenagers. Cameron Fuller and . . ." Mr. Anderson is looking at me. "Cameron?"

"Sienna. Sienna Walsh."

"Anyone else in the house?" He's hesitant, quiet, and the question doesn't register. I'm mesmerized as I watch the streams of water make impact. Everything I've ever owned is engulfed in a giant, flaming water fountain of destruction. "Cameron?"

"My parents are out of town," I say. "Maggie's at school."

"*Yes, just the two,*" he repeats, visibly sighing in relief.

"*Sienna's phone number, son?*"

I have no idea. Her cell's in the house and I don't even know if she has a house line. If she does, I've sure as hell never called it. We're more texters.

"*I don't—*" I look to Sienna, who is still sobbing, her head slumped down onto the seat.

She rattles off ten digits that are barely recognizable between her sobs, and Mr. Anderson relays them to the dispatcher.

"*They're both injured . . . yes . . . third-story jump.*" He shakes his head. "*One seems to be worse. Broken bones . . . yes . . . yes, I'll meet them. I've got them in a boat. I can dock a ways down . . . one can't walk. Okay . . . thank you.*"

Mr. Anderson presses buttons and the phone is back at his ear. There's a long moment of silence. "*Trevor, it's Mike Anderson. Listen, there's been a fire. Cameron's fine, he's with me. Fire department's on the scene, but it's bad. You'll want to head home as soon as you can. I'll leave my phone with Cameron so you can reach him. Give him a call when you get this.*" Then he hangs up. I guess it's not a "talk to you later" kind of phone call.

Mr. Anderson hands me the phone and backs the boat away from the dock once again. We make our way down the river, pulling along the bank a safe distance from the fire. The boat is close to the bank, and I take the wheel while he fishes under the cushions, pulling a large metal anchor out. Thrusting it onto shore, he pulls it until it digs into the soft grass. Moving to the back of the boat, he does the same, the boat now pinned parallel to the shore. The water is choppier here, and as we crest each wave and slam against the shore, Sienna lets out breathy grunts.

I see the lights of an ambulance cutting across the grassy yard, closing the distance. The flames are smaller now, and from this side, I can see that most of the top level of the house has collapsed.

I can see the charred stone shell of the house, the melted strips of siding along one side that used to be a dark red, and there, in the driveway—illuminated by the fire trucks—my parents' red BMW.

CHAPTER TWENTY-FIVE

NOW

CAM

The bus is always a million degrees, especially at night. Most mornings when I wake up covered in sweat, I'm not sure if it's just the sweltering heat, or if the nightmares are back. I'm not sure if they ever stopped. So when I wake up with something hot coiled against my legs and chest, I'm even more confused than usual. And my confusion turns to shock as I open my eyes and realize the coils of heat wrapped around me are Vee's arms and legs. She has one arm slung over my stomach, a leg across mine. Her head is resting in the crook of my shoulder. *What the hell. I must be dead, because no way is this my life.*

When I brought her onstage to sing with me last night, at the very least I wanted to give her some sort of positive memory of the tour. Of our time together. I wanted to give her the push she needed to pursue her music. And I wanted her thinking about me when she left in a few days to go back to Riverton. *Vee in my bed?* That's not at all what I expected.

The bus is still quiet, and no one else seems to be awake yet. I reach for the curtain, pulling it closed slowly, careful not to move her. Whatever has come over her, I know she'll be mortified if someone finds her this way. I don't want this moment to end with an obnoxious comment from Anders. *Or* with another scandalous video clip. I don't want this moment to end at all. Even though it's barely six and we didn't go to bed until well after two, I can't bring myself to go back to sleep. I don't want to waste a single second of having her with me like this. A million reasons run through my head, explaining why she would end up in my bed: Was there some sort of family emergency? Maybe she and Logan had a falling out. Or she found a pair of Reese's old boxers in her bed, and mine is a last resort? I can think of a thousand reasons she would end up in my bed. Not one of them has anything to do with me.

At seven o'clock I begin to stroke her arm with my fingertips. "Vee," I whisper against her ear, "wake up." She comes out of it slowly, nestling down into my shoulder before she fully wakes. The moment she realizes where she is, I know it. Her eyes are huge, like soccer balls. Her arm, which had lain loosely over my chest, is now rigid.

"Shit."

I keep rubbing circles into her arm and laugh. "You got into *my* bed." I shift to my side, so we're facing each other, and slide my arm over her hip. "Can't be mad," I say, tucking a piece of hair behind her ear, letting my hand drift behind her neck. Her body relaxes and her eyelids flutter shut again.

"I'm tired, Cam." Her eyes are glossy and wet as she stares at me. "Hating you is exhausting."

I run my finger across her cheekbone, trapping the tear that has escaped. "You don't hate me."

"I should."

I nod. *Maybe she should.* We're pressed up against each other in the tiny bunk, and I think of the two of us under a blanket, on the sand. "I'm going to kiss you."

A barely perceptible nod, and then my lips are on hers. The

kiss is soft at first, hesitant even. *This feels wrong. Undeserved. Am I actually allowed to do this?* She isn't pulling away, isn't stopping me. I can taste the salt of her tears, and I can't help but think of our first kiss. What a different place we were in then, how different we were. And also, how similar it all is now; being with her, wanting her, loving her. *We're destined to kiss at inappropriate times.* Maybe I did condition her to cry when we kiss. Maybe she always will. I don't know if I even care, as long as there's an always to worry about. I pull her closer to me, press us together, feel her warmth against me. I suck her lower lip, and then our tongues are meeting, twisting and tangling. Our bodies move in sync, our hips pushing, hands pulling.

Vee wraps one leg over my hips, bringing us even closer in the small space. She makes a sound like a single guitar string being plucked, a soft, tinny hum. The only thing that separates us is two thin layers of cotton and even that feels like too much, and also not enough. Being with her is like being wrapped around an exposed wire, like baring all of my raw nerves. My hand slips from her waist down to her hip, slipping under her pajama pants and resting against her warmed skin. I leave it there, letting her decide where it goes. She twists toward me, and my hand drops further, following her leg all the way down to her knee before slowly running my fingers back up. I'm waiting. This is all too good, too surreal. She'll stop this.

She doesn't. My hands continue to wander and explore, and our breath is loud in the small space. Her hand wraps tightly in my hair as she kisses me fiercely, roughly, like it's the last time. Like she wants me as much as I want her. Which isn't possible, because since I met her, I've wanted her more than air. The humming still fills my ears; a song, soft and low. Her lips are stilled against mine, before she captures my mouth again. The song continues, grows louder, is muffled by our mouths. It ends like it starts, with a single note, a hum. The sound of our breathing, our chests pounding in rhythm between us. The bunk above us squeaks and Vee tenses.

I kiss her hair, letting my lips rest there, as her body begins to relax again.

Her face is pressed against my chest. "You have nightmares."

"Yeah."

"I usually just stay until they stop."

"You've done this before?"

"Most nights." Her voice is soft, muffled by my shirt. "I must have fallen asleep."

She's been treating me like an inconvenience for weeks; barely speaking to me. And at night she's been crawling into my bed. She's been holding me. I don't like the little seed of hope that's growing in my chest.

I pull the covers back up around us. "So when people have nightmares your first thought is to climb into bed with them?" I'm trying to lighten the mood. "I sure hope Reese never gets lucky enough to have night terrors." I kiss her on the forehead and she laughs against my chest. "Thank you."

I kiss her again, because I can't get enough of touching her and I don't know how long it will last. How long I'll be allowed to be near her whenever I want.

VIRGINIA

The fans are in love with "This Girl," so at the next show—my last show before I leave for the wedding—Jenn tells me I'm going to play it with them again during a special off-camera encore. It doesn't sound like a request; it sounds like a task. Like when she tells me to set up a promo contest, or to prep Anders for an interview, so he doesn't sound like a mumbling idiot (her words, not mine). "This Girl" and "Purple Shirt" have become fan favorites, and the second time I go out onstage it's still terrifying, but it's easier.

Logan hasn't gotten me a present since I was ten, but when he goes off-script during a radio interview to mention that he and I aren't actually together, I know it's an "I'm sorry," wrapped in a box, with a bow on it. He casually mentions to the deejay that the seriousness of our relationship has been "inadvertently misconstrued," and I wonder if Jenn prepped him, because the words don't sound like him. The whole thing has a bit of a "friends with benefits" vibe, but I'm not about to get picky. He's the one stepping in front of the firing squad. I wonder if people hear the underlying truth in his words: *We lied; we got caught.*

When they ask him about the photo of me and Cam, Logan actually does tell the truth: he doesn't know—it's no one's business but mine and Cam's. But the band and me, we're like family, he says. It's sort of shocking how well Logan handles the whole thing. He gave the interview this morning, and by afternoon, the clips of his statement are everywhere.

The response from fans is mixed—some think Logan's explanation makes perfect sense. He's perfect, they love him, and of course they knew it was lies all along. Others aren't so trusting. They think he's protecting me—the girl he's still in love with. Either way, Logan has come out unscathed by the whole twisted situation, which is all that matters to me. I don't care anymore if nameless people on the internet think I'm horrible. *What do I care?* By next month I'll be old news. I just don't want the band to suffer because I'm on tour. With everything I have to think about with Cam and me, I'm suffering enough for all of us.

CHAPTER TWENTY-SIX

THEN

CAM

It's almost midnight when my phone rings. It's Vee's house phone calling, and I can't help the bubble of hope that's rising up in my chest.

"Hey."

"Cameron?" an unfamiliar voice says.

"Um . . . yeah, sorry . . . this is Cameron."

"Honey, it's Millie, have you seen Virginia?" She's talking so fast, it's like all of her words are running together.

"Um—she's not here. Did she say she was here?"

"No, I was just hoping. We got some upsetting news and she left about an hour ago. Call me if you hear from her, please?"

"Sure. Of course." The line goes dead before I can even finish. I pull on my socks and then my boots, my knit cap and gloves, my thermal shirt and polar fleece, then my ski coat. I shove an extra pair of gloves in my pocket and make my way outside.

Vee is sunken down into the snow, sitting on the wood planks of the boardwalk. She's a purple smudge on a clean canvas. The wind is fierce, biting and cold, but I can still see her footprints. She hasn't been out here long. I'm glad to see she has her big puffy winter coat on, but the jeans she's wearing are already covered in a fine dusting of white. She has tennis shoes on.

"Vee?"

She waves me off like I'm bothering her. "Go away, Cam."

"Not likely." I bend down and scoop her up before she can fight me. Walking through the snow-filled parking lot with her in my arms like a little kid, she kicks her legs and smacks at my chest. "Stop it, Vee. It's freezing out here. I'm taking you home."

"I don't want to go home." Her words are practically a scream.

"Fine. I'll take you to my apartment," I say, and she nods, leaning her head against my chest and closing her eyes. Once we reach the road, I deposit her on the passenger side of my car, which is running and warm.

Inside my apartment, I set her down on her feet, unzipping her jacket and pulling it off of her shoulders and down her arms. She kicks off her snow-covered shoes. Her whole lower body is caked in snow.

She stands stiffly as I try to brush snow from her hair, but it's melting and wet. "Go in my room. Take off your clothes and get in bed."

"Cam—" She gives me a glaring look and I can't help but smile.

"Get your mind out of the gutter. Grab some clothes and wrap yourself up in the covers." I kiss her on the forehead, and after weeks without touching her, she lets me. "Call me when you're done." She looks at me questioningly one more time, but makes her way into the bedroom, closing the door behind her. A few minutes later I hear my name.

The covers are twisted and tucked around her, but she's still shaking. I lie next to her, pulling her as close as I can, with the covers still between us. We lie, wrapped around each other, completely silent, until her shivering finally stops.

"You want to tell me what happened?" I say, brushing the damp hair away from her face and up onto the pillow. It's torture being this close to her after so long. We still feel a million miles apart. "Something with your parents?"

A tiny gasp slips past her lips, and the tears follow. I kiss her head, draping a leg over her cocooned body. I wish I could absorb her. There's no getting close enough.

"Nonni . . ." Vee lets out a jagged breath. "She had a st-stroke. It's really bad."

My stomach clenches, then drops, like one of those free-fall amusement park rides.

"I should have seen her more. I've been horrible. I mean, what—what if this is it?" She sucks in a long breath. "What if I don't get to fix it?" She sobs and shakes against me and I hold her tighter. I'm not sure if it's for her benefit or mine. "She'll be fine. Right? She'll be fine . . . she's tough. Nonni's the toughest old lady I know." She's rambling, like she needs to convince me it's true, so she can believe it herself. Maybe she does.

I should say something. I should tell her it's all going to be okay. Of course Nonni will be fine. Not to worry. I know I should say it, but I can't. Even with my nose pressed up to her hair, all I can smell is the flowery scent of the funeral home, like a million cheap scented candles have been burned. My ears are filled with the soft classical songs that barely break through the bustling noise of people. *Say something.*

I feel hands on my back, arms around my shoulders. Instead of Vee's cold skin, I feel the cold, smooth metal of the caskets under my fingertips. The soft drop of roses on dirt, the squeak of my crutches with each step I take toward my aunt and uncle's car. *Say something.* I hear the slam of car doors, smell the unfamiliar scent of a home that isn't mine. I feel the coldness from my sister, who has been silent; feel the gaze of her eyes, which are filled with tears. Eyes that won't look at me. Cold blue eyes I haven't seen in almost a year now. *Say something.*

I should be comforting Vee, telling her it will be okay, but all I can think about is how bad shit like this happens all the time. People die. It happens every day, to good people. Strong, tough people. And we can't do anything about it. It doesn't matter how much our families love us, or how many friends we have, or if we're rich or poor. It's not up to us. We're helpless. There are so many things going through my head that I know I should say, but only one thing comes out of my mouth: "I'm going to take you home."

She struggles to turn toward me, trapped by the blankets and my arms. Her breath is warm against my face. "What?"

"You should go home." I can see it in her eyes; the moment she realizes I don't want her here. It's the same moment I realize that I can't do this. I can't be what she needs.

"O-okay." She slowly slips out from under the covers and for just a second it feels like déjà vu, seeing her in my St. John's sweatshirt, a pair of my pajama pants rolled down at the waist, so they stay on her hips. She stares at the door and not me. "Let's go."

My phone vibrates, buzzing across the nightstand. I ignore it, letting it buzz until it finally starts ringing. LOGAN flashes across the screen. I let it ring, until it finally becomes impossible to sleep through the incessant sound.

"Hey—"

"I need you to come over here." Logan sounds fully awake.

"It's 1 A.M. I'll call you in the morning."

"I don't want to talk, idiot. Vee is here—"

I try to push away the question of why she's at Logan's. It's none of my business.

"She's crying and shit, and Cort can't get here for a few hours." His voice is a harsh whisper. "I don't know what to do. Can you just come over? I need backup. I need help, man." He sounds like he's dealing with an active burglary taking place in his house, instead of a frantic girl.

"Call Anders."

"Be serious." He snorts. "I need to *stop* the crying."

"She doesn't need me, Logan. You're her best friend." Even as I say the words, I hate them. And I know they're not entirely true. Not anymore, at least.

"She's not even talking to me. She showed up crying." Logan sounds panicked. "And I've tried everything. I sat with her . . . I held her. I thought maybe she'd tell me what was wrong, but she's just crying." I'm pissed thinking of him holding her, his hands on her, comforting her. *I should have said something.* I can't do it.

"It's Nonni," I say. "She had a stroke or something. She's in pretty bad shape, I guess."

I dropped Vee at her house, where she clearly didn't want to be, only so she could run to Logan. I can't even blame her, as much as I want to. I know I can't give her what she needs. I can't just lie and say it's all going to be all right, and I can't be honest and tell her that I understand what she's going through. I'm useless. She doesn't need to hear my truths. The truth is, everything ends. Things go wrong, people die. There's nothing you can fucking do about it. It doesn't matter if you saw them two days ago or two weeks ago, there's no way to prepare for it. *God, I'm messed up.* Logan can reassure her. He can tell her everything will be fine, and he'll probably even mean it. He doesn't know any better.

Logan is what she needs. Maybe, deep down, he's what she's always wanted, too. *And he'd have to love her back, wouldn't he? How couldn't he?* I've only known her for months and I love her. He's known her for years—how could he not? He's good for her. Logan's her best friend. Part of her family. The history they share is complicated, but she knows everything about him. She will never—could never—know me like that. Vee deserves Logan. More importantly, I *don't* deserve her.

I hear my name in the distance and realize that I dropped the phone on the bed when I began stuffing clothes into the canvas duffle bag that lies beside my bed.

"You coming, Cam?"

"I can't." I press the END button and shove my life back into bags and boxes.

CHAPTER TWENTY-SEVEN

NOW

VIRGINIA

I spent the first seventeen years of my life in Riverton, but every time I come back it feels a little less like where I belong. When I arrive on Friday night, I go straight to the little chapel that will host the ceremony. Cort is waiting for me in front of the giant wooden doors, holding a dress bag in one hand and a paper plate covered in ribbons in the other. When she sees me, she does her best backwoods country impression. "Well, there she is, our little Virginia Miller. Television star!"

I can't help but laugh. Cort's hair is a vibrant shade of red on top, with a thick layer of blond underneath. Mom must be thrilled. I throw an arm over her shoulder and pull on a strand of hair. "You're going to look like a fry dipped in ketchup." Our dresses are a hideous shade of yellow. "It's going to be hot."

"So hot." Cort loops her arm around my waist and we walk into the chapel. "Almost as hot as that duet last week. You want to tell me about that?"

"I'm sure you saw it," I say. "It was on national television, if you didn't notice."

"Trust me, I noticed. Was it amazing, being out there?"

"It was—" I don't even know how to describe it. There are no words in my vocabulary, no other experience to compare it to that could do it justice. Being on that stage was like drinking freedom. *It was like breathing in my dreams.* "It was incredible." The description is so lacking it feels like a lie. I can see my mother and father through the little square window in the door of the sanctuary when we stop outside the doors.

"Do you want to tell me about it?" Cort says.

"There's nothing to tell." And it's sort of true. It's forty-nine percent true.

"Okay. I'll drop it," she says.

"Nothing to drop."

"So it was just a blink then? That's the story you're going with again?" She gives me a playful smile and a wink as we push through the doors. We're still linked arm in arm as we walk down the long aisle. I'm not sure what to say to her, because I don't even know what I want. Worse yet, I don't know what I *should* want. Since kissing Cam on the bus I've felt like a disappointment to strong, independent women everywhere. *What was I thinking?* When a guy abandons you during one of the most upsetting times of your life—and then disappears—you're not supposed to take him back. You eat ice cream by the pound for a week, and you swear off all of his favorite bands. You write angry songs. You go out and create an amazing life for yourself, so you can rub it in his face. You are definitely *not* supposed to crawl into bed with him—nightmares or not. But there's this voice in my brain that I can't seem to turn off. It's the same one that whispered in my ear in high school, saying "trust him," "protect him," "love him."

Attention, strong, independent women of the world: Please tell me how to shut this stupid voice off!

"And if it wasn't a blink? If it was a wink?" I say.

"Then it was a wink."

I know she's not letting me off the hook this easily. "And?"

"And . . . I hope it works out this time. Otherwise I'll hunt him down, and that pretty little face of his won't survive." She's smiling while she slices her hand through the air like she's a jungle cat.

After the rehearsal, which seems totally unnecessary since the bride and groom have both been married before—*to each other*—Cort and I head to a viewing party at a local sports bar, to watch the band's performance. Sitting at a corner table, away from the masses of local fans, it's surreal to see it this way. Caustic Underground performs first, and Pax and the guys are on point. As the commercials play halfway through their set, I imagine Bri standing backstage, running bottles of water out to them, like she always does. Right now my guys would be going over their set list one final time.

Cort points out all of her band crushes while we watch, giving me a list of guys she expects to be introduced to. *Like I'm qualified to be a matchmaker.* During the segment between bands, when they play footage from the tour, they show a clip of me and Cam sitting in the back of the bus, holding our guitars. It's from the first few weeks of the tour. I'm sitting with my back to the camera, holding my guitar, while Cam sings "This Girl" to me. He looks like he's serenading me. Maybe he was. Seeing it this way, on the outside looking in, it's impossible not to see the look on his face as he plays, willing me to join in. Pleading. My eyes are on the table, but his are on me. They scream an apology. He might not have said the words until that night backstage, after our first performance together, but his eyes told me he was sorry weeks ago. I just didn't want to see it.

Your Future X has a rough night; Cam comes in too early on a verse of "Purple Shirt," which throws off Logan. They're visibly flustered, and not at all the confident future-rock-gods they usually are. It's the first time I've seen them falter onstage.

I look down at the purple shirt I pulled on over my sundress. *Maybe it doesn't count if I'm not there.*

"Don't be stupid, Vee," Cort says, when I tell her my theory. "It's not the ugly-ass shirt. It's you that's missing."

My parents have been back together for less than six months and are once again living in the beach house. And even though it's where I grew up, everything about it feels surreal now. The house is the same, but all of the furniture is new. "New furniture for a new life," Dad said. Being in this house feels like being on the set of a movie about my childhood. Except they didn't get the details quite right. My most recent memories aren't here; they're in the little yellow house I shared with my mom.

Mom is sitting at the kitchen table when I get home, stuffing mints into tiny yellow bags. She smiles when she sees me. "Have fun, sweetie?"

I nod, taking a seat next to her at the giant oak table. "I've missed Cort." I touch one of the shiny bags. "Can I help?"

She pushes a bowl of mints toward me and I grab a handful of the tiny, pastel bricks. The house is quiet; my dad must be in bed already. Or they're keeping up the charade of a traditional wedding and he's sleeping somewhere else. Mom and I sit in silence, stuffing bags and eating mints. The windows behind us are all open and I can hear the gentle rhythm of the waves outside.

"Can I ask you something?" I say.

She nods, stuffing another bag. "Sure."

"How did you forgive him?"

Mom looks up from her bowl of mints. "Who?"

"Dad. Why did you take him back?"

She laughs.

What the hell is wrong with her? I watched her suffer for two years. Going to night classes to finish her nursing degree; working nights at the nursing home, constantly exhausted.

"I never really wanted to get into this"—she's tying bows onto a pile of bags—"but it's probably time you hear it. I realize how it looked and I should have said something a long time ago." She folds her hands on the table and picks at her nails. "I resented your father for a long time. You're the best thing I've done, but you weren't in my college plan. And I always planned to go back, but life was busy. Your dad was successful, so I didn't need to work." She picks up a bag and starts tying bows again. "It didn't make any sense to put you in daycare so I could go back to school. I thought I was fine with that, but it ate away at me."

"Dad didn't want you to go back?"

"He never said that, but he never supported me. He never pushed me. And the more successful he was, the angrier I became." She drums her fingernails on the table and lets out a long breath. "*I'm* the one who asked for the divorce."

I can't believe what I'm hearing. My father has been the villain of my mind's story for years. "But he left."

"*I* left," she says. "I went back to school, I got the job at Lake Terrace. I finally felt like I had my own identity. I had to do it on my own before your father and I could work again."

"And he just waited for you?"

"No. He went on with his life and he gave me space. I had things to work out myself . . . I couldn't give him what he needed. He didn't like it, but he loved me enough to accept it. When I was ready I went after him and hoped like hell I still had a chance."

I'm staring at the pile of pink and green and yellow mints on the table in front of me, picking out all of the green ones. I can't look at my mom.

"When someone hurts you the way I hurt your father"—she reaches across the table, and her fingertips barely graze my arm—"it isn't easy to forgive. I don't know if I even deserved it."

"But you went after him."

"I couldn't *not* go after him," she says.

And *this*, I realize, is the problem.

The wedding was beautiful. And now that it's finally over, I'm lying on the sandy beach, slightly buzzed from the bottle of champagne I monopolized. In my bridesmaid dress. I close my eyes, listening to the waves as they greet the shore, and I finally feel at home on this beach again. When Cam left, the tiniest things—things I didn't even know were connected to him—reminded me of him. I couldn't sit on the beach without thinking of our nights under the stars, couldn't hold my guitar without hearing his voice. Everything I owned smelled like him. It both hurt and healed me, being constantly confronted by those memories of him.

Even the nursing home, where he had never set foot with me, became tarnished by his memory when I caught a glimpse of him as I sat next to Nonni's bed one day, in late spring. Cam had been gone for months by then, and I spent an increasing amount of time at Lake Terrace. Because it was such a beautiful day, and Nonni wanted some sunshine, I pulled back the curtain that normally divided the room. There was a small cluster of photos on her roommate's nightstand, and a gleaming silver frame with ornate curls at the corners had caught my eye.

When I picked it up, Cam stared back at me. He stood next to a girl who must have been a few years older, and an older couple who were clearly his parents. They were outside, in what looked to be a backyard, and all wore khaki shorts and white shirts. Cam and his father wore ball caps, and the only way to describe the way they looked was happy. His dad had one arm around Cam, who had a huge smile across his face. His mom and sister both had long blond hair that was blowing in the wind and wrapping around their faces. The picture was filled with joy, and Cam didn't look much younger than he'd been when I met him; maybe a few years.

"My parents aren't in the picture." Cam's simple explanation had clawed at my brain.

"Hi," I said, taking a seat between the two hospital-style beds. "It's Grace, right? I'm Vee." I smiled as I placed my hand on hers. I picked up one of the frames and turned it toward her. "Is this your family?"

As the wind brushes past my hideous yellow silk dress and the cold sand seeps between my fingers and toes, I wonder if I'm as forgiving as my father. Or as strong as my mother. I think I'm probably just a watered-down version of both. Maybe I'm not cut out for this kind of love at all.

CHAPTER TWENTY-EIGHT

VIRGINIA

It all starts with an internet search. One I've thought about doing ever since I met Sienna. I couldn't then, though. Deep down, I knew if we were going to work, Cam needed to tell me. Now it's too late. He's gone, and it's over, and I'm sitting in front of my laptop in my dark room, feeling like I'm breaking a rule.

When I hit the SEARCH button, I feel like my heart is going to break through my chest. I sort through page after page, clicking on links to real estate agents, teachers, and doctors. By page eight, I'm thinking about giving up. *Maybe it's better that I don't know anyway.* I have nothing else to go on because I don't even know what city he lived in. Again, I'm caught off guard by the realization of how little I actually knew about him. Funny, it's hard to track someone down based on stories about their childhood pets, or their favorite candy. *But I know his sister's name.*

All of my searches come back full of strangers. I strip off my jeans, about to give up and go to bed, when I see the sweatshirt lying on my bed. Cam's sweatshirt. I've been sleeping in it every night, as the smell of Cam slowly seeps out of it. I run my fingers over the rough "St. John's Prep" embroidery, before hitting SEARCH again.

There's an image of Cam in a soccer uniform in an article from middle school; Cam's hair is short and darker and his face is fuller. I pick him out in another photo, onstage at a school contest of some sort. It's an online school newsletter. This one is from high school, two years ago. He doesn't look much different, but his clothes look nothing like the Cam I know. He's in an old concert tee and tattered jeans, a giant, almost unfamiliar smile on his face.

I click on the article results and it's finally in front of me— what I've been waiting for, hoping for, and also dreading. Tears well in my eyes as I skim the headlines, "Overnight Fire Claims Two," "Two Escape Deadly House Fire," "Two Dead and Two Injured in House Fire." The articles feature a photo of a large home, engulfed in flames, or charred and roofless. One simply includes two headshots—Cam's parents—and my breath catches in my throat at the words "two dead."

Cameron Fuller, 17, was home with a friend when a fire broke out in his family's three-story home in a rural area along the river. The two teenagers jumped from a third story window to escape the blaze. Rescue crews on site were told the house was empty, but later found that the owners of the home, Trevor Fuller, 49, and Margaret Fuller, 45, were also victims of the fire, which claimed the lives of both. An investigation is under way. Both minors were taken to Municipal Hospital for treatment. Injuries are said to be extensive but both are expected to recover.

Seeing the wreckage of Cam's past doesn't make me feel the way I thought it would. I wanted an excuse. Something I could tell myself, to explain away why he left. Instead, the new knowledge shifts everything inside of me. It hurts more, knowing that this is what he couldn't tell me; what he didn't want to share. A secret this big can't be hidden forever; it has an expiration date. I can't help but wonder what Cam had thought ours was. High school? College?

The newspaper articles are wrong. *One of them will never recover.*

I'm sitting cross-legged on my bed, picking at the chipped glitter polish on my toes, when I hear my bedroom door squeak open.

"Vee?" Logan's voice creeps into the room cautiously, and then he does.

Ignoring my visitor, I continue to focus on my dilapidated toenails. *Is it normal that my second toe is so much longer than my big toe? Maybe it's some sort of genetic defect. Is this why my balance is such shit?* I pull on my toe, comparing my long, skinny toe to the short, fat one.

Logan takes a slow step toward my bed. "You didn't answer any of my calls. And you missed practice again last night."

I gouge my thumbnail into a clump of glittery polish.

"He's not answering his cell." He doesn't have to tell me who. *I can't believe how badly he wants to be done with me.*

Logan shoves his hands into his pockets. "Have you heard anything?"

I shake my head.

"Figured." I think he mutters "asshole" under his breath, and I can't help but agree. "We're going to put up posters, see who we can find. We've got that big Winterfest gig coming up." He's been edging toward my bed one slow step at a time, until he's standing with his knees against my mattress. "I heard Nonni's doing a lot better. Your mom said she'll be back at Lake Terrace in a few weeks? That's awesome." Logan is obviously nervous and rambling and I know I should talk, to put him out of his misery, but I can't make myself do it. I don't want to talk to him. Not about Nonni or college or Cam—not about anything.

"Your mom's worried." The bed sags under him as he sits on the edge. "She said you've been holed up in here since . . . everything went down." More painful silence as I continue to pick at my toes, and Logan swipes my hand away, keeping it in his. "Come on, Vee. Talk to me."

Staring at Logan—his concern-filled eyes and his drawn brows—I can't help but feel like the world's biggest jerk. I've pushed our friendship aside for months. There have been so many secrets; lies even. He hasn't deserved any of it. And now, after keeping it from him for so long, I feel like I'm finally cracked open, ready to be poured out. *Things are changing.* Everything ends. People leave, life marches on. With or without me. With or without any of us.

"Vee, you've got to talk to me."

Tears leak out as I drop my head into my hands, trying to wipe them away before they get out of control. "Sorry I've been such a bitch."

"Hey, not any more than usual." His voice is light and teasing. Emotionally charged situations are Logan's kryptonite. I'm shocked he didn't run that horrible night I showed up in tears.

I reach over, taking his hand in mine, lacing our fingers together as I stare at them. "I've been avoiding you." This probably isn't the time for this conversation, but I can't hold it in any longer, and for once, it isn't the last thing I want to talk about. I look at our interlaced fingers in Logan's lap. Logan deserves the truth. "What you said about college—about us drifting apart—"

Logan squeezes my hand. "Was crap. It was bullshit and I shouldn't have said it." Logan shakes his head and as he speaks he focuses on our hands in his lap, playing with the tips of his fingers like he always does when he's nervous or uncomfortable.

I know Logan so well; every habit and favorite, every family secret.

"I don't want to go to State."

"Then you should have told me that."

I smile at him. "I didn't want to face the reality that things are going to change when we leave for school. I might lose you." I suck in a breath before I can keep going. "Ten years from now, we could pass each other on the street like complete strangers." The thought of not knowing Logan someday has tears stinging my eyes again.

"I shouldn't have said it, Vee. I wanted you to come, that's all."

"But you were just being honest. I get that now. You've always told me the truth. You're always honest with me. And the truth hurts sometimes"—I'm looking at my glittery toes again—"but empty promises hurt a lot more. And you've never given me those."

"Hey," Logan waves his hand in the air and I look at him again. "We're never going to be strangers, Vee. That will *never* happen, okay? You're stuck with me. Someday you'll have to compete with a crazy-ass girlfriend."

I laugh.

"You know it's true." He smiles. "I'll say the wrong thing and she'll burn my shit in the front yard. I'm going to call you for help when it happens." For the first time in months, we feel like us again. No awkwardness, no strange tension.

I nod, but it's still hard to imagine. A new picture of the future has formed since Cam left, and it hangs in my mind like a grotesque garage sale painting that's been nailed to the damn wall.

"Look at me," Logan says.

My eyes lift reluctantly to meet his, tears spilling over and onto my cheeks.

His thumbs brush across my hot cheeks. "We"—his finger darts between us—"will never be strangers. Maybe we won't talk every day, or every month or year, but you're family. And you'll always be my best friend. Some things might change, but that won't. Okay? I'm always going to be around when you need me."

I nod fiercely as hot tears once again spill down my cheeks, and despite them, I can't help but smile, choking on my breath as it comes out as part sob, part laugh.

"I'm sorry." *For so many reasons.* "I'm sort of messed up."

He pulls me until I collapse into his chest and his arms wrap around me. "You may be batshit crazy, but I still love ya."

I have my best friend back. And something about telling him the truth—getting it all out between us—it unleashes all of the pain I've stuffed away, and I feel it washing over me again. I sob and gasp for air, my face shoved into Logan's chest as I curl up against him. And if I try hard enough, I can almost imagine it's *him* holding me.

Step Four: Dakota Gray Sings for the World

It doesn't happen on the streets of Chicago, on a stage, or under bright lights. I'm sitting in a corner of my bedroom, with one of my old purple curtains hung up behind me. My wig is itchy and my palms are slick with sweat. I've set this up twenty times over the last week, trying to get the lighting and angle just right, so you can make out my silhouette, see the movement of my mouth. But you can't see my face. The camera I bought has a remote, and as I push the red RECORD button, I adjust the microphone one last time before my fingers finally find the strings.

"I'm Dakota Gray." I'm still not looking at the camera. "And this is a song I wrote about having your heart broken. It's called

'Catastrophic Love.' I hope you like it." I feel like a complete idiot talking to the camera like anyone is actually watching this, but telling myself there are people out there who will see this makes me feel heard. And every time I upload a video, it feels like a confession. Soon, I even have a few people listening, absolving me of my pain.

CHAPTER TWENTY-NINE

NOW

VIRGINIA

I make it back to the bus two hours before it's scheduled to leave Pittsburgh and head to Cincinnati. The guys are out getting food when I arrive, and within minutes of setting foot on the bus, I have a text from Jenn: *Production bus. Now.* "Please" isn't in Jenn's vocabulary, but still, something about her message seems more urgent than usual. I've never been summoned like this before, and the weekly marketing meeting I usually attend isn't until tomorrow. I haven't climbed the last step of the bus when I'm assaulted by Kaley's whining voice announcing my arrival with a halfhearted "Here she is."

"Here I am," I mutter, taking a seat in the lounge area. It's identical to our bus, except in place of our small coffee table, there's a large fold-down one that blocks the aisle and turns the front of the bus into a pseudo–conference room. There are papers spread across the table. They look like printouts of internet articles, and they're slashed with yellow streaks of highlighter and adorned with pink and green sticky notes.

"What is all of this?" I take a seat at the table next to Priya, and slide one of the papers closer to me with the tip of my finger. When I see the title of the article, I can't breathe.

Overnight House Fire Kills Two

I run my fingers over the rest of the papers, pulling each one aside, and they're all the same. There are pictures of the house, the twin headshots of Cam's mother and father, the school photos of Cam and Sienna. I knew they wanted to feature Cam's past, but this isn't what I had imagined. I didn't think about all of the details being laid out for the American public. Or maybe I had been so mad, I just didn't want to think about it.

"I've got footage from the girlfriend," Kaley says, smiling proudly. "James emailed the raw footage this morning."

"Girlfriend?" I'm confused about what they're talking about.

"Sienna Walsh," Kaley says, sneering at me like I'm stupid for not knowing the answer. Sienna. Of course.

I give Kaley a tight smile. "*Ex*-girlfriend."

I can't believe she'd do an interview against Cam's wishes. But why wouldn't she? Why would she assume that cameramen would show up and it *wouldn't* be approved by Cam? He's on national television; *of course* she'd think he had approved this.

"Why are you doing this?" I don't think it through before the words tumble out of my mouth and roll around on the table like a handful of loose marbles.

Jenn looks up from the pile of papers in her hands. "I assume you saw the last performance." It's not a question. "It was their first time in the bottom three. They could have been cut. We need to drum up support, give them a boost."

Kaley holds her laptop up for us all to see. "There's a dicey-looking mug shot of Gary we can leak," she says. "It's from years ago, but you can tell it's him." Gary is the oldest performer in the competition. He's in his late fifties with peppered hair. He's not half bad looking for an old guy, and he's been a fan favorite from the start.

Jenn is still looking at the pile of papers. "Do it."

"But if Future X isn't who the fans want—" I don't know why they're doing this. I can't understand why they give a shit if it's Your Future X who wins, or Caustic Underground, or Gary and his Merry Band of Old Guys (also known as Broken Sparrow).

"The fans don't know what's best for them," Jenn says. "Sure, they love the band with the quirky sound now. Or the band of fifty-year-old accountants and financial advisors making a comeback. But six months from now, when their album drops? Fans won't care. That loyalty goes out the window when they have to put their money where their mouth is." She taps one fingernail roughly on the table, like she's testing the shiny black lacquer. *Tap. Tap. Tap.* "Marketing. That's what sells albums. Catchy lyrics, pretty faces." She looks at me apologetically. "Don't get me wrong, your band makes amazing music."

Not *my* band.

"They *should* be the ones to win this," Jenn says. "We just need to make sure America makes the right choice." *Tap. Tap. Tap.* "This isn't personal, this is just how it works. A high school love story . . . a love triangle . . . it's not what we want to do, Vee, it's just the business we're in." *Tap. Tap. Tap.* "Don't you *want* your friends to win? That's all we're trying to do here."

I nod. "When?" The next show is three days from now in Cincinnati.

"We need some time," Jenn says. "We'll run a special segment before next week's show in Chicago."

I cringe at the thought of this train wreck happening so close to home. "And what if there's another way to create buzz?"

Jenn doesn't look at me. "There's not."

"But if there was?"

"Like I said, I don't care what does it. If you can somehow

prove that Reese is the modern-day Mother Teresa, I'd be more than happy to run with that story." She smiles and straightens her jacket before standing. "I'd be shocked. But I'd do it."

"What do you need from me?"

"Prepare him." Her face is sympathetic. "It's going to come out eventually. Make him see it's better this way. He can make the most of it and get something good out of all that pain and suffering."

Something good. I can't believe she just said it. I nod, and excuse myself, because she's right about one thing; I do need to prepare Cam. I know what I have to do, and I'm going to need a lot of help to make it happen. I pull out my phone. Luckily, I know 1.5 million people who will be happy to help me, and all it takes is one posting:

SURPRISE LIVE SHOW FRIDAY IN CINCINNATI.
VENUE ANNOUNCED AT 6:30.

CAM

I'm sitting backstage, scribbling some lyrics down, when Vee sits next to me. She's been back from Riverton for a whole day, and we've both been so busy we've barely spoken. The three days she was gone from the tour somehow felt longer than the year I went without seeing her before all of this. Maybe I had gotten used to the dull ache after so long. Now the feeling of having her close to me is fresh in my brain, and her absence—even this distance between us since her return—feels like it's amplified. When she sits down next to me, I feel like the breath I let out has been trapped in me for days.

"We need to talk," Vee says.

I nod.

"It's about your parents."

I swallow. Take a deep breath. Fidget in my seat. I set the guitar next to me, so I can turn to face her. I've been preparing for this since the day I met her, and I still don't feel ready for it. For this moment when she sees me differently, treats me like the broken asshole I know I am. "I don't really know where to start."

"They're going to run a story about the fire."

They shouldn't, but her words shock me. "You know about the fire?"

"I have the internet, Cam." She looks at me apologetically. "And I was heartbroken and curious when you left."

I nod.

"I'm sorry."

I nod. I've been reduced to a heavy-breathing, choked-up bobblehead. They should sell me at the merch tables outside. *I'm sure that would be a huge hit.* "I broke my arm in two places. A few ribs, my collarbone." I pull down the collar of my shirt, showing her the tiny raised scar, and she runs her finger over it.

Vee shakes her head. "You don't have to tell me about it."

"I do, actually." And it's true, because I know she needs to hear this just as much as I need to be able to say it. If nothing else, she needs to know that my leaving had nothing to do with her. Or how much I loved her. It had everything to do with me. She nods, and I continue. "I had first-degree burns over most of my body. Like a really horrible sunburn."

"It was Sienna with you?"

She's obviously read articles, and I wonder which ones. *Which pictures has she seen?* I nod. "My parents were out of town for the weekend and Sienna stayed over." I'm not sure if now is the time to elaborate on my relationship with Sienna, but I don't. "She was in worse shape than I was." I shake my head, remembering how much pain she had been in. "She broke most of the right side of her body; shattered her hip, broke her leg in a couple of places, fractured her wrist. She was in a wheelchair for months, couldn't walk for months after."

Vee glances up at me, her eyes full of questions I know I have to answer. "This was six months before you came to Riverton," she says. It isn't a question. "Eight months before we met."

I nod and twist the leather band around my wrist. "I finished the semester at St. John's, and when I turned eighteen, I left. I couldn't be there anymore." She nods like she understands, but I don't know how she could. "I was different afterward. And everyone had expectations . . . of how I should feel . . . how I should act."

"And your sister?" The question catches me off guard.

"We're not close, but she's fine. She was at college when it happened."

She nods again, but never asks the questions I'm waiting for. The questions everyone asked me after it happened: *Why did you say the house was empty? Did you know your parents were in the house? Were you fighting with them? Were you angry? How could you not know?*

"And you left because you didn't want to tell me this?" Her features are tight, and I can tell she's trying not to cry. "Why?"

I jerk my head toward Jenn and Kaley, who are headed our way. "Not here." I grab Vee's hand and pull her up. I lead us to one of the small dressing rooms and lock the door behind us. Vee's breath catches in her throat as she takes another step backward into the dim space. I grab her face gently in my hands, feeling the warm wetness of her cheeks against my palms.

"You were never the reason I left." I feel like the words have been caught in my throat since the day I left Riverton. They feel rough coming out. "I just couldn't be what you needed. I was messed up, Vee. I *am* messed up." I brush tears away with my thumbs. "When stuff happened with Nonni, I didn't know what to do. All I could think about was what happened with my parents. All I knew was worst-case scenario. How everyone dies." She sucks in a choked breath and I regret saying it; bringing up her own hurt. "And I didn't deserve you. I didn't deserve to be happy."

"Why didn't you tell me?"

"I spent six months with everyone looking at me like a broken, second-rate version of what I used to be. That's the whole reason I moved to Riverton. I didn't want anyone looking at me like that anymore. Especially not you."

She nods, but she doesn't look at me. Her eyes look past me, over my shoulder, and she's rigid, stone in my hands.

"I love you, Vee. Then"—I kiss her forehead, and my lips are still brushing against her skin when I speak—". . . now. That's the one thing I never hid from you. That's the truest thing about me."

A statue come alive, Vee is suddenly in motion. Her hands on my chest, lips on my mouth. Warm hands run up my neck, and mine twist in her hair. Slowly, I push her back against the counter, pinning her in place with my hips. Our hands are grabbing, our limbs tangling, our mouths searching. And we fit. It feels like we were out of gear, stuck in neutral, and now we're together and we've clicked into first. We're taking off. Racing toward something, but I'm not sure if it's the starting line or the finish. Maybe what we had before was a false start.

Finally, breathless—after seconds or minutes, or maybe hours—she pulls away from me. I feel the loss immediately—the cold space that used to be filled with her warmth.

VIRGINIA

When I finally break free from the centripetal force of Cam's body, the space around us feels charged. I have to pull my hand out of his, because I can't think when we're touching. I need to prepare him for what's going to happen. I tell him about Jenn, about the articles and the interview with Sienna. How they'll run a special next week. He doesn't say anything, he just stares at me, motionless; breathless, I think. Hopeless. *"I didn't want anyone looking at me like that anymore."* Cam's words ring in my head and I know, more than ever, that I have to do something. Even if it doesn't work, if I'm a complete failure, I have to try.

"Cam, listen to me." I dip my head into the path of his eyes, which are fixed on the floor. "I've got a plan, and I'm going to do everything I can to stop this, but I need you to go along with this. Just for now. I need you to trust me."

He nods and pulls me against his chest. We stand there until Logan knocks on the door, announcing the start of their rehearsal time. "We learned a new song while you were gone," Cam whispers into my hair. "It's a surprise. I can't wait for you to hear it." He kisses my head. "But for now, can you let us practice it? Maybe hang out in the bus for a while?" His voice is sweet and pleading.

I nod, and head for the exit. I have things to do, anyway. There's already a checklist forming in my mind. I need to talk to a few friends I've made on the crew. And I need to convince Tad to help me if I'm going to pull this off. I only have two days to make this happen.

I've convinced Jenn to let me set up an encore concert in the park across from the venue. The guys are thrilled with the idea, and thanks to a fame-hungry mayor, I managed to get the last-minute permit and security needed to put on a free public concert after we tape the show tonight. Your Future X will be playing his daughter's high school graduation party next spring, but it's worth it. Most of the next two days is spent on my computer and my phone, and when I have free time I sneak away to practice. Only Tad ever bothers me.

"You're really going to make this happen?" Tad pokes his head—for once camera-free—into the small room I've found on the second floor of the theater where we'll be performing tomorrow.

I nod. Letting them lay Cam's past out for the country like a buffet of pain isn't an option. "You'll take care of Jenn?"

"I'll do my best," he says. Tad is an integral part of my plan. I need someone behind the scenes to manage things while I'm out onstage with Cam, performing a new song. Cam and I have decided to keep the new tune—which I wrote—a secret. Reluctantly, Jenn agreed. After the success of "This Girl" I guess she figures a duet between the two of us can't go wrong. Boy, is she going to be surprised.

Step Five: Expose Dakota Gray

At 6:30, just as the guys are taking the stage for their set, I fire off the message I promised.

> CANONSBURG PARK @ 9:00. BRING FRIENDS!
> SEE YOU THERE.

The band's new song is called "Dakota," and it's a rock ballad about falling in love with a girl before you even know her. It's loud, a little punky, and the audience loves it. I couldn't have planned the song choice better myself. The crowd is loud and rowdy as the guys rearrange for our final song of the night. Cam is already perched on his stool, making adjustments on his acoustic. Usually I just walk out on the stage and Cam introduces me, but tonight, thanks to Tad's friend (and lighting tech) Becca, we're changing it up. And because we're on TV, and dead air is a major no-no, we've got to make this quick. The curtains close across the stage and I walk behind them, almost running as I bring my own stool alongside Cam's. Behind me, a gaffer has a can light, and angles it behind my stool. I give her a smile and a nod.

Cam whispers in my ear. "What's with the wig tonight?"

"All part of the master plan." I lean over, whispering my instructions in his ear.

He's surprised; I knew he would be. "Really?" I smile and nod, urging him on.

"When it's time."

Less than a minute has passed, and already Jenn is pacing stage left. The curtains are still closed and she's taking a step onto the stage when the lights go out, covering us all in darkness.

And it begins.

I take a deep breath as I hear the curtains peel back with a creak. I've gone over this at least ten times with the crew. When the curtains are parted enough to reveal us, I start picking the first few notes of the song to cue Cam. He's close enough that I can see him, even in the darkness, and I nod, letting him know it's time.

"We have a new song for you tonight. Please welcome back Vee Miller." The backstage lights come on, sending a soft glow over the purple backdrop that hangs behind us. I take one final breath and turn to face Cam as the spotlight comes on behind me. It's bright, and hot on the side of my face, and I know exactly what the audience sees now. My silhouette.

The microphone is pressed against my lips. "Dakota Gray," I say, and behind Cam, Jenn takes a step toward the stage.

Tad grabs her by the wrist, and she jerks as he holds on.

Shit.

She pulls her arm from his grip and I can see her mouthing, "Who the hell is Dakota Gray?" The audience has erupted and she's just standing there, stunned. Her head is down as her fingers fly across her phone and when she sees it—when she knows—I can't help but smile at her. I give her a wink, because that's what Dakota Gray would do.

Dakota Gray is a sassy bitch. Dakota Gray is fearless. Dakota Gray is an internet *sensation*. There's nothing people love more than a mystery. And in the year since her videos started posting online, no one has known her real name. They've never seen her face. She's never played in public. She's never been found, because she didn't want to be.

Until now.

I continue to play the intro, and when I start to sing the first verse Cam joins me, just like we practiced. I'm lucky Cam is *not* one of Dakota Gray's 1.5 million fans, because we're singing one of my first songs. My best-known song. I had to modify it to make it a duet—and a little less angry. It's an homage to love and heartbreak. The lights come up slowly and the darkened crowd explodes with bursts of light as cameras go off.

I'm exposed.

My hand is in Cam's as we exit the stage and he pulls me to a stop when we reach the darkness of stage left. "I can't believe you just did that," he says. It's hard to hear him over the roar of applause.

I laugh. "Jenn's pissed." I throw my arms around Cam and squeeze him like I'm trying to crush him. It feels like I'm going to explode with adrenaline right now, like I could put on an entire concert by myself. And then I remember that's exactly what I have to do. This was just part one of my master plan.

"That's not what I mean. I can't believe you just did *that*," Cam points to the stage.

I don't know why he's surprised, because Dakota Gray fears

nothing. Not even getting her heart broken. She crushes her lips into Cam's, keeping them there as he lifts her up off the ground.

We're startled out of our embrace by Jenn's angry voice. "What the hell was that? I didn't approve any of that." She holds up her clipboard, and points to the show logo. "This isn't the Virginia Miller hour!"

"Dakota Gray," I correct. "And we have an encore concert to put on now." The band is all around us and I pull Cam's hand, leading us all toward the exit. Jenn is following behind us, still yelling as we make our way out to the parking lot.

"I don't give a shit about your little concert," she says, as we walk along the side of the building. "You had two days. Don't get your hopes up," she says snottily.

Dakota Gray tosses her hair over her shoulder and pins Jenn with a smirk that says, *We'll see about that.* Dakota Gray is confident. She's been listening to the constant buzz of notifications all day, until she finally had to turn the phone off. She had to send her final location message to her fans using Tad's phone. But I, Virginia Miller, am less confident. I think about crossing the road and seeing an empty park. I think about failing Cam, because an auditorium full of people isn't enough to create the kind of buzz we need. There's no time for my insecurities right now, because up ahead, Tad is coming around the corner with two more camera guys. They walk ahead, filming us from every angle like usual. But when we finally reach the edge of the building, and turn toward the park, we all stop. Things are anything but usual.

"Holy fu—lipping—" Anders mutters behind me.

"Oh, my—" I look at the scene around me. *Am I officially kicked off of this tour?*

I'm not sure how many people are in the park. There were five thousand in the auditorium tonight, and this looks like four times as many. Every available surface is covered in bodies. Trash cans, picnic tables, and bike racks are being used as chairs. There are a few people sitting in a tree on a little hill to one side. People are still winding down the sidewalks, seeping into every crack of space on the grass.

Jenn has stopped behind me and her phone is pressed to her ear. "Get the rest of the crew out here. Now."

A pair of warm arms wraps around my waist, and Cam's lips are at my ear. "You're amazing."

"Well?" Jenn rushes ahead of us and waves toward the stage. "Don't just stand there."

Cam kisses my temple, his lips lingering against my skin. "Thank you."

At this moment, I don't regret it at all.

CHAPTER THIRTY

NOW

CAM

The official body count for our encore concert in the park was 19,274. That's what the police report says. Jenn taped it to the bathroom door of our bus and circled the number and the fine (a much bigger number), but she hasn't said anything else about it. I have a feeling the press we're getting will more than make up for the cost. We've barely sat down since we stepped off the stage last night.

We're on a plane to New York the next morning, and by afternoon we're on our third talk show interview. Most of the shows ask Vee to sing by herself, but she's refused. And for once, I don't think it's her nerves. She tells them it's not just about her, it's about the band. On the first show she and I play "This Girl" and at the second the band plays "Dakota" with Vee joining us on vocals. It's fucking unbelievable that she did this for me. I'm not at all surprised that people around the world love her. That's easy to believe. But after everything I put her through, I can't believe she put herself out there for me. Especially when I haven't answered the one question I've been waiting for her to ask: *Why didn't you come back?*

I thought she'd need to know the answer to forgive me, but she still hasn't asked, and I wonder if maybe she doesn't want to know. The answer is easy. At first it was too hard. How could I ever make it up to her? How could I explain myself? And the more time that went by, the more impossible it seemed. The more I panicked. Could she ever forgive me? Why would she wait for me? I never went back because deep down, I always knew she deserved better.

We're sitting on a production stage, around a big white table with three very loud women. *They're* asking us entirely different questions. Clips of Vee's videos play on a screen behind us. One of the hosts—a fifty-something retired Olympic something-or-other—is reciting a laundry list of facts.

"You made your first video less than two years ago."

Vee nods.

"You've performed over fifty original songs. Plus covers."

Vee smiles. "Yep." She's holding my hand under the table. I'm losing blood flow.

"You posted this video just last night." An image of me and Vee sitting on the tour bus appears on the screen behind us. It's the duet we played at the last show. We weren't allowed to use the official tour footage, so we re-recorded it on the bus. The video is shaky and grainy. At one point you can see Reese's finger drift into the shot.

"Do you know how many views it has so far?" the host asks.

Vee shakes her head. We've basically been in a bus, plane, or cab for the last sixteen hours. Behind us a string of numbers appears.

"Two point four million," the host says, shaking her head. Vee smiles, but doesn't say anything. She's breathing hard and slow, and I can tell she's overwhelmed.

The second host, a petite blonde, turns to face us at the table and smiles. "My teenage daughter is a huge fan, Dakota. Or do you prefer Virginia?"

"Either is fine."

"She says you're the Queen of the Breakup Anthem." Vee tenses, and crosses her hands on the table in front of her. "Most of your songs, especially the early ones, are obviously about heartbreak." She taps her talking cards on the table and gives Vee a conspiratorial look. "Can you tell us who inspired those?"

Shit. I can tell you who inspired them. I'd raise my hand if I thought the joke would cheer Vee up.

The other host chimes in. "Maybe you want to put a warning out there?"

Vee fidgets nervously in her seat. "Oh. Hm. That seems kind of rude." The hosts all laugh. They think she's joking.

The Olympian turns to Vee again. "Someone *obviously* broke your heart." She lists off some of Dakota's most popular songs, which include titles like "Catastrophic Love," "Bleeding Hearts," "Love's a Mistake," and "Over You Under Him." Vee fidgets in her chair when they read the last one and I snake my hand along the edge of the table and put my hand on hers.

"Obviously," Vee mutters, when the laundry list of songs has finally ended.

"No comment?" the blonde says, giggling. "You're a better woman than me. If some guy treated me that way, I'd be screaming his name from the rooftops."

"I think you've actually done that," the Olympian offers and they all laugh. The women launch into a discussion about Sidney Montrose, an A-list pop star who *does* put all of her exes on blast. The women seem to think Sidney could teach Vee a thing or two about well-played vengeance. Vee laughs along, but she's fidgety. Uncomfortable.

The host announces we'll be performing and says, "Well, we

wish you all luck." Then her eyes fix on Vee's hand in mine, and she looks at Vee again. "It looks like it all worked out for the best, anyway."

Vee pulls her hand away from me slowly and tucks a piece of hair behind her ear. She doesn't smile. We make our way to the small stage, where we play "This Girl" again, but for the first time, she doesn't look at me while she sings it.

VIRGINIA

Before I had even started the Dakota Gray frenzy, I think I knew that I needed to leave eventually. I can't stay on tour indefinitely and leave my life on pause. And it's no longer an option to continue acting like what has been going on between me and Cam is normal. We've fallen asleep together every night since he found me in his bed. Every morning, I wake up and wonder if he's still there, or if he's disappeared. My being on the tour is convenient, and he could be out of my life at any moment.

Plus, a million opportunities have opened up for me since coming forward as Dakota Gray. I need to take advantage of them while I'm still relevant. Because let's face it, I'm only *internet* famous. Without a camera pointed at me, I'm a nobody. I need to make an *actual* name for myself. I need to learn to play on a stage by myself, without a disguise or a fake name.

Am I seriously doing this?

I'm going to pursue my music. And I'm not going to be a publicist or manager, or even a songwriter. I'm going to perform. I decide what I deserve, and I deserve to chase my dreams. *I deserve not to wake up in a panic every morning.* Once I decide I'm leaving, a mental countdown begins in my head, and each minute and hour seems to rush by. At first, I decide I'll stay until the next show in Chicago. I'll have a free ride home. *Four days.* I tell myself that's how much time I have to spend with Cam, and Logan and Anders, and even Reese—before their lives change. Because there is no doubt that they'll win this thing. In another six weeks, they'll officially achieve the rock-god status they've been dreaming of. They'll go back to LA to record their album, and then they'll go on tour. And that tour will be *all* about them. The groupies will all be there for them. The fame and the fans, all theirs. It's only a matter of time—six weeks— before they trade in their normal lives for something that is so much more. The more I think about how much I'll miss them, the more I think that in four days I'll lose my resolve.

I need to leave tomorrow.

One more rehearsal, one more night with Cam, one more day of this imaginary life.

CAM

We spend our last night in Cincinnati at a rowdy dance club. Vee and I are back in my bunk, lying pressed up against each other, still in our sweaty clothes. I run my finger along her arm, mesmerized by the bumps that rise up on her skin in its wake. I might be slightly buzzed.

Vee's voice pulls me out of my trance. "I have to go back."

"Did you leave something? Give Logan a call." We left the club early, but Logan stayed. He's been embracing his official bachelor status. "He can bring it back in the morning."

"No." Her voice is tiny and she turns onto her side, so she can look at me. "I need to go back . . . to Chicago."

I don't know what to say. *Don't go.*

Is it school? Or her way of ending things? Does she just need space? Maybe we're moving too fast. We're practically living together, when you think about it. *We're moving too fast.*

"I can't stay here." Her words are barely decipherable as she whispers through tears. Her breaths are coming out in tiny gasps.

"Come here." I shift my arm under her and she tucks herself into me. I kiss her head and run my hand down her arm.

"I can't just leave my life," she says. "And I can't go backward. This thing with us . . ." She takes a few slow breaths like she's trying to compose herself. "I forgive you for leaving, Cam. I can even understand why you left. But I can't keep acting like it never happened, because you never came back." She takes a deep, ragged breath. "You never came back, and then I popped up in your life again. And if I hadn't . . . if I hadn't ended up on this tour? You'd still be on one side of the country and I'd be on the other. I didn't know how to find you, but you knew how to find me." She takes a deep breath and I can feel the warmth of it against my chest. "You could have found me whenever you wanted, and you didn't. We can't live in this little bubble and act like it's moving forward."

"Vee, please." I kiss her head again, unable to find the words to tell her exactly how I feel. "I lo—"

"Please don't." Her face tilts up toward me, her eyes pleading. "It's already hard. And I know you do, but it's not enough." She smiles at me, in a way that has me expecting her to say, "It's been fun." In the last year and a half she's obviously become more like Dakota than even she realizes. I can't help but respect her, even though it's my turn to be left behind now.

I don't say anything because I know every word I say will just hurt her more. And she's right; I didn't come back. After I left that night I never had even one moment of hope that she would end up in my arms like this again. I'm thankful she did, though. Even if it was just for the short time that we shared this bus. Because even if she's gone forever—off to live her own life—I know there's no way she can forget the songs we sang, or the words I finally said to her. This may not be the encore I'd hoped for, but at least we'll always have this one unforgettable summer. I'll take it.

CHAPTER THIRTY-ONE

NOW

VIRGINIA

It's the third time I've played at Monte's, a small music venue on the North Side of Chicago. The room is long, narrow and dark, with a small stage at the far end. The walls are covered in vintage newspaper articles, plastered like wallpaper. The first two times I played here I was the first act, going on before a local singer who sang a lot of folksy ballads. But each time the crowds insisted on calling me back up to the stage after her set, since so many fans came late. *I have fans.* It's surreal to think that people are actually coming to see me, and after the second show the manager told me I'd be taking the main spot. I knew a huge reason for my popularity was all of the tour coverage, but it still felt amazing and I decided it didn't matter why they came to see me. Maybe they just wanted to see Dakota Gray, internet sensation. Or Vee Miller, reality TV star. I didn't care. Either way, I'd just have to win them over with my music.

Each week I felt more comfortable onstage, talking with the crowd, sharing little stories about the songs. When I'd written them, and why. I told myself I was playing for friends and started to treat them that way. After the first show I stopped wearing my Dakota Gray wig. When I sit on the stage I imagine I'm sitting on Cam's bed playing a show for one. And every time I play, there are chants for "This Girl," but I can't bring myself to play it by myself. Something about it feels wrong, so I always apologize, playing something upbeat to wrap things up.

Four weeks after getting back to Chicago, I'm waiting off-stage as my opening act—*my opening act!*—finishes her set. I don't care that I'm playing in a bar that only holds three hundred people and not an auditorium that seats five thousand. I'm playing my own shows, facing my fears, moving forward. *I'm chasing something.* As my opener exits the stage and I enter, she gives me a strange, nervous smile. *I'm* the one who should be nervous. Taking a seat on the vintage wooden chair, I'm tuning my guitar, just about to begin, when a voice interrupts over the house PA system.

It's the club's music manager, Kevin. "Before we hear the musical talent of Vee Miller, aka Dakota Gray, we have a quick presentation to make."

What the hell?

The crowd is lighter than usual tonight, and I sit in my chair—continuing to fiddle and tune as I wait for the go-ahead from Kevin—while a steady stream of people begins to enter. They're all wearing white. White tank tops, white polos. *Is this a tour group of some sort? Maybe a nearby convention?* I squint, trying to look for a name badge or logo, but don't see anything. The small tables are quickly filled and by the time everyone has entered, the entire bar area is standing-room-only. Other than my performances with Cam on tour, this is the biggest group of people I've ever played for. It's far from small and intimate, and I begin to feel my nerves building. *Deep breath.*

The PA system crackles to life again, but instead of Kevin's voice, music begins to play. It's a guitar, and it sounds live, not recorded. *Are they seriously playing another musician right before I go on? It's probably the manager's girlfriend, who has been pushing for a spot in the lineup for weeks. She's practically tone deaf.* I don't recognize the song, but then Cam's voice pours out of the speakers and I'm frozen in place. I look around the room, straining to see over and around people. He must be here somewhere, but there's no sign of him. Except for his voice. It feels like it's been ages since I heard it, even though it was less than twenty-four hours ago that I heard him sing on national television. The last words I heard him speak were words of thanks, to everyone that made it possible for the band to win. I had screamed and shouted, dancing in Cort's living room like a maniac, when they won. And when he thanked his parents for watching over him, through it all, I lost it. The words drifting out of the speakers right now are even better. As the first verse begins, all I can do is listen to the words that I know are only for me:

> *She's the high and the low,*
> *the waves and the shore.*
> *She's nights in the dark,*
> *and toes in the sand,*
> *she's the voice in my head*
> *saying try it again.*
> *Try it again.*

As he finishes the chorus, a girl in the front row, center stage, turns her back to me, revealing the black letters across her white shirt that say: "When we met," and as Cam keeps singing, another person turns around, revealing a second message: "I was broken." As the song goes on, person after person shows me their messages as I listen to Cam's words:

WHEN WE MET I WAS BROKEN

She's the words on the page
that tell me to stay.
She's the start and the end
to all my favorite days.
She's the start and the stop,
she's the start and the stop.
Don't make me stop.

AND THE FIRST TIME I HEARD YOUR VOICE
I FELT ALIVE AGAIN

This is my serenade,
this is my second chance.
This is my serenade,
my second chance.

YOU STARTED PUTTING ME BACK TOGETHER
BEFORE YOU EVEN MET ME

She's the cure to my pain,
she's the sun and the rain.
She's the sun and the rain.

I SHOULD HAVE STAYED
BECAUSE YOU ARE THE ONLY FUTURE
I HAVE EVER IMAGINED

This is my serenade,
this is my second chance.
This is my serenade,
you are my second chance.

I'M NOT GOING ANYWHERE
WITHOUT YOU

As the song ends and the last girl turns back around, another approaches the stage with a gift-wrapped box. She hands it to me with a giant smile. It's wrapped in shiny purple foil, with a silver bow and a tag that says OPEN ME. When there are hundreds of eyes on you I don't know that there's really a choice, but at this point I want nothing more than to know what is in this box. I shake it just a little for effect and it rattles like it's full of glass. *What the hell is it?* I choke back the building tears as I rip open the paper and pry open the box flaps, revealing a pile of tissue paper. I fish each piece out, dropping it around me on the stage like it's Christmas morning.

Folded up neatly on top is a purple Future X shirt, and I pull it out, wondering why on earth I need another one of these. As I begin to fold it to shove it back into the box I notice something on the back of it and hold it up to see THE ORIGINAL written in white lettering across the back. *I'm the original Girl in the Purple Shirt.* Embracing the fact that it feels like Christmas, and I'm a complete dork, I pull the T-shirt on right over my dress.

I reach into the box again, and pull out another layer of tissue paper, revealing a pile of . . . change? There are hundreds of quarters and nickels and dimes, like someone has dumped their loose change jar into the box. I look at it all, confused, and notice there are also small plastic cards mixed in. Blue and white and black; they're bus cards and train cards. As I pull a few out, completely bewildered, a guy in a white shirt approaches the stage and hands me an envelope. The music has stopped and I wonder if Cam is here. *Where is he?* I scan the crowd and don't see him. But against the back wall, hiding behind a camera, I see Tad. *Cam has got to be here somewhere.* I smile, and Tad nods back, his usual grin still in place.

"Open this," the man standing in front of the stage says, before taking his place in the crowd again. Every eye is fixed on me as people lean forward and look around each other for the best view. Everyone seems to be just as curious as I am about what is going on.

I pull out the card, which is scribbled on in a handwriting I recognize from a million napkins and scraps of paper that have littered the tour bus, adorned with lyrics.

Vee,
I fell in love with you years ago. I made you a promise then and I'm finally keeping it. I promise to ride the trains with you, and make sure crazy taxis don't run you down in the street, and to refill your Metro card so you don't get kicked off the bus.
            I Love You,
            Cam

Tears fall onto the card as I choke back a sob, and as I finally look back out to the crowd, Cam is standing in front of me at the edge of the stage, his guitar in one hand. He's wearing a white shirt too, and when he turns his back to me it says PROPERTY OF CHICAGO in big black letters.

"I don't—" I can barely talk through the tears. "—What are you doing here?"

Cam sets his guitar on the edge of the stage and pulls a red, white, and blue Cubs ball cap on. "I live here." He takes a step up onto the stage, standing between the crowd and me.

"In Chicago?"

He nods.

"Since when?"

He squats down in front of me so his face is level with mine, and his eyes bore into me. "Since the girl I love moved back here." The crowd erupts in muffled gasps. "Since I realized that you are the only future I've ever seen for myself. I'm going to do whatever it takes to make sure you're the only—" Flashes are erupting throughout the crowd and muffled whispers fill the air.

Someone in the back of the club yells, "Marry him or I will!"

Cam freezes in place. "Shit." He swallows and bites his lip. "Vee, I'm not—" He shakes his head frantically and I choke back a laugh. "Shit. I mean . . . not that I wouldn't. But I wasn't—I just—" He starts to stand up and I grab him by the elbow, holding him in place.

"Settle down. I know." Strangely, the idea of being with Cam—even forever with Cam—hasn't sent me into a tailspin. There's no way I'm ready, but it doesn't plunge me into a complete panic. I smile and lean forward, pressing my lips to his as he grabs my hands and pulls me toward him. My guitar is wedged between us and the crowd breaks into applause as we fumble with the instrument keeping us apart, shoving it to my back to get closer. Cam's hands are snaking up the back of my shirt and wrapping around my ribs when whistling pulls me back to reality. *We are onstage. In front of a very interested crowd.*

I lean into his ear, "Sing with me?"

He kisses me on the forehead, and a giant grin spreads across his face. "Always." I raise the mic stand and we take our places around it.

"You guys want to hear a song?" I ask the crowd. "Or did you all just come here to help embarrass me?"

The crowd erupts in cheers and whistling and I begin to play "This Girl," feeling for the first time like the words are a declaration and not a wish.

There's this boy, oh this boy,
who's got me all tied up
in the best kind of knots.
There's this look you've gotta see,

when he's starin' at me,
it's his hands on my hips,
and in the way that we kiss.
I can't help but smile
'cause he's lookin' at me,
oh he's lookin' at me.

There's this boy, oh this boy—
I think he's the boy for me.

EPILOGUE

CAM

As I step through the giant automatic doors of Lake Terrace with Vee, I consider—for maybe the hundredth time—how I'm going to handle this. Vee hadn't given me a choice when she said, "You're going to meet Nonni on Sunday." There was no question asked. I had known it wasn't optional by the way she scrunched her eyebrows together and squeezed her lips into a thin little smile, daring me to argue with her.

That was two days ago, as we sat in standstill traffic on the interstate, trying to make our way to Riverton. To spend the weekend with Vee's parents. Back in the day, Vee's mom took me in with open arms. Fast-forward, after I ran off with no notice, broke their daughter's heart, then inadvertently made her look like a cheater on national television—and I don't quite know what to expect. I've basically been covered in a cold sweat the last forty-eight hours. Since the moment she told me we'd be making this trip. She told me that if "whatever this was" between us was going to work, I would have to face her family eventually. *Face her family.* The way she said it hadn't exactly done wonders in assuring me that I wasn't being driven straight to the firing squad.

But eating dinner with her parents and making awkward small talk with her aunt, who spent most of the meal ogling me—*I am a rock star now, after all*—had been *nothing* compared to the crush of panic I'm feeling as we walk down the floral-papered hallways of the nursing home. I'm not sure if it's just in my head, but I swear I can smell the familiar scent of room 207—eucalyptus, baby powder, and lavender—before I even see the door. While Vee enters, announcing loudly, "It's VA Day, Nonni!" I stand frozen in the doorway.

There are so many memories wrapped up in that room: the first day I showed up to visit Gram and told her about the fire, and she cried for the strangers that were my dead parents; the loneliness and emptiness I felt when I came to Riverton, feeling like I didn't deserve anything else. And then there was Vee and the strange curiosity I had felt when I heard her that first day; the way she made me want to be a part of something again, the burning pain I feel every time I think about how much I hurt her and almost lost her in the end with my secrets. Will she think I'm a total stalker when she finds out how I *actually* met her?

Then I hear a raspy voice inside the room.

"Is he going to come in, or is he just going to stand over there?"

"Nonni, be nice," Vee scolds.

"Hush. I'm teasing. Come over here." She's waving her hands in the air, ushering me over.

Hands in my pockets, I join Vee next to Nonni's bed. "Nice to meet you, ma'am." I hold out my hand and she swats it away.

"Pshh, you call me Nonni. And give me a hug." She puts her arms out and I lean into them, hugging her awkwardly as she sits in her bed. As I stand up she grabs my arms in her hands, squeezing my biceps. "Nice arms on this one," she says, winking at Vee.

Vee bursts into laughter and I can't help but join her. "Stop harassing my boyfriend, Nonni." Her smile falters and she gives me a sideways glance. Neither of us is used to saying it—we never used to. I slip my hand around hers and squeeze.

"Don't listen to her," I say. "You can harass me any time you want, Nonni." I give Vee a smile that she returns.

Nonni distracted me and I've completely forgotten about the problem at hand, until Vee reaches behind her and pulls the curtain across the room in a flash of blue fabric. We're engulfed in sunlight, and there in her bed is my Gram. She claps her hands together in excitement, but she isn't looking at me, she's looking at Vee. I stand in shock as Vee bends down and gives my grandmother a hug full of familiarity.

"Hey, Grace." Vee is holding one of her hands as she speaks to her. "How are you feeling today?"

Gram pats Vee's hand slowly. "Good, honey, I'm good."

Vee turns, pressing her mouth to my ear. "See, I have secrets too." She takes Gram's hand and nods toward me. "Grace, I think you already know my *boyfriend*, Cam." She smiles at me as I stand staring at the two of them, completely thrown by what is happening.

"He looks like my grandson." Gram reaches for my hand and I step forward to hold it. Vee takes my other hand, keeping it by her side.

"He sure does." Vee reaches up and rubs her hand over my hair like I'm a little boy. "I think he's a little cuter, though." She grabs my face roughly in one hand, squeezing my cheeks together. "Don't you think?"

"That *is* your grandson," Nonni offers in a firm voice. "See over there." She nods toward the dresser. It's lined with photo frames—the large one of my family is still there, but there are others, too. There's a photo of me onstage, playing my guitar—taken at one of the small clubs we played in Houston; and a photo of Logan, Anders, Reese, and me, sitting on a couch backstage before a performance. And a heart-shaped frame with a photo of me and Vee sitting side by side, playing "This Girl" onstage the first time. Every photo has a little white sticker across it with everyone's names printed out.

Gram just looks at the pictures and nods her head as Vee squeezes my hand.

"Thank you," I whisper in her ear as I kiss her temple.

"How's the apartment search going?" Nonni asks.

Vee and I sit down in the plastic chairs between the two beds. "It's not, really," she says. "I forgot how ridiculously expensive everything is. It's too late to get anything on campus. And I'm still looking for a new job. Money from my online videos is just enough to pay my bills at the moment. Until I find something, swinging an apartment by myself isn't an option."

I take Vee's hand in mine, lacing our fingers together on top of the armrest. "I wanted to talk to you about that, actually."

She looks panicked. "We can't move in together." Her voice is quiet, like she doesn't want our grandmothers to know she's rejecting me.

"Vee, just—"

She's giving me a shut-this-down-or-I'll-shut-*you*-down look. "Cam."

"It's just an idea. I thought—"

Vee slides forward in her chair. "Let's talk about it later?"

"I'd like to hear this idea," Nonni says, and I officially love her.

"Nonni, we're—"

I cut Vee off before she can finish. "Nonni, excuse us for a second while I calm down your neurotic granddaughter." I turn

Vee's chair toward me and put my hands on her shoulders. "Stop panicking." I smile, amused by how worked up she is, and she glares at me. Her face is etched with irritation. "I'm not asking you to move in with me."

"You're not?" She looks confused, and it may be the optimist in me—because I *will* ask her to move in with me someday—but I think I see a little disappointment, too.

"I'm not." I squeeze her shoulders and take her hand again, as I turn her chair back around.

Nonni smiles at me. "I like this one."

"See, she likes me." I give Vee a cocky smile.

"She's always liked you," she says, matter-of-factly.

"She just met me."

Vee raises her eyebrows at me and Nonni laughs. "I might be old, but I remember a face when I see it every day. And you spent a whole lot of time lurking behind that curtain while this one"—she nods toward Vee—"was visiting with me."

I open my mouth to speak, but don't know what to say. Vee bursts into laughter beside me.

"I always joked about you stalking me, but really"—she's trying not to smile and failing—"at a nursing home?"

"What can I say?" I raise one of her hands to my lips. "The two people I love most spend a lot of time at nursing homes."

The air around us feels charged, and I'm acutely aware of the fact that we are sandwiched between our grandmothers. In a nursing home. I clear my throat dramatically. "So, about the job hunt." My eyes settle on Nonni, hoping that bringing this up in front of her is the good decision I had hoped it would be. "We actually found you one."

"Who exactly is 'we'?"

"Logan and I. Well, the whole band, really." Vee pulls her hand out of mine, folding her arms across her chest.

"I've told you both a hundred times, I'm not qualified to

manage the band." She sighs, and I think she wishes it weren't the truth. "Especially now that you're going to be negotiating the record deal, and planning a major tour. There's all sorts of legal issues. You need someone professional."

"Right," I say. "We actually hired a manager a few days ago. Should be finalizing the paperwork next week," I say.

"Oh."

"We were thinking you could be involved in a different way, actually. Play a bigger role with the new record and the tour."

"A bigger role than manager?" She rolls her eyes at me again, and I know I should just spit it out and tell her, but I'm having fun riling her up. "Seriously, Cam, I'm not qualified to be your publicist, either. I'm not qualified to do *anything* for the band anymore." She punches me gently in the shoulder. "Face it. You're a big deal now." She's so adorably proud of us, I can't help but kiss her. After a quick peck she pushes me away, darting her eyes at Nonni. *Right. Still in a nursing home.*

"We're going to need help when everything starts up again. Recording the album, working out the tour details, writing new songs—we're going to need you there."

"Of course. You know I'll help," she says.

"Yeah, you will. You'll have to, actually. Because we were thinking you could go on tour with us." I wait a second for it to sink in. "Definitely *not* as our official groupie." She's still silent. "A co-headlining tour, Vee. We'd play songs separately *and* together."

I'm waiting patiently for her to say something, but she just stares at me like I told her I was going to cut my arms off and let Anders use them as an oversized set of drumsticks. I'm not sure if it's a good-silent or bad-silent. I'm hoping she's just in shock, overcome with emotion. She's still staring at my shirt, not meeting my eyes, when tears start to run down her cheeks.

"Vee?" I tilt her head up to look at me, and swipe my thumbs across her cheeks. "Are these happy tears or sad tears? Because I'll be honest, I'm worried you and I have too many sad tears." She laughs and looks over at Nonni, who is beaming at her, her own eyes glistening. *Maybe it's genetic.*

"Everyone is okay with this? Anders and Reese, too? You're not just trying to find an excuse to take me on tour with you?"

"It was actually Jenn's idea, but she told me I could pitch it. It's an official offer from the label, but the band is definitely on board. Reese hopes to use you as a wing-woman on tour, just so you know." She looks between me and Nonni, tapping her fingers on the armrest of her chair. I *do* want her on tour. But more than anything, I want her to have everything she wants. I want the world to see how amazing she is. And yes, I want to be able to see how amazing she is every single day. Even if it's on a stuffy, cramped tour bus.

"So what do you say, are you ready to officially become a rock star?"

Vee looks at Nonni then me, and she smiles. "Can I really say no?"

ACKNOWLEDGMENTS

The list of those who made this book possible is long and filled with people I could never gift with enough hugs.

A gigantic I Love You to the likely suspects: my husband, for letting me obsess for a year, and not trying to peek over my shoulder. My sweet, wonderful Rory, for loving me back "big time," despite some missed bedtimes while editing. To my mom, for believing I was a writer way before I ever did, and my dad, for being unbelievably proud. Thank you for raising me to be a dreamer, and to always believe those dreams are within reach.

To my amazing agent, Michelle Wolfson, thank you for believing in me and wanting this book in the world as much as I did. You deserve ALL the chocolate, and our first phone call will forever be one of my favorites.

To editor extraordinaire Amy Stapp, I am so thankful for you, your love for this book, and our twin-like brains. You took this story to all of the best places, and I adore you for loving these characters as much as I do.

To my fantastic publisher and the whole Tor Teen team—thank you for making this experience better than I could have ever hoped for.

To my beloved NIAY group: Emily, for planting the seed of

confidence I didn't know I needed and reigniting a very old dream; to Angie and Jaclyn, for being my two very first (and very enthusiastic) readers; and to Ellen, Mary, Sarah, and Lisa for your year of cheers and edits. *Love Songs* would never have happened without the keen eyes, cheerleading, and side-by-side determination each of you offered.

Big thanks to my "first" editor, and friend, Lara Willard, for helping me get my baby ready for querying and always being a helpful pair of eyes on everything from my query letter to my book title.

Thank you to everyone who helped guide me through the publishing process: my lovely critique partner, Jenn P. Nguyen, my rambling-in-an-awesome-way mentor, Harriet Reuter Hapgood, and my fantastic Swank-Electrics. Your cheerleading, insight, and commiseration were sanity-saving!

Heartfelt thanks to Maggie (you'll always be Mrs. Mendus to me) and all of the teachers who plant and nurture that very first love of words. You are so very important, and so very special.

And a bigger-than-the-sky Thank You to every reader who picks up *Love Songs;* having this book in your hands makes me happier than I could ever describe.